The Gifted Child

The Gifted Child

PENNY KLINE

Published by Accent Press Ltd 2016

ISBN 9781783757763

For Jason and Tammy

1

He moved his head and the trees whirled past, green and white, dappled, waving. Drifting in and out of consciousness, he opened his mouth, not knowing if any sound came out. How far had he fallen … landing so hard, hurting his shoulder, his cheek … An arm stretched out on the grass. Easing it, slowly, carefully, his fingers reached his face, touching the pain, feeling the sticky dampness. Then a noise from a long way off, coming closer, rustling, scrabbling, warm breath on his skin, a smooth, dark shape, the smell of a dog. It was getting dark. A coldness touched his neck, his hair … licking, moaning; a voice calling his name.

The pain eased; he was falling, spinning. 'I'm here,' he murmured, 'I'm here', then his body floated and he opened his eyes, saw the flickering lights and heard the wind.

The dog jumped to the ground and stood still, sniffing the air. Perhaps it had picked up a different scent. Perhaps it was lost. When it started to howl perhaps it had nothing to do with the man on his back on the grass, who could have been sleeping but for his vacant, lifeless eyes.

2

Theo had his back turned, fiddling with the zip on his bag of games. Kristen tried to imagine the expression on his face. Anger? Fear? Perhaps a part of him he could never show was relieved. Relieved that it was over, that the day had arrived, even glad that he was going back to where he belonged.

'She might have changed her mind.' His voice was thick with unshed tears. 'When Dad died she pretended she wanted me. Why didn't you tell her? Why didn't you say I had to stay with you?'

'Oh, Theo, if there was anything I could do.' Kristen balanced on the bed, trying to prise his football poster off the wall. The corner came away and it started to tear.

'Leave it,' he commanded, 'I don't want it.'

'All right.' She spoke softly, wanting to calm him. 'When you're in London you'll be able to support Chelsea. Their ground's not far from Putney.'

'I won't,' he shouted. 'If Dad was alive none of this would be happening.'

If Dad was alive they would be playing football in the park, or buying food for a picnic, or planning a trip to the Gower Peninsula. 'I'll see you often,' she said, 'I promise. Please, Theo, don't look like that.'

His arms hung limply by his sides. 'You said you'd have to

find a flat where the rent's cheaper. There won't be room for me.'

Tears streamed down her face. 'What does it matter where I'm living? You can have my bed. I'll sleep on the sofa.'

'When?' He was frightened, blaming himself for making her cry. 'When can I come?'

'Soon. Very soon.' Kristen allowed herself a flicker of hope. Perhaps Ros had changed her mind, had second thoughts. Combining an acting career with looking after an eight-year-old child was going to be too much. Already she was wishing she had decided to let him stay in Bristol, at least until the end of the year. But even if she had, it was too late, there would be no going back. Ros was someone who would never risk losing face.

The basement flat – the only place they had been able to afford when they returned from America – had been pleasantly cool in May but now, in August, it felt like a hot, stuffy burrow. She and Theo were the rabbits, weak and defenceless, and Ros was the fox. Any moment now she would nose her way down the steps and tear them apart.

She was late. People like Ros always were. Being late was a way of showing how terribly busy she was, how important, how much in demand. A recent part as a social worker in a soap opera had only lasted for three episodes, but convinced Ros she was on the brink of the breakthrough she had been waiting for ever since she left drama school, the year before Theo was born.

In the five weeks since William's body had been found, Ros had only been in touch three times. Once after the police had broken the news, once to arrange to collect Theo and a third time – a text – to alter the day from Friday evening to midday Saturday.

Theo had switched on the television, turning down the sound until it was barely audible, a thin wail of pop music accompanying the gyrating figures on the screen. Looking up at the pavement, Kristen recognised familiar scraggy legs in wrinkled stockings. They passed the iron railings, and disappeared, and she heard Mrs Letts put her key in the lock of the ground floor flat and slam the door behind her. *He's going*

4

back to his birth mother? Mrs Letts had heard the expression in a documentary about adoption. *It's all wrong. They're supposed to put the kiddie's happiness first.*

A car slowed down, then accelerated with squealing tyres. Kristen put an arm round Theo's shoulder but instead of responding as he usually did, his body stiffened.

'You should have told her I've got thinner,' he said, 'and about my bad dreams. If I was older they'd let me choose and I'd tell them she drinks.'

'Being caught over the limit doesn't mean you're an alcoholic.' Kristen listened to herself defending the woman she hated, but it was Theo she was thinking about, not Ros.

'Yes it does,' he said. 'She's a criminal. She ought to be in prison.'

'She's getting her licence back at the end of the month. She'll be able to take you out, bring you down here to see me.'

When he turned to face her, his pale cheeks had two bright red spots. 'If it's true, if she does want me, that means it could have been her. She could be the one who killed Dad.' Then his whole body sagged. 'She's here.' He gazed up at the street. 'It's a sports car. They'll make me sit in the back and I'll feel sick. D'you think he lives with her?'

'The man who's driven her down? No, he's a friend, another actor.'

Ros was wearing a linen trouser suit and a pale orange T-shirt. Her glossy shoulder-length hair gleamed in the sun. She was holding a pair of designer glasses, swinging them round her finger, smiling, but not too much, just enough to convey the appropriate mixture of friendliness, compassion, and pleasure at seeing her son.

'This is John.' She moved her head in the direction of the man coming down the steps. 'Sorry we're late, we got lost in a one-way system, took a wrong turning up by the Downs.'

So far, everything had been addressed to Kristen. Now she bent to kiss Theo on the head. 'Hello, darling. I saw your face at the window.'

'Coffee?' Kristen asked, half hoping her offer would be turned down, half desperate to put off the moment when Theo's

5

luggage was carried to the car.

'Coffee would be lovely.' Ros touched her companion's arm. 'You probably recognise John. If you don't he'll be rather upset, won't you, my darling?'

Kristen shook his hand, feeling a slight warmth towards him simply because he wasn't Ros. His face *was* vaguely familiar. He could have been in any recent hospital or police series. He was probably about ten years younger than Ros.

Over the coffee, Ros kept up a stream of chatter while taking care never to mention William. Every so often, she gave Kristen a sympathetic little smile and, while her cup was being refilled, she inquired about the new job Kristen was starting in two days' time. 'Something with gifted children, you said.'

Kristen had explained on the phone but she would have to do it all over again. Pleasantries had to be exchanged. Everything had to be carried out as painlessly as possible.

'A holiday course at a tuition college,' she said. 'One of the staff's been taken ill. Brigid Howell suggested me for the job. Her husband, Alex, was in charge of the research project William worked on before we went to the States.'

Ros examined her shiny apricot nails. 'The man who was instrumental in finding William the post in Ohio. As I recall, when you first moved to Bristol he was working for someone else.'

'That project came to an end, but by then Alex had met William and wanted to take him on.'

'Nice to be so much in demand.' Ros gave a beaming smile, almost as if she had forgotten for a moment that William was dead. 'And Brigid Howell runs this holiday course, does she?'

'No, it's a man called Neville Unwin. Brigid has a four-month-old baby but the classes are only for two hours, three mornings a week.'

'And you'll be instructing them in the great philosophers.'

'Neville Unwin wants me to teach them how to think.'

'Really? How clever. John's interested in all that kind of thing, aren't you, my darling, brainstorming, lateral thinking. Of course, how stupid of me, the thesis you're writing on children with exceptional ability. I remember William telling me about

6

it.' She glanced at Theo, flinching when her son's stony eyes stared back at her.

'Shame Theo won't be able to attend the classes,' said John, trying to break the tension, then, Theo stood up and left the room, looking at Kristen with a rueful expression.

Ros sprang up to follow then changed her mind and sat down again. 'Gone to the loo, I expect.' She leaned towards Kristen until their heads were only inches apart. 'Have the police been in touch recently? Are they still as sure as ever they know who did it?'

Kristen nodded. 'Someone they call "the dog man". He's a pickpocket who pretends he's lost his dog, then steals bags, wallets, whatever he can take.'

'I told you how a rather charming policeman called Tisdall came to see me?' Ros pushed back her hair with both hands. 'Just a formality, I mean, what could I possibly tell him? You know, it's the randomness of it I find so hard to bear. William just happening to be in that particular place at that particular time. It makes you realise how little control we have over our lives.'

She was talking too fast and for the first time it occurred to Kristen that she must be wondering how Theo was going to react when it was time to leave.

'How's he been the last few weeks?' she whispered, 'I'd have come down sooner, only as I mentioned on the phone I'm not sure it would have been much help.'

Kristen could hear Theo outside his bedroom door. 'I'll check his luggage is ready.'

Ros started to say something then decided against it, but a few moments later she joined them in Theo's bedroom, hovering in the doorway as if she was afraid she was intruding on a private conversation. 'Listen, I just want to say … I know … well, of course I don't, how could I? What I mean, Theo can come and stay here whenever he likes, whenever you can get time off work, Kristen, or at the weekends of course. I do hope we can all be friends, keep things informal, be guided by Theo, really. What do you think, darling, does that sound about right?'

For the first hour, Kristen felt nothing. Floating, muzzy, a tiny insignificant speck in a world where nothing mattered because nothing lasted, she drifted from room to room, switching on the radio and listening to the weather forecast, the news headlines, but without taking anything in. First William. Now Theo. To lose the two people you loved had something clean, clear-cut about it. Her life had been wiped out, there were no messy leftovers to be attended to. She was nothing, a blank sheet.

The sight of Theo's football shirt draped over the back of a kitchen chair jerked her out of her false euphoria. He would unpack, or Ros would, and notice straight away that it was missing. Then what? Ros would phone – or Theo would – and she would promise to send the shirt, and the ugly-bug stickers she had found down the side of the sofa, and he would tell her how unhappy he was or – if Ros was in the room – he would be brave, even sound quite cheerful, but she would know, they would both know.

Picking up the crumpled red shirt, she carried it to the washing machine, pushing it in on top of his sheet and pillow case, the duvet cover with its pattern of sheep, and feeling the weight of misery descend on her. Ros would buy him a new football strip, as many new strips as he wanted, and try to take an interest but do it badly. *You know what I'm like, darling, can't tell which team is which, and what on earth do they mean when they say the ball's offside?*

No, it was no use pretending Ros was the distant, alien creature Kristen wanted her to be. Half of Theo's genes came from her and she had looked after him for the first four years of his life, or at least employed a succession of au pair girls. When the last of them took a day off and never returned, William had given up his research post at London University and taken over the care of Theo himself. It was something that had gone in his favour in court.

During the four years since the divorce, Ros had seen far less of her son than William thought she should, although he admitted to Kristen – after she moved in with him a few months before the judge gave him custody – that his secret wish was that Ros would go to California and Theo would only have to see her once a year...

By now, the three of them would have reached the M25, unless they had stopped at a services for something to eat. With a lurching sensation, half dread, half hope, it occurred to her they might still be in Bristol. *I tell you what, darling, while we're here we might as well buy you some decent clothes. It'll be easier than trying to shop in London, less of a stampede.*

Returning to the other room, she stared up at the street, almost expecting to see them coming back. Ros had only reclaimed her son because doing anything else would have meant people thought badly of her. After all, she could hardly allow herself to be accused of putting her acting career before her own flesh and blood. Besides, there were compensations. Showing Theo off to her friends might be rather fun.

A policeman was strolling past. He looked down at the basement flat, as if he sensed Kristen watching him, or perhaps it was his job to keep an eye on the place where William had lived.

The job of breaking the news had been given to a policewoman and when Kristen answered the door she and an older male colleague had been talking in hushed voices. *Was she Mrs Frith?* No, but she knew what was coming next. *A member of the public, walking near the River Frome ... a dog yelping ... the body would be need to be identified.*

Later, two CID officers had called round to tell her they suspected foul play, that it seemed likely William's death was the result of a mugging that had gone wrong. They were looking for a person whose activities were already known to them. William's wallet was missing and the mugging had all the hallmarks of someone they had nicknamed 'the dog man'. It had taken place in an area where previous thefts had been reported, a dog could have been used as a decoy, and a man, answering the description provided by several previous victims, had been seen in the vicinity around the time of the attack. They would, of course, keep her informed.

At the inquest, cause of death was attributed to a blow on the head with half a brick, followed by a second injury to the skull when William fell from the bridge and landed with his legs in the water but the rest of him on dry land. Damage to the vertebral artery had led to subarachnoid bleeding. Subarachnoid. The word had stuck in her head like a mantra.

The doorbell rang and Kristen's heart started to thud. Theo had broken down in uncontrollable sobbing. Unable to handle the situation, Ros had decided to bring him back. *Just until he's had more time to adjust. I'm so sorry, Kristen, but I think for Theo's sake …*

'Oh, it's you.' When she opened the door, DS Tisdall had his back turned and was moving his head up and down as if in time to a tune going on in his head. She'd recognised him by the dead straight line of his hair on the back of his neck. That and the grey folder under his arm.

'I just need to clear up a few anomalies. Is the boy with you?'

'He's gone back to London – to live with his mother.'

'I'm sorry.' Tisdall followed her into the flat and sat down. 'Is that what he wanted, or didn't his wishes come into it?'

'So you're no nearer finding the man who did it.'

'We're making some progress,' he said, conveying the impression that exactly the opposite was true. 'I just need to ask a few supplementary questions about the six weeks between the time you came back from America and the date of the crime.'

'I told you before. Theo returned to his old school. I stayed at home and worked on my thesis. William looked for a job.'

Tisdall wrote something on a slip of paper he had taken from his pocket. 'You and Mr Frith and the boy went to Ohio eight months ago but Mr Frith found it difficult to settle?'

She opened her mouth to protest that Tisdall knew all this already but he held up a hand. 'What kind of job was Mr Frith looking for after you returned to Bristol?'

'Anything he could find to tide him over. In the autumn there was a possibility of another research assistant job in –'

'Why not a full lectureship?'

The first time she met Tisdall she had warmed to him. Not that he had been particularly sympathetic, but there was something world-weary about him, something that made her

10

think he had suffered and grown kinder because of it. Now all that had disappeared.

'I get it.' She met his gaze and frowned. 'Better to be a research assistant in a good department than find himself with a full teaching load somewhere less auspicious. And you had to give up your teaching post when you went to America, and since returning to Bristol you've been unable to secure another. So both you and Mr Frith were here in the flat a large part of the time?'

She hesitated, and Tisdall, whose eyes rarely left her own, noticed the slight pause. 'Unless he was out looking for work.'

'But he was here in the evening?'

Her hand moved up to her mouth. 'Sometimes he went to see friends.'

'Leaving you to do the babysitting.'

Anger rose in her, anger that Tisdall had chosen this day of all days to call round, pretending he wanted to keep her up to date on the investigation when in fact he had come to ask more questions. Or repeat the ones he had asked before.

'Why are you so sure this dog man person killed him? Hasn't it occurred to you that someone who knew him…' She broke off, afraid she was going to cry.

'When I asked if he had any enemies you –'

'Not here in Bristol.'

He pressed his lips together. Controlling a smile? 'Oh, you mean the boy's mother. Mr Frith's ex-wife. As I think I mentioned before, Miss Richards has a watertight alibi.' His voice became softer, gentler. 'Just the same, if you think there's something we should look into. As I'm sure you're aware, it has been known in a domestic dispute for a third party –'

'A hired killer?' she said sarcastically. 'I don't need humouring. I just want you to find who killed him.'

3

During her first visit to the college, six days ago, Neville Unwin had explained that the classes for gifted children were held on Saturdays during term time, and three mornings a week in the school holidays. To Kristen's surprise, he had treated the interview as if her temporary post was a foregone conclusion. After all, he had told her, word of mouth was normally far better than a formal reference and if Brigid Howell thought she could do the job then that was good enough for him. In any case, who else would they find at such short notice?

After a few token questions about her teaching experience, and her thesis, followed by murmured condolences about William, he had returned, with obvious relief, to the business of telling her exactly what the job entailed. Tall, grey-haired, with bags under his eyes and a beer gut that hung over his tightly belted grey trousers, his manner had been friendly but detached. The classes, he said, had been running for a little over two years. At first he and Brigid had done most of the teaching then, when Brigid left to have a baby, Sarah Pearson had taken over. Gradually the numbers had increased and now Brigid's baby was four months old she had agreed to return to her old job. Unfortunately, a few days later Sarah had been taken into hospital with peritonitis and would need to convalesce.

The house, in a street off Redland Road, might once have been an imposing family home, but an ugly extension had been added and a fire escape with peeling black paint wound its way down the side of the building next to a small parking area. Kristen manoeuvred her car into a narrow space between an old grey Rover and the privet hedge, switched off the engine, took a deep breath, and reminded herself that, like a member of Alcoholics Anonymous, she had given herself only one aim: to get through one day at a time.

The backpack in the shape of a koala bear that had been hanging on a hook inside the front door on her last visit was still there. She put out a hand to touch the thick brown fur and at the same moment – Neville Unwin must have seen her through the window – a voice called, 'Hello there, come along in.'

When she entered his office, he was making a strenuous effort to finish a phone call, suggesting whoever it was ring back later and pursing his lips as the caller insisted on having the last word.

'Right then.' He replaced the receiver with a bang and smoothed back a lock of thin grey hair. 'Kristen's an unusual name. And Olsen, that must be Scandinavian. It's all Christian names here, staff and kids alike.'

'My grandfather was Norwegian, but he came to live in England when he was a boy.'

'Good, got that straight then.' He opened a drawer and pulled out a sheaf of papers. 'As I mentioned last week, Sarah Pearson's a science graduate, but it won't do the kids any harm to study something different. I'm hoping you'll teach them how to brainstorm rather than seeing the path to true enlightenment in terms of logic and mathematical reasoning.'

'I've prepared some short assignments.' Kristen took a folder from her bag, returning it when Neville waved a hand, indicating there was no need for him to check.

'Just the ticket.' He glanced at a clock on the wall. 'I'll take you to where you'll be working. The gifted kids use a different entrance from the other students, round the side where they can go straight through to their classrooms.'

Brigid Howell had put her head round the door and Neville gestured to her to come in. 'Just telling Kristen about the organisation of the place.' His swivel chair swung from side to side. 'Kids arrive at ten. The parents of the ones who live relatively close by have arranged a carpool. Then there's Shannon Wilkins who comes on the bus.'

Brigid's face had an odd expression, perhaps because she was making an effort to acknowledge how Kristen must be feeling. They had spoken on the phone, but the last time they had actually met had been nearly ten months ago.

Shortly after William became Alex Howell's research assistant, they had been invited to dinner at the Howell's house, and Alex and Brigid had come round to their flat once, before William took the job in Ohio. For a time, Kristen had hoped she and Brigid might become friends, but they had been too busy to see very much of each other and when they did meet up, Brigid had seemed a little reserved.

Since there had been no contact between them for nearly a year, Kristen had been surprised when Brigid phoned to ask if she would like her name put forward as a temporary replacement for Sarah Pearson. *Only if you feel up to it, Kristen. I just thought it might help and with your experience and your research you'd be ideal for the job.* At the time, Kristen had been touched by the warmth in Brigid's voice. Now she was back to her old self, pleasant enough but formal.

'Lovely to see you again.' Brigid gave her a brief hug and sat down, crossing one leg over the other. Last time they met, her hair had been parted in the middle and hung loosely, covering both sides of her face. Now it was swept straight back, in a style that accentuated her jutting cheekbones and pointed chin. She had lost weight, probably the effect of combining a part-time job with looking after a young baby.

Neville was talking about how it was not his policy to administer intelligence tests. 'Most of the gifted children are referred by their schools and if their teachers think they'll benefit from the classes that's good enough for me. The large proportion tend to be middle-class, but we have two or three, one particular girl who –'

'Shannon,' Brigid interrupted, 'Neville's star pupil.'

He turned a frown into a smile. 'Yes, well, I'm not sure I'd pick her out in quite that way. She's exceptional at maths but some of the others are probably just as gifted in other areas.'

The phone started ringing. Neville sighed, lifting the receiver and putting his hand over the mouthpiece. 'Brigid, would you mind? If you could take Kristen to her room.'

Out in the corridor, some of the strain left Brigid's face. 'Neville used to do some of the teaching,' she said, 'but lately he's been given more admin and A level work, so now he provides individual tuition for particular children he thinks might benefit.'

'Shannon, the maths genius.'

Brigid nodded. 'There's something about her that appeals to him. The working class girl who, but for an observant teacher, could have ended up deliberately underachieving. Incidentally, no mobile phones are allowed, apart from Shannon's. She travels on the bus alone so Neville's made an exception.'

They had reached the room at the end of the corridor where Kristen was to do her teaching.

'You'll have about eight or nine.' Brigid tucked her shirt into her denim skirt. 'One group before break and another from a quarter past eleven. I should spend this morning getting to know them. Coffee's at eleven.' She opened a cupboard. 'Paper, paste, felt pens…'

'How's your baby?'

Brigid had her head in the cupboard. 'You must come and meet her. The first six weeks were hell. She slept all day and cried all night. Probably knew she had two geriatric parents who hadn't a clue what they were supposed to be doing.'

Kristen laughed, although the tone of Brigid's voice suggested she had found it hard going. How old *was* she? William had said Alex was in his early forties. Brigid was younger, but not that much, probably thirty-seven or eight.

'How are you?' Brigid put an arm round Kristen's shoulder. 'Are the police any nearer to finding …' She broke off, unable to say 'the murderer'. 'A mugging that went wrong, am I right? Alex and I were so shocked. If there's anything either of us can do.'

The children were starting to come through the side door. Brigid gave Kristen's arm a squeeze. 'I'm so glad you decided to take the job. We'll talk later, right?'

Five girls and four boys came into the room together and sat down quietly, following Kristen with their eyes as she put down her bag and joined them at the circular table.

'Hello, nice to meet you all.' How could such a small group be more intimidating than a class of thirty-plus? 'My name's Kristen. I expect Mr Unwin – Neville – has told you I'll be filling in while Sarah's away.'

She was wondering how much they knew about her, if they had been told she had lived with the man whose smiling face had been on the front of the evening paper, once after the body was found, and again when the police were appealing for information.

'I'm Hugo,' said a dark-haired boy with the kind of face the people who make television ads would have snapped up in an instant, 'and he's called Barnaby.' He nudged the boy on his left.

The rest of them started to tell her their names until a girl with a worried expression and a strong Bristolian accent asked if they would be continuing the work Sarah had started.

'I expect Sarah will complete that particular course when she comes back. In the meantime, Neville has asked me to do something different. We'll be learning how to think.'

She expected them to exchange glances, raise their eyebrows, but no one did.

'I'm Shannon,' said the girl who had asked about the course, and one of the boys whispered something to his neighbour that Kristen failed to catch.

The last child to join the group closed the door behind him. He looked a little like Theo, only a couple of years older and without Theo's slightly protruding ears. Kristen glanced at the clock on the wall. Five past ten. Two hours to get through until she could return to the safety of her flat.

Ros phoned at ten that evening. Theo was tucked up in bed, she said.

'Tell him I've posted his football shirt.'

'Yes of course.' Ros's voice was indistinct. Then the sound

returned loud and clear. 'I just wanted to let you know he's fine, seems to be settling in well.'

'Good.'

'As I said, Kristen, I want you and Theo to see as much of each other as possible. We'll all keep in touch. I do understand.' She sounded like a character in a badly scripted television series.

'Yes. Thank you.' Kristen replaced the receiver and started walking round the room, picking things up and putting them down: the clay rhinoceros Theo had made during his first term at school, the Rastafarian doll William had found in a skip parked down the road, the photograph of the three of them, taken by a friend on Theo's fifth birthday, eight months after she had moved into William's flat in Chiswick.

How could she and William have been so stupid, thinking they led a charmed life? But what difference would it have made? William had been given custody, but Theo was still Ros's son. He had gone back to her because in legal terms Kristen hadn't a leg to stand on.

Wandering into the kitchen, where the curtains were still drawn back, she saw the cat from the first-floor flat with its face pressed to the window. Its mouth was open, yowling to be let in. Kristen ignored it then relented and unlocked the back door, feeling it slide past her legs.

What did it want? Food, milk? It looked far too well fed. Theo had wanted a cat, or a rabbit, or even a gerbil. *Please, Kristen, please. You could tell Dad children are meant to have pets so they learn to look after them.*

Bending down to offer the cat the unappetising remains of her supper, she tried to pick up what Theo was feeling at that precise moment. Like his father, if there was something he wanted badly enough he usually managed to get it. Even now he would be planning a way of making sure he came back to live in Bristol. He was clever. He knew he had to live with Ros for a time so everyone would see how unhappy it was making him.

The cat sniffed the food and decided against it. Now it was asking to be let back into the garden. Kristen opened the door and stared into the darkness, remembering the expression on Theo's face as he waved goodbye from the back seat of the yellow sports car. No tears, no trembling mouth, just a faint smile combined with a look of grim determination.

He had made up his mind and he wanted her to know it. By Christmas he would be back.

4

'Worst case scenario,' Tisdall said, 'victim meets the killer only minutes before the crime so it makes no odds how much forensic's been collected.'

DC Brake nodded his agreement. 'If that's how it happened, if Frith's death *was* the result of a mugging. No defence injuries so maybe he knew his attacker.'

'Or whoever it was came up behind him when he was looking over the bridge. I'd say that's more likely.'

'Why d'you suppose Frith had gone there?'

'A walk. A run?'

'He wasn't wearing the right clothes.'

Tisdall laughed. 'Not everyone dresses up in Lycra to take a bit of exercise.'

'If it was the dog man he's not going to try his pickpocketing trick again. He'll be lying low. Of course, it's likely he's none too bright.'

They were on their way to interview Ros Richards or, in Tisdall's case, to re-interview her. Something about the case made him uneasy. The dog man as prime suspect was too easy, although settling on the most obvious person frequently turned out to be correct.

Brake, who lived on the other side of Bristol, had driven to Tisdall's house in Henbury to pick him up, and the two of them had joined the M5 at Cribbs Causeway. It was fortunate, thought Tisdall, that Julie had already left for work otherwise she would have invited Brake in for a cup of coffee and a chance to show off her new sofa. Brake would have been an easy prey to her charms, just as he would be when he met Ros Richards.

'Been checking the computer like you said.' Brake's crisp, efficient voice interrupted Tisdall's musings. 'Body temperature plus the degree of rigor mortis indicated Frith had been dead for eight to ten hours when the body was found.'

'Spotted by a jogger at six in the morning.'

Brake sighed. 'That's what I'd like to do but Kelly would never stand for it.'

'Find a body that had been there since the previous evening?'

Brake laughed politely. 'Keep fit. Go to a gym. Work out.'

'Ah, well, that's the trouble with getting married. How long is it, a couple of months?'

'Seven weeks, coming up to eight.'

Tisdall nodded. Marriage had a bad effect on some – they started worrying about the hours, about working weekends, getting home late – but in Brake's case it appeared to have given him new confidence. 'And your Kelly didn't mind sentencing herself to a lifetime of late shifts and overtime?'

'Wouldn't mind joining the force herself. Took an interest in the Frith case even before I got involved. Doesn't go for the dog man theory any more than you or I do. Feels really sorry for Ms Olsen.'

'I'm keeping an open mind.' Tisdall had overheard Brake in the canteen talking about his A level in psychology, and he'd gained the impression the DC thought he could see beneath the skin, pick up the hidden agenda. Just the same, he'd be taken in by Ros Richards' polished performance. Not that Ros was a genuine suspect.

'There's the two witnesses,' Brake was saying, 'people who saw someone answering to the dog man's description, close to the scene of crime. And the fact that his wallet had gone. If Forensics had matched up hairs, clothing fibres and –'

'Every contact leaves a trace,' Tisdall murmured, closing his eyes for a couple of seconds although, like most people who are used to doing their own driving, he felt obliged to open them again to make sure they were not in imminent danger of running into the coach in front.

Brake made a clicking sound with his tongue when the boys, sitting in the back row, scratched their armpits in a poor imitation of a colony of apes. Brake had just completed an advance driving course and Tisdall, who had enough on his mind to occupy him all the way to London and back, was happy to let him demonstrate his new proficiency. Proficient, competent, everything about Martin Brake smelled of neatness and order, from his immaculate hair and well-cut suit to the faint whiff of his aftershave. Tisdall wondered what Brake thought of him, what he'd said when Liz Cowie told him the two of them would be working together. *Ray Tisdall? How old is he? Forty-five and happy to remain a sergeant. Hasn't looked too hot lately. What's his problem, d'you suppose, on the booze?*

A drink problem, thought Tisdall, I should be so lucky. He caught a glimpse of himself in the wing mirror that had been incorrectly positioned – or perhaps he had knocked it when he climbed into the passenger seat – and felt reasonably pleased with what he saw. Decent head of hair, gaining more grey by the month but so far losing none of its thickness, whereas some of his contemporaries had already started moving their partings. His gums hurt. He had brushed them until they bled but they still felt hot and swollen. One of these days he would have to make an appointment. His last dentist had gone private, which had given him the perfect excuse for putting off a check-up. Now he was paying for it.

Brake had a good head of hair *and* perfect teeth. He was humming under his breath, which probably meant he was finding the silence embarrassing.

'No particles of skin under the victim's nails,' Tisdall said, 'so it looks like the attack must have been unexpected, no preceding argument.'

'They found an asthma inhaler.' Brake changed to the left lane, to avoid going on to the Midlands, then to the right one, joining the traffic travelling east. 'Is that what first put them onto this dog man?' Mirror, signal, manoeuvre, and he'd joined the M4, pulled into the middle to pass a heavy goods vehicle then returned to the slow lane that was surprisingly free of traffic for a Friday.

'Asthmatics are two a penny,' Tisdall said. 'They found an old collar too but it didn't fit the stray. And a deflated football, part of a radio, and a dozen ice lolly sticks.' He gazed through the passenger window and thought how simple life was when you were Brake's age. If he told him about the God-awful mess his own life was in, the poor bloke would be shocked rigid. Well, maybe not, but it was best not to take the risk, even though he could have done with a sympathetic ear.

His thoughts returned to Ros Richards and the flat in Putney, on the top floor of a purpose-built block with an entrance phone and a foyer with a tankful of depressed-looking fish. Ms Richards had worked hard at giving the impression her life was a hectic social and professional whirl, with long days at the television studios followed by parties frequented by showbiz celebs, together with a smattering of Premier League footballers, rich entrepreneurs, and minor politicians. Tisdall had assumed most of what she told him was wishful thinking – after all, until Frith's body was found neither he nor anyone else at the station had ever heard of her. Still, even if she did live in a world of make-believe, hiring a hitman because her ex had been given custody of her child was a bit over the top, quite apart from the fact that the boy had already been living with his father and Kristen Olsen for the past four and a half years.

A splosh of brown and white bird shit landed on the windscreen and Brake swore under his breath, spraying a liberal amount of washer but with only moderate success. 'Typical,' said Tisdall without meaning anything in particular. He was imagining what it would have been like if he'd made a fight of it and Grace had been faced with losing Serena. Not that he'd have had a hope in hell of the judge coming down on his side.

As far as he could tell William Frith had handed over most of the day-to-day care of his son to Kristen Olsen. Tisdall wondered how Grace would have felt if Serena was being brought up by someone who wasn't even linked by blood. But Kristen seemed to be under the impression Ros had been happy to leave the boy with his father since that left her free to pursue her career as an actress. How much did Kristen really know about her? Only what Frith had told her. Even if, and in his opinion today's trip was pretty much a waste of time, even if it was remotely possible Ros Richards had been involved in Frith's death, would that mean the boy would be returned to Kristen as of right? There could be other relatives, a grandparent or aunt.

'Inspector Cowie still seems stuck in the same way of thinking.' Brake smoothed his immaculate hair.

'She does.' Tisdall was watching a hot air balloon. It looked in danger of coming down on the motorway, but drifting over a hill they always looked lower than they actually were.

'You've a family, haven't you?' asked Brake. 'Kelly and I are hoping to have kids, but not for a year or two.'

'One daughter,' said Tisdall, 'from my first marriage.'

'Right.' Brake glanced at him, afraid he might have touched a raw nerve.

'I see her once a week,' Tisdall explained, letting him off the hook, 'more often in the school holidays although she's in a volleyball team and plays seven-a-side football so she's out a fair bit. Anyway, she'll be thirteen next month, won't want to spend time trailing round Bristol with her dad.'

'Oh I don't know,' Brake said tactfully, 'girls are usually close to their fathers.' Then, checking his watch against the digital clock, said, 'Should reach the M25 by half past. Not due at Ros Richards' until three and Putney's only a stone's throw from the Hammersmith flyover.'

'Time for a fry-up,' Tisdall said. 'Stop at the next services, or are you and Kelly health food freaks?'

When they reached Ros Richards' flat, Tisdall had to admit he had misjudged Martin Brake. Far from being impressed by her designer clothes and the flashy way her flat had been furnished, Brake looked as if he had taken an instant dislike to the woman. He kept fidgeting with the knot in his tie and glancing at the window, then at Tisdall.

'Hot in here,' he said, speaking too loud for fear he sounded tongue-tied, intimidated. 'Would you mind if I opened a window?'

'Go ahead.' Ros gave Brake the kind of smile people usually reserve for a young child. 'The bottom ones are sealed but if you manage to open one at the top you'll be my hero for life.'

Tisdall stood up to study a large photograph of Theo. The boy was spending the afternoon with a friend, something that made talking to Ros considerably easier although Tisdall would have been glad of a few words with Theo, mainly so he could report back to Kristen Olsen that he was all in one piece. Is that what she would want to hear? In her position he would have had mixed feelings.

'So,' he said, cutting short Brake's inquiry about the workings of the window catch, 'the last time you saw your ex-husband was a little over a year ago when he brought your son to spend a long weekend with you here in Putney.'

'That's right,' Ros drawled, 'but I told you all that the last time and I do wish you wouldn't keep calling him my ex. William and I were on perfectly amicable terms. After he died, I've no idea why, but I suppose a psychologist could explain it, I started thinking about the good times we'd had, the first year after we got married, and before that. The friend's house where we met, how long ago was it? Did I ask you before, what was it that actually killed him?'

'A head injury that led to a brain haemorrhage.'

'Before or after he fell?'

'There was an imprint of half a brick on his left temple, but it was probably the stone he hit when he fell from the bridge that proved fatal.'

'I see,' she said slowly and he got the impression this was no play-acting, that getting the facts right was important to her. It was for most people, the people closest to the victim.

'And I suppose you did the usual house to house inquiries,' she continued, 'tell me, did you fix on this mugging theory right away or did it occur to you it could have been a crime of passion, or even the result a gay man approaching William and

26

reacting badly when he was rebuffed?'

Brake was giving her his whole attention. 'Any particular reason for thinking it could be a crime of passion,' he asked, giving up on the window catch and joining Tisdall on the over soft sofa.

Ros shrugged. 'What else did you want to ask me? All the same questions as before I imagine, in the hope that I'll contradict myself and that will look highly suspicious and we'll have to go through the whole rigmarole all over again. Well, I'm not in any rush.'

'Correct me if I'm wrong,' Tisdall said, 'but Richards isn't your maiden name, just the one you adopted while you were at drama school.'

Ros laughed, running her fingers down the arms of her leather chair. 'Did I tell you or did someone look it up in the records? Higgs didn't sound quite right somehow, although I've sometimes wondered if it might have been better to stick with it. "Ros Higgs" has a certain earthy bluntness about it, what do you think?'

Tisdall made no comment. The way she played at 'being an actress' was tiresome but also rather pathetic. She was 'resting' – must be or she would have told them how desperately busy she was, how she could only spare half an hour because of having to work on her script.

'We checked what you were doing the day Mr Frith was killed,' he said. 'No problem there, all the names you gave us backed up your account.'

'What a relief,' she said without a trace of sarcasm. 'That must have saved you a lot of bother. Presumably there's been no sight nor sound of this dog man person or you wouldn't be here now. Are you sure he exists?'

'Your ex-husband,' Brake said, 'I wonder if you can tell us what he was like, Ms Richards. Sergeant Tisdall probably knows already but I'd be grateful if –'

'My pleasure, Constable. Let me think. He was charming, those sorts of people always are, and good-looking although he never took much trouble with his appearance. Expensive shoes but didn't bother to keep them clean. Could be a little moody but that sometimes adds spice to a relationship, provided you don't allow yourself to be thrown off balance. And of course he was a genius.'

Once again there was no sarcasm in her voice. Brake removed two cushions from behind his back and placed them on the floor. 'When you say "moody" do you mean he had a temper?'

'Not particularly.' Ros looked amused. 'What I meant was, he tended to be unpredictable. Life and soul of the party on most occasions but if someone did something he didn't like he could go into quite a sulk, sometimes for several days.'

Tisdall had been afraid Brake was going to make a fool of himself, but he was persuading Ros to give them a picture of William Frith that was considerably at odds with the one Kristen Olsen had provided, and also the one Ros had supplied during his first visit to Putney. Of course, it was possible Frith had behaved differently when he lived with Kristen. People did change, although in Tisdall's opinion the change was usually superficial. When they returned to Bristol he would make more effort to look into Frith's life before he left for America. From what Kristen had told them, most of his time was taken up either working at the university or helping to look after Theo, but the man Ros had just described sounded the type who would have valued his freedom, enjoyed a night out with the boys.

It would mean another visit to the basement flat in Bishopston, more upsetting questions which might or might not be answered honestly. Kristen Olsen was as keen as he was to find out who had killed her lover and deprived her of her 'son', but only if it came out the way she wanted it to, if Frith's image remained intact.

'Right then,' Ros said, 'have I told you all you need to know? You're aware, I expect, that William saw himself as a bit of a philanthropist. No, that's the wrong word, an altruist. Good works, helping the poor and needy. When he lived in London he enjoyed mixing with the down and outs, hearing their life stories, offering practical advice. I imagine there's plenty of opportunity for that kind of thing in Bristol. If you ask me they ought to round them all up and enrol them in the army.'

'We know Mr Frith worked two evenings a week at a hostel for the homeless,' Tisdall said.

Ros gave him a beaming smile. 'There you are then. You know, there's a kind of person who's fascinated by dirt and squalor. A friend of mine, one of those analyst people, says it means they're fixed at Freud's anal stage of development. Clever people are like that. I suppose it was his intellect that attracted Kristen to him. She's an expert on "the gifted child"; that's rather a good description of William, actually.'

5

'I'm going to give you two objects to think about.' Kristen handed out sheets of paper. 'A paper clip and a blanket. Make two headings and try to think of six ways each object could be used, apart from the more normal one.'

'I don't get it,' Barnaby said.

'Yes you do.' Hugo put his hands round Barnaby's neck and pretended to throttle him, 'like you could use a paper clip to scrape dog shit off the bottom of your trainers.'

The girl called Becky giggled. 'My Dad fetched a blanket when the barbecue fell over. Mum nearly murdered him. It was her best rug.'

'I've heard of this before,' murmured Shannon, 'Only it was six ways to use a brick.' She glanced at Kristen, taking a small bottle from her pocket and squeezing a drop into each of her eyes. The rest of them gave her a wary look and set to work writing the headings on their paper.

Six uses for a brick. Right up to when they pulled back the sheet Kristen had hoped. William had promised to be back before Theo's bedtime but it was not until well past midnight that she had contacted the police. *Could he be with a friend, madam, or a relative? Have you contacted the local hospitals?*

Bruising on the left temple, a deep gash on his forehead but the rest of his face was unmarked. His thick, straw-coloured hair had been brushed to one side, making him look different, younger. *He could have been asleep. He looked so peaceful.* But it wasn't true. He looked terrible. She heard the policewoman ask if it was him and felt herself nodding jerkily, as if she had a stiff neck, then a hand took hold of her arm and guided her out of the cold. 'We'll drive you home, Miss Olsen, or would you prefer it if we dropped you off with the people who are looking after your son?' *He's not my son*, she had started to say, then stopped as her eyes and the policewoman's met and she took in the woman's concerned, sympathetic face …

Every so often, Kristen checked to see how the children were getting on and each time the frown marks between Shannon's eyes deepened. On the third occasion, Kristen asked if something was wrong but the girl shook her head, returning to her work. She was wearing a white cotton sweater and a red skirt – the others were dressed in jeans or shorts – and she had badly bitten nails. She worked hard, but now and again Kristen had caught her staring into space with a puzzled, anxious expression. Was something bothering her, something to do with the classes? She seemed older than the rest but perhaps it was the rows of studs in her ears, or her slightly patronising attitude, particularly towards the boys. Apart from Hugo, they gave the impression of being a little afraid of her.

The door to the classroom burst open and Neville strode towards her, taking an envelope from an inside pocket. 'Arrived on the morning post.' He paused for a moment, studying the envelope. 'Addressed to Mrs Frith.'

'Frith?' The room felt hot, airless.

'I'm sorry.' Neville's discomfort was obvious. 'I thought it had been delivered to the wrong place. I hadn't realised you sometimes used William's name.'

'I don't.'

He hesitated then handed her the letter. 'Anyway I thought you'd better check.'

It was addressed in capitals to MRS FRITH, THE COLLEGE. Then the name of the road but no postcode. 'Thank you. If it's not for me …' But Neville was already halfway through the door.

The letter was written on one side of a sheet of plain white paper, and was unsigned. *The police have got it all wrong*, she read. *It wasn't the dog man killed your husband. I can promise that.* 'Promise' had been written with two m's, then crossed out and written again correctly, and the writing was spidery, as though it had been done with the wrong hand. So the dog man – if he was the one who had written it – thought she and William had been married. She would have to talk to Neville and he would dislike the fact that the person who had written the note knew where she worked. Questions would follow, an offer of help, but underlying the offer would be irritation that the letter could herald the start of problems that might affect the reputation of the college. By the end of the morning Kristen was so exhausted she had to turn down Brigid Howell's offer of lunch.

'I'd love to, Brigid, but I'm feeling rather…'

'Yes, of course. Another time. I wasn't going to say anything, Kristen, for fear of upsetting you, but that's stupid, how could anything I said make you feel worse? Have the police been round again? Have they told you any more?'

'Not really.' Kristen stifled a yawn. She was grateful, hoped they would get to know each other better, but she longed to be on her own, in the car, cocooned against the world. So far she had managed to restrict her intake of alcohol to two or three glasses of wine each evening. How long would it last?

Brigid left and, knowing she would have to talk to Neville, Kristen stood in the corridor, working out what to say. As she was about to knock on his door, Shannon appeared, breathing hard, and asked if Kristen had a book she could borrow.

'Yes, of course. Actually, you might like this one.' She searched in her bag, found a book of lateral thinking puzzles and handed it to the girl who held it against her chest.

'Miss?'

'Do call me Kristen.'

'Sorry.' Shannon hesitated. 'Only I … like, I was wondering … is Sarah any better? I don't mean …' Her face was contorted with anxiety. 'What we're doing is good. Bye then.'

When Kristen tapped on Neville's door it opened immediately, almost as if he had been watching her through the keyhole. 'Problem?' He was holding an apple, eaten down to the core.

'I just wanted to explain about the letter.' She had decided to tell him the truth. After all it was hardly her fault if whoever sent it had found out where she worked. 'It's anonymous, says the dog man didn't kill William. A crank, I expect.'

'Let the cops deal with it.' Neville tossed the apple core into his waste paper basket. 'My wife's idea. Light lunch to help me lose weight.' He smiled, then his face became serious. 'My only concern was that it might not be for you, or it might be …' He broke off, hitching up his trousers. 'Any problems you know where I am. Incidentally,' his voice had the over-casual tone of someone who has been planning to say something but wants it to appear as if the idea has only just occurred to him, 'I was telling my wife about your thesis and she wondered if you'd like to have a chat.'

'With your wife?'

'Vi Pitt – you may have heard of her. She had an exhibition not long ago, that gallery near the floating harbour. Didn't take up painting and drawing till she was in her forties, joined a class just for fun and discovered … I was going to say she discovered she had a talent she'd never known about, but Vi doesn't believe in innate ability, thinks it's all a question of hard work. Anyway, we're not too far from where you live, top of the hill going down to Westbury. If you're interested she'd love to meet you.'

He started writing his address and phone number on a pad then looked up a little uneasily. 'Vi's agent, the man who sells her stuff to a London gallery … Cameron Lyle, you may have come across him.'

'Lyle? I don't think so…'

'No? The reason I mention it … he knew William. That's why I thought you might be familiar with Vi's work. Perhaps they were just acquaintances.' He tore a page off his pad. 'Vi would be delighted to see you. Tomorrow afternoon would be a good time unless you're tied up with something.'

'Perhaps you should check...'

'No need. I'll be having a round of golf. She'll welcome the company.'

'If you're sure.' Kristen tried to sound more enthusiastic than she felt. Still, it would pass the afternoon. She hated Saturdays, they brought back too many memories. And Vi's agent had known William...

Tisdall called round first thing. The previous afternoon, Kristen had been to the police station and shown the letter to a Detective Constable Brake who had assured her she had done the right thing, getting in touch, although it was likely it would turn out to be the work of a nutter. Now, standing with his back to the window so it was impossible to see his face, Tisdall repeated DC Brake's observation.

'Both the note and the envelope have gone for fingerprinting.' He began walking round the room. 'Using his own handwriting, rather than cutting letters out of a newspaper, suggests the sender was not concerned about covering his tracks. You'd be surprised how much rubbish we get. Some people will stop at nothing to get themselves involved in a criminal investigation, making up evidence, providing false sightings. Fortunately most of them are well known to us, but there's always the odd newcomer to join the ranks.'

'You don't think it was the dog man?'

He ignored her question, picking up a photograph of Theo and replacing it exactly where it had stood. 'The letter was posted in Bristol, reasonable quality paper, available in most stationers, newsagents, and the like. How many people know where you're working?'

'I've no idea. Hardly anyone. The fact that it was sent to the college doesn't mean you'll have to go there, does it?'

His face showed nothing. 'How many kids attend these classes?'

'About twenty altogether, but there are adults at the college too, being coached for A levels.'

He thought about this for a moment, as if she had told him something important. 'Sooner or later someone will pass on a conversation they've overheard. Once we've identified the man, we'll either be able to charge him or eliminate him.'

Kristen raised her eyebrows. 'I'd have thought if anyone was going to pass on information they would have done it by now. Why wait all this time? What would be the point? Your colleague said it was a dog that first drew attention to William's body.'

Tisdall had resumed his journey round the room. Now he stopped in his tracks. 'DC Brake told you that?'

'What kind of dog was it?'

'Black mongrel.'

'Did you find out who it belonged to?'

He shook his head. 'It went to one of those rescue places. Only young, probably let loose by someone who was going on holiday and couldn't be bothered to put it in kennels.'

'Then what happened?'

'Sorry? Given a home by an elderly lady, I believe. Now, the envelope the letter came in was addressed to Mrs Frith so whoever sent it thought you and Mr Frith were married.'

'I worked out that much.' With an unpleasant sensation in her stomach, it occurred to her that Tisdall thought she could have written the letter herself. Any minute now and he would start asking about her state of mind, whether the doctor had given her something to help her sleep. 'If it turns out it was the dog man,' she said slowly, 'will he be charged with murder or could it be only manslaughter?'

'To secure a conviction for murder, it's necessary to prove intention – either to kill or inflict bodily harm that proves fatal.'

Manslaughter. She pictured the word in her mind's eye. Manslaughter. Man's laughter. 'But you'll never know exactly what happened.'

He flashed a brief encouraging smile. 'Don't worry, we will. Incidentally, when Mr Frith and his wife split up, was it by mutual agreement?'

'No, it was Ros's idea.'

'That's what he told you?'

'She walked out, leaving Theo with his father, and moved in with another man.'

'But it didn't last.' Tisdall looked at his watch. 'When William was given custody she must have taken it pretty hard.'

Kristen shrugged. 'She's an actress, she needs to be free to go wherever the work is.'

He gave an unconvinced nod. 'I saw her on TV not long ago, series set in a timeshare holiday home, shown on another channel the first time round.' He had his hand on the door. 'None of my business, I know, but are you up to doing this teaching? So soon, I mean?'

'What do you suggest?' she said angrily, 'I need the money.'

He held up his hands in mock defence. 'I was only thinking the job sounded quite a taxing one. Anyway, DC Brake's got the address of the college and if I need to talk to anyone I'll keep it as discreet as possible, you needn't worry on that score.'

Kristen followed him to the bottom of the steps leading up to the street. 'Why did you want to know how William and Ros's marriage ended?'

'No particular reason.' His hand tested one of the points on the top of the iron railings. 'I'll be in touch again shortly and it goes without saying, if you receive any more anonymous communications you'll pass them on to us straight away.'

Mrs Letts from the ground floor flat had come out, pretending she needed to water her window box. Tisdall squeezed past her, gave Kristen one last questioning look, and climbed into his car.

'Any news?' Mrs Letts lowered her voice to a breathy whisper. 'You can always tell when it's a policeman.'

'They're working on various lines of inquiry.'

'Really?' The old woman's deeply lined face lit up then, sensing she was not going to be told any more. 'How's poor little Theo?' She put her head on one side and adopted a sorrowful expression. 'Must be missing Matthew, his friend from school. Thick as thieves, those two. Such a shame.'

The letter, Kristen was thinking. The dog man. The inquiry about the break-up of William and Ros's marriage. She felt sick, shaky, and desperately needed someone to talk to, a close friend, a soul mate. *William*. But had she been William's soul mate?

6

Neville and Vi's house turned out to be an ugly bungalow, hidden behind a tall privet hedge. A short strip of concrete, leading to a detached garage, meant there was room to pull off the road and park, although if Neville came back before she left her car would block his way. While she was debating what to do, a voice called out something she failed to catch and a large, grey-haired woman appeared from round the back of the bungalow, clutching a black polythene bag in one hand and a garden trowel in the other.

'You must be Kristen. Leave the car wherever you like. Nev won't be back for ages.'

Vi was wearing a green skirt that barely covered her large knees, and a grey cardigan with sagging pockets. 'I hope he didn't twist your arm. For some odd reason he thinks I must be lonely here on my own.' Then, seeing Kristen's face, 'I'm sorry, that came out all wrong. No, of course you're not interrupting my work. You go ahead while I get rid of this.' She swung the bag. 'Neighbour's cat managed to relieve itself in three different places. My studio's the room built on, old outhouse converted by Nev, bet you never guessed he'd be the handy type.'

The back of the bungalow was more attractive than the front and the garden was a mass of flowers with a single tree that threw a shadow across part of the lawn. Seeing it reminded

Kristen how Brigid Howell had once had her own landscape gardening business, and it had done quite well until some of her customers failed to pay up and she had a cash flow problem.

Vi's studio door was open wide. Kristen stepped inside, expecting to see a jumble of jars, boxes, drawing books, and rags, and was surprised to find it looked more like a study belonging to an obsessively tidy academic. A finished painting of a suburban garden had been propped on a shelf alongside several smaller pictures, mostly of dolls and other toys. One wall had fitted cupboards and a sink unit, then a space where more paintings had been stacked on the floor. The two windows were small but it was clear Vi preferred artificial light. On the only easel stood a painting, done in bright acrylics, of a tabby cat with round, green eyes and a red collar.

Vi appeared in the doorway, took a packet of cigarettes from a pocket in her skirt, and lit up, taking two long drags and screwing up her eyes against the smoke. She was solidly built, with the round shoulders of someone used to working in a hunched-up position.

'What d'you think? Small but beautiful – the room, not that thing.' She jerked her head towards the cat painting and pulled up a basket chair. Her feet slopped in and out of fluffy slippers that had once been pink but were now a dusty grey. Balancing her cigarette on the edge of a table, she gestured to Kristen to sit down and laid a large, blue veined hand on her wrist. 'Now, what would you like to eat?'

'Oh.' Kristen had forgotten about lunch. 'Actually, I'm not very hungry.'

'Me neither. Wait a bit, shall we?' Vi hoisted herself up onto a stool. 'Before we talk about anything else, I wanted to say how desperately sorry … If there was anything I could do but of course there isn't. Life's so unfair, so …' She searched for the right word then gave up and pointed at the cat painting. 'I can't get the eyes right. I detest sentimentality. On the other hand, people who think a love of animals is sentimental have lost touch with their own humanity.'

Kristen stood up to get a better view. 'What's wrong with the eyes?'

'The way they're positioned makes the face look too flat. After all it's not one of those ridiculous Persians bred to look like a human baby covered in fur.'

There was something fresh and original about the picture. Vi had achieved the level of realism, the attention to detail, that the gallery obviously demanded but had still managed to keep an almost childlike quality. No wonder this Cameron Lyle person that Neville had mentioned was happy to act as her agent. She had only been painting seriously for a couple of years but Lyle must have realised he was on to a good thing. 'Show you some more later on,' Vi said, 'now tell me how you're getting on with the gifted ones.'

'You make them sound like Midwich Cuckoos.'

'Before we go any further, you did want to come here, it wasn't some awful ordeal, something you felt you had to do to keep Nev happy?'

'Of course not.' Kristen wondered if Neville had told her about the letter addressed to Mrs Frith. 'He mentioned the thesis I'm working on?'

'But I imagine taking a job needed every ounce of courage you possess. Enough of that, you're trying to work out how someone like me comes to be living with a chap like Nev.'

Kristen started to protest but Vi stopped her. 'Everyone always does. He's got a degree in Maths – *Pure* Maths they call it for some reason – and I left school without a qualification to my name. We met when his sister was alive. I used to visit her, take her out in the car, poor love.' She noticed Kristen's expression and broke off. 'Brigid Howell hasn't told you. Jane was an invalid, born with a syndrome, not Down's. Devoted to her, Nev was, wouldn't dream of having her put in a home even though it was hard with his job. She had her good days but sometimes ...' She stared through the window, scratching the back of her neck. 'I've a daughter, Jen, had her when I was still at school, or would have been except the headteacher found out when I was five months gone and threw me out. What a pillock, me, I mean, and to make matters worse I married the father.' She was talking very fast. 'The little boy – Theo – how is he? He must be missing you, poor lamb.'

'He'll be coming for the weekend quite soon.'

'Good.' Vi caught Kristen's eye and looked away, sorting through the pile of unframed paintings. 'I was going to say children are resilient, adaptable, but it's not true.'

She gave Kristen a sympathetic smile. 'And you loved him. William. Loved each other. And the little lad of course.'

'Being with William was always so … Difficult, sometimes, but never boring. He liked to do things on the spur of the moment, go to Pembrokeshire for the day or …' Kristen gave an involuntary gulp. 'I *think* he loved me.'

'I'm sure he did.' Vi gave her a brief hug. 'I'm so glad we've met. Tragedy freezes you, puts you in state of shock. You're keeping a tight grip on yourself and if I were you I'd be exactly the same. People expect floods of tears, but it's not like that, is it?'

'Thank you.'

Finding the picture she wanted, Vi balanced it next to the one of a garden and moved back a few paces, twisting her head to take in Kristen's reaction. It was a portrait of a girl of about nine or ten, holding a pet rabbit with its ears laid flat against its back, and as with the painting of the cat, extreme care had been taken with the whiskers and the soft pink nose.

'Never completed it,' Vi said, 'not a good enough likeness.'

'One of your grandchildren?' Kristen asked.

Vi shook her head. 'Jen's two are both boys. Child of a neighbour … the family moved away … it was all rather unfortunate. Still, it was my first attempt at a portrait apart from a really shocking one of Brian.'

What was unfortunate? And who was Brian?

Vi stubbed out her cigarette in a saucer of pencil sharpenings and tipped the lot into a metal bin. 'Nev mentioned Brian, I expect, he runs a class at the adult education centre, taught me everything I know, believes painting's like anything else, you have to start from scratch, learn the basics. Drudgery it was at first, mixing shades of grey, learning about tones and the effect of one colour on another.'

She picked up a stiff sheet of paper and started fanning her face. 'Women's bodies, eh? What a money-spinner for the pharmaceutical companies, but they won't get a penny out of me.'

Kristen laughed – the afternoon was turning out better than she expected – then she noticed Vi's face.

'You're here because of Cameron.'

'No, I wanted to meet you –' Kristen began, but Vi interrupted her.

'Spends half his time buying and selling old toys and the rest persuading galleries to take paintings by people like me who haven't a clue how to go about selling their stuff.'

'You must have worked very hard,' Kristen said.

'Oh, I did that all right.' Vi bent to search through a pile of drawing books on the floor. 'You have to find one thing that really matters to you. Not one person. How could a single individual give you everything you need? I've no illusions my paintings are going to change the course of art history, but I'm clear in my mind what I'm aiming for and the beauty of it is I'll never achieve that aim so I can carry on till I drop.' She held up a painting of a Yorkshire terrier. 'Woman down the road let him sit for me. Trouble is they're all fur, no bones to speak of.'

Kristen took a deep breath. 'Neville said Cameron knew William.'

Vi had her back turned. 'I believe they met a few months before you went to America.'

'William did voluntary work at a hostel for the homeless in Fishponds.'

'Did he?' Vi sat down heavily and found another cigarette. 'Wouldn't have been where they met, not Cameron's style, not unless there's a side of him he's kept well hidden. Next time I see him I'll tell him I've met you but if you wanted to speak to him yourself, he's got a stall in that antique market down near the river, open all day Tuesday.'

'He lives in Bristol?'

'Kingsdown.' Vi gave her a slightly anxious look. 'I've never been there but I believe it's a one-room flat, quite high up, a kind of artist's garret.'

'He paints too?'

'Heavens no, nothing artistic about Cameron.'

'I thought you didn't believe in natural talent.'

Vi pulled a face. 'I don't, it's just the thought of Cameron painting. Footloose and fancy-free, that's how he likes it, always on the move, no plans, no commitments, but for all his casual air when it comes to business matters he's as tough as old boots.'

She sighed. 'As usual, I've been talking far too much. I'm going to make us a snack and you can tell me all about yourself, or if that doesn't appeal …' She paused halfway through the door that led into the rest of the bungalow. 'If you do decide to contact Cameron … only he can be a little … No, what am I saying? Make up your own mind. Only I wouldn't want you to pin your hopes…'

'That he'll tell me who murdered William? How could he possibly know that?

7

Back home, Kristen made herself a sandwich and sat, watching the news, while thinking about her conversation with Vi. She had stayed at the bungalow longer than she intended then noticed the time and left quickly in case Neville came back. For reasons she couldn't explain to herself she wanted to keep the two of them separate. Neville at the college. Vi in her studio. She liked Vi, there was something warm and comforting about her, although as soon as Cameron Lyle was mentioned Kristen had sensed Vi starting to choose her words with care, and her tone of voice had become deliberately casual. Had Lyle told her something about William, something she thought Kristen might not want to hear? If she contacted him herself would she come to regret it? *I wouldn't want you to pin your hopes* ... Why had Vi assumed she would be setting such store on meeting the man?

When she pressed her to explain what she meant, Vi had changed the subject, suggesting again that she made them something to eat. Anything Vi and Neville knew about William, they would have to have learned from Brigid – or from Lyle. If Vi knew something, why not tell her there and then? Why suggest she visit the antique market, then issue a veiled warning? What was it about this Cameron Lyle? And why had William never mentioned him?

It was not until she was on her way home that Kristen

realised she had forgotten to ask Vi if she would be willing to be interviewed properly about her views on artistic talent, childhood influences, and learning to paint relatively late in life.

The newsreader was talking about a bomb going off. Somewhere in the Far East. Kristen hadn't been listening properly. Someone out in the street was whistling a snatch of a hymn – 'For those in peril on the sea' – and suddenly, the flat that had seemed so safe, so familiar, felt alien, even menacing.

Standing looking up at the pavement, she allowed her thoughts to drift back to her first meeting with William, soon after she came down from university. She had been out of work, considering the possibility of registering for a higher degree but not sure if she would be able to obtain any funding. The academic she had been consulting had taken her for lunch and William, who had once worked as a research assistant in a different department, was in the same pub, meeting a friend. Who had been looking after Theo? Ros? A childminder? It was stupid to pretend she had been attracted to William immediately but when they left the pub he had accompanied her to the underground, saying he was on his way home. It was a lie, something he admitted while she was buying her ticket, and they had arranged to meet in two days' time, provided he could find a babysitter. He was divorced, he said, but had custody of his four-year-old son, neither of which statements turned out to be strictly accurate although both had come true by the end of the following year.

During the next few months she had got to know Theo, as well as William, spent an increasing number of nights at the flat in Chiswick, and finally moved in at the beginning of December. What was it that had made her fall in love with him so quickly? He was clever, funny, sexy, but the best thing of all, he was sweet with Theo, gentle, patient, loving … Within two years, the court had given him custody and the three of them had moved to Bristol.

The bare facts, but just now that was all she could manage. Night after night since it happened, she had tried to work out what he had been doing by the river that evening. Where was the man he was supposed to be meeting? Who *was* the man?

She should have asked him before he left the flat. Why hadn't she asked? But it was not the first person he had arranged to meet in the hope of finding a job. *Contacts, Kristen, it's all about making contacts.* It was Tisdall who had put doubts in her mind, dropping round to keep her up to date on developments, although there never were any. Had William been doing something dangerous, something he didn't want her to know about? What was the last thing he said to her?

Following his father's death, Theo had kept a tight grip on himself, been over solicitous towards her, then watched babyish programmes on television, asked for junk food, and left most of it. Moving towards his bedroom she forced herself to face the feeling she had been pushing away for weeks. She had loved William more than anything in the world, still did, but another part of her hated him – hated him for being so careless, so irresponsible, hated him for dying.

The postman was late and when the letters finally dropped onto the mat, Kristen only had two. The first was a bill, tossed aside to open later. The second was from Theo, written on expensive paper, and with the help of a drawing of an iguana he had managed to fill both sides.

Dear Kristen, I hope you are well. We went to the Natural History Museum and I saw a dinosaur's bones only they were not all real ones because some of them were missing. It was very interesting. After we had tea with cakes and ice cream. Mum says I can come and see you quite soon if you are not too busy. Love from Theo.

It was the first time Theo had referred to Ros as 'Mum' and seeing it was like a punch in the stomach, a betrayal, until it struck her – how could she be so stupid – that since there were no spelling mistakes, the letter had been dictated by Ros, word for word. Theo's spelling was fairly good but he would never have written in such a formal style. Kristen imagined him asking Ros for an envelope and a stamp and having the letter snatched out of his hand. *It's a bit messy-looking, darling, I'm sure we can do better than that for Kristen.* The final transcript was perfect apart from two attempts to write "natural" that had been crossed out and turned into round black spots. Presumably

Ros had grown tired of making him copy it out yet again. The paper smelled of Calvin Klein's Obsession. What would Theo be doing at this precise moment? Meeting Ros's theatrical friends or alone with a childminder? Kristen imagined him refusing to eat properly, losing weight. In September when he started at his new school his progress would suffer, and he would fall behind, and an educational psychologist would be in brought in. Every time she allowed herself to hope, something happened to take it away. This time is was the Natural History Museum. If Theo had been there with Ros he was unlikely to be getting on too badly. Except, at this stage, it would feel like previous times when he had spent a long weekend with his mother.

Anger against Ros merged with the anger she now allowed herself to feel against William. She had been unable to give the police any idea as to who the man he was meeting could have been. Did Tisdall think she was covering up for him? No, it was William they suspected of lying.

When they first moved to Bristol, William had met up with a group of rock climbers and spent two weekends scaling Clifton Gorge. The third time, trying a more difficult ascent, he had fallen, breaking his ankle and injuring his back and, to make matters worse, been annoyed by her anxiety. Think about Theo, she had said, afraid he would stop loving her if he thought she was trying to control him. Was that what Ros had done? No, it had been Ros who decided to end the marriage. But was even that true? She could ask Ros, but she never would.

During the evening, Ros phoned to ask how she was and if she had received Theo's letter.

'It came today. Thank you.'

'Would you like to speak to him?'

'Yes, please.'

'I think I mentioned how that Tisdall came to see me again, plus a younger one, bit of a smart arse but quite nice-looking.'

'What did they want?'

Ros cleared her throat noisily. 'Tell me I'm imagining it, but just before they left the young chap said something that gave me the feeling he actually thought *I* might have something to do with it.'

'You?' Kristen sounded convincingly astonished.

'I know, isn't it ridiculous. Listen, Kristen, I'm not sure how to put this, but I'll say it anyway and you must take it as you will. I wanted to thank you for everything you did for Theo. He's a lovely boy, so well-mannered, no trouble at all.'

'I'm glad.' What else could she say? *So well-mannered, no trouble at all.* Didn't the stupid bitch realise that meant he was miserable, was in a bad way?

'Anyway,' Ros breathed, 'I'll be in touch again soon. Bye for now, take care.'

She had forgotten to put Theo on the line. Or perhaps she had looked at him and he had frowned, meaning he didn't want to talk. It was too hard for him, adjusting to his mother while still keeping in touch with her. No, surely that couldn't be right. He was in another room and Ros had forgotten to call him. Kristen would never know. In her mind, she would go over and over, speculating uselessly. Her and Ros, and Theo caught in the middle. How could the law be so cruel? Should she have contested it? Is that what Ros would have preferred? But what about Theo? How could a boy his age be expected to choose between his two "mothers"?

The entrance to the hostel for the homeless was down some steps. Tisdall paused for a moment, deciding on the exact nature of his inquiries. So far almost everything they knew about William Frith was concerned with the period of time between his return from America and his murder. Kristen Olsen had given a rough description of the family's way of life before they left, how Frith had worked at the university, she had taught at a comprehensive, and on the days when she was late collecting Theo he had stayed behind at an after-school club where he could wait for her until five o'clock.

Forensic had found a couple of glove prints, small ones, on the anonymous note sent to Kristen. Brake thought they must be a woman's prints but Tisdall thought he was clutching at straws. The gloves had been made of wool.

As far as Tisdall could tell, Kristen had been besotted with Frith. He was brilliant, good company, a wonderful father, and no doubt highly satisfactory in bed. Ros Richards had provided a slightly different picture.

'Detective Sergeant Tisdall.' He held out his card to a pasty-faced woman, standing at the top of the steps that led down to the hostel. 'If I could have a word with Daniel Joseph.'

The woman said nothing, expecting Tisdall to follow, and walked towards an open door on the right of a dimly lit corridor.

'Someone to see you.' She stood back for Tisdall to pass. 'Looks like the Old Bill.'

The name Daniel Joseph conjured up a picture of a larger than life Old Testament character, complete with bushy beard, but the man sitting on the desk, swinging his legs, was small, almost gnome-like, with a soft pink face and sandy hair.

'Hi.' He jumped down and held out his hand. 'How can I help?'

'I'm making inquiries about William Frith,' Tisdall said, 'I believe he worked here about a year ago.'

'That's right. Someone came round before when I was away.'

Tisdall referred to his notes. 'A man called Simon Greenfield was in charge. Is he here this evening?'

Joseph shook his head. 'Gone back to Christchurch. Christchurch, New Zealand, that is. He was over here for six months, has a job back home organising voluntary work. When I went on holiday he agreed to stand in for a couple of weeks.'

'So he didn't know Frith.'

'None of us had seen William since he returned from the States. In fact, until I read about what had happened I thought he was still in Ohio. As you can imagine we were pretty cut up.'

Tisdall had not been offered a seat but he sat down anyway. 'So this Greenfield must have had to ask someone else who works here to confirm what we needed to know.'

Joseph frowned. 'What would that have been?'

'Which evenings Frith worked here, and for how long.'

'It should be on file. Not computerized, I'm afraid.' Joseph

50

pulled out a drawer in his filing cabinet, took out a battered folder, and started shuffling through a sheaf of papers. 'Here we are.' He ran his finger across the page. 'Except it was never amended. William used to come on Tuesdays and Fridays but in May of last year he cut it down to just Tuesday, said he needed to spend more time with his family.'

'But it's possible your stand-in told my colleague he'd been doing two nights a week up to when he left for America.'

There was a smell of dry rot. The office window looked on to the back of a garage that sold retreads and carried out on-the-spot MOT's. The brown and orange curtains could have done with a wash, or better still replacing altogether, but the place was probably run on a shoestring.

'What would Frith's duties have been?' Tisdall asked. 'Signing people in, talking to them, giving practical advice?'

He nodded. 'He was here from eight to eleven, sometimes a little later.'

'What do you suppose he was doing down by the river?'

'Sorry?' Joseph fiddled with the pens on his desk. 'Oh, you mean … I've no idea, haven't a clue, wish I knew.'

'It's not far from here.'

Joseph thought about this for a moment. 'There was a time he used to go down there with a client. He and Clive used to run there and back, time themselves. Usually took them about twenty minutes. There's a rough track, steep, muddy in wet weather.'

Outside in the corridor, two men were arguing. Joseph left the room to find out what was going on and while he was away Tisdall jotted down a few notes. Frith had lied to Kristen Olsen about where he went on Friday evenings. How many other lies had he told her, and where did he go? When the family returned from Ohio they had some money saved, enough to last them a few months if they were careful, but Frith was starting to sound the type who disliked being careful, watching what he spent. Had he been involved in some kind of criminal activity, something that required him to be out on Friday evenings, something that had led to arguments, trouble? Tisdall realised he was indulging in wishful thinking, hoping he could make the

51

investigations last considerably longer than Liz Cowie had allowed him. More than likely Frith's Friday evenings were spent somewhere perfectly harmless, a pub or a club.

Julie liked clubs, had stated complaining how they didn't go out enough, and if he said he was too tired she pointed out how her job was just as demanding as his, if not more so. He'd taken her out the previous weekend and they'd been sitting in a pub when she'd dropped the bombshell. Better make the most of our freedom, Ray, better not waste the chance of an evening out. For an appalling moment he had thought she was pregnant. But it wasn't that bad. *Well, you'd like a baby one day, wouldn't you? When we've moved to somewhere with more space.* So the plan to buy a house was back even though he'd explained it was impossible until the mortgage on Grace's house had been paid off.

Daniel Joseph had returned and was fussing around, opening and closing drawers. 'Is there was anything else you need to know?'

'Not for the time being. Oh, there was one thing.'

Joseph straightened a picture on the wall, a framed poster with one of those awful little homilies Tisdall couldn't stand. *If life gives you lemons make lemonade.*

'Present from a well-meaning neighbour.' Joseph laughed at the expression on Tisdall's face. 'In this business you can't afford to be too picky, have to take whatever's thrown at you, sometimes quite literally. Bit like your job, I imagine.'

'This Clive,' Tisdall said,' the man who used to go running with Frith, how often does he turn up here? Have you any way of finding out where he is at present?'

'Couldn't say, I'm afraid. Travels all over, sometimes has a spell in hospital if things get bad. He's bi-polar, manic-depressive. William had this idea the best treatment was strenuous exercise.'

'What's his other name?'

Joseph opened a filing cabinet and started flicking through cards.

'Jones.'

'Jones,' Tisdall repeated, 'is that his real name?'

Joseph shrugged. 'Could be. Unless there's forms to fill in, benefits we think they're entitled to, we don't do rigorous checks or ask awkward questions.'

'Maybe not,' said Tisdall, 'but one day keeping accurate records may turn out to be important, for your clients' sakes and possibly for other people too.'

Joseph gave a snort. He thought he was being accused of incompetence, although in reality Tisdall wasn't much bothered how the hostel was run. His mind had wandered, or to be precise, something Joseph had said had triggered off a series of questions that had been forming in his head. Had Kristen Olsen really spent the whole of that fateful evening alone in the flat? Was it pure chance that Theo had been staying with a friend? And why, since it would have been a good opportunity for the two of them to go out for the evening, had William picked that particular day to meet up with the mythical bloke he hoped might give him a job?

8

It was almost time for morning break but to fill up the remaining ten minutes she decided to give the children the Draw a Person test.

Handing out paper, she started to explain what she wanted them to do. 'Take trouble, draw the best picture of a man or a woman that you can, with as much detail as you like.'

Some of them screwed up their faces and she heard Hugo complain to Barnaby that it was 'kids' stuff', but when she told them it was a kind of test their expressions changed dramatically. They liked tests. They were used to doing well.

Later, she would use the drawings as a method of assessing their intellectual maturity. If Neville Unwin found out he would probably disapprove but he was unlikely to hear about it since, apart from the extra work he did with Shannon Wilkins, most of his time was taken up with the A level students.

When she agreed to help with the classes, what had she expected? Children with IQs of a hundred and fifty plus, perhaps the odd genius or two? They all appeared bright enough but most had the advantage of a home with plenty of discussion about the world, and plenty of books.

Amy had her hand up. In spite of the classes being voluntary and relatively informal, some of the children still behaved as though they were at school.

'What is it, Amy?'

'I can't draw hands.'

'Don't worry, it's not a test of how good at drawing you are.'

Theo loved drawing. She had bought him a box of pastels and shown him how to mix the colours. Had she remembered to pack them, and if she had, would Ros let him use them or would she be afraid of marks on his clothes or the carpet? Theo was clever. He could have attended the gifted children classes, but would she have wanted him to? Once she had heard a teacher say, 'God spare us the gifted child'. She knew what he meant. 'Gifted child' often meant pushy parent with unrealistic ambitions. Ros had said nothing about the school Theo was to attend in the autumn. Would it be a private one? If it was he wouldn't like it. Or perhaps she was wrong. *Stop trying to plan his future. He's not your child.*

Most of the children had drawn one or other of their parents but Shannon had produced a picture Kristen found disturbing. The man had bushy eyebrows and heavy bags under his eyes. His hair had been sketched in quite roughly, as had his nose and eyes, but much attention had been paid to his open mouth which contained two rows of large, uneven teeth.

'Someone you know,' Kristen inquired, 'or an imaginary person?'

Shannon shrugged, pushing her paper aside defensively and murmuring something about how she had never been any good at art. During the weekend, her dark brown hair had been cut even shorter, revealing several superficial scratches on her neck, and the studs in her left ear had been removed, leaving a row of red pinpricks.

Kristen looked away for fear of embarrassing her but it was too late. 'One of them got infected, Miss, I mean, Kristen.'

When the rest of the group left for their morning break, Kristen asked Shannon to hang on for a minute and was alarmed to see the expression on the girl's face.

'Did I do it wrong?' Her voice was high-pitched with anxiety. 'You see, like I didn't really know what we were meant to do.'

Kristen moved towards her but Shannon took a step back.

56

'Your drawing was fine. I just thought you looked rather pale, wanted to make sure you weren't worrying about something.'

'No, nothing.'

'No one's been picking on you, teasing you? Do you have friends from school you see during the holidays? It can be difficult being singled out as "gifted".'

Shannon looked relieved but her hand was on the door handle, she wanted to escape. 'It's, like, I'm only good at Maths.'

The coffee room was crowded and Kristen noticed that Brigid was deep in conversation with one of the A level teachers, and it was not until it was almost time to return to the classroom that Kristen managed to catch her on her own and ask how much she knew about Shannon's background.

'Shannon Wilkins? Only that she's exceptionally good with figures. Actually, I don't see that much of her these days. On Mondays and Fridays she has individual tuition with Neville while I'm taking that group.'

'Do you know anything about her family? Something seems to be bothering her.'

'Neville does all the interviewing.' Brigid was halfway through the door. 'I think he met the parents when she joined the classes. As I recall, they're still together and she's got an older sister. Why not have a word with him? They're often a bit moody at this age, especially the girls. By the way, don't forget your invitation for lunch.'

'Thanks.' But there was something a little off-putting about Brigid's manner and Kristen knew she was unlikely to take up the offer without a definite invitation. Perhaps she resented the questions about Shannon, thought since Kristen was only filling in until Sarah Pearson returned she should stick to the teaching and not involve herself with any problems the children might have.

At the end of the morning, she stayed behind, studying the drawings before placing them in a folder to take home with her. Most were more or less what she had expected but Barnaby's was surprisingly immature. Was he gifted in the usual sense or had he joined the classes because he and Hugo lived next door to each other in Sneyd Park? Surprisingly – it was where the rich had their houses – William had wanted to live there, high above the Gorge, somewhere where it was possible to see the Welsh coast and beyond it, the Brecon Beacons.

The flat in Bishopston had been a temporary place to stay while they looked for somewhere better. A temporary place. William had only lived there for six weeks and Theo for another five. Later she would drive to Fishponds and walk by the River Frome, look for the bridge. She could never be certain she had found the exact spot, but for several weeks the feeling had been growing that until she forced herself to stand looking down at the water …

Someone was in the passage outside the classroom. The children had left fifteen minutes ago but when she opened the door, Shannon was standing a few feet away, chewing her nails.

'I left my book behind.'

'Which book was that?'

'The one I read on the bus. Only, like, I was going to ask you something.'

So the book had been an excuse. She had started walking to the bus stop then changed her mind and returned to the college hoping Kristen was still there.

'Could you …' Shannon broke off, frowning. 'Could you do a bad thing but it was for a good reason? Supposing you knew something but telling someone would, like, make things worse, would it be better not to say anything even if, like, it meant a bad person got away with it?'

'Are you thinking about someone in particular?'

Shannon hesitated. 'Oh, I've just remembered, I didn't read my book on the way here so, like, I must have left it by my bed.'

Instead of driving straight home, Kristen followed the signs to Fishponds and turned left down a road she hoped would lead to the river. From the small amount Tisdall had told her, she knew she would have to leave her car and walk. Pulling up in a cul-de-sac she found her street map in the glove compartment and attempted to work out where she was. She should have studied the map at home, but what she was doing was a spur of the moment decision, not something she could have planned.

After several wrong turnings, she found what looked like a path that led down to the river. Two boys sat together on the grass doing something with matches and a polythene bag. They looked more or less the same age as the children she taught, but there the similarity ended. One had hair dyed two different shades of blond, the other had the pale, unhealthy appearance of someone who lives off a diet of junk food.

Kristen considered asking them if she was going in the right direction, then changed her mind. A third, older boy had joined them from behind some trees and as she hurried on she thought she heard them following her, but when she stopped, steadying herself on an exposed tree root, everything was silent apart from a swishing sound as a squirrel scooted through the long grass and disappeared up the trunk of a scrubby tree.

Brigid had said squirrels ran along the wall at the end of her garden. She loved the garden and sometimes complained how she had too little time to tend to it now Rebecca had arrived. Was she out there now, playing with the baby? Kristen hoped if she took up the invitation to lunch, she would be allowed to hold Rebecca, smell her skin. The loss of Theo was becoming more acute, not just his presence, the games they had played together, their conversations, but the feel of him when she tucked him up in bed, the soft silkiness of his hair.

Turning a bend, she could see where the track joined a narrow road, and beyond that a small parking area with space for two or three cars. A map of the Avon Forest had an arrow and "You are here" painted in a bright green box. Next to the map was a "No Fouling" sign, with the silhouette of a dog spattered with mud, and on the grass below it a collection of old drink cans and chocolate wrappers. Considering it was so close to a heavily built-up area, it was a beautiful place and Kristen was surprised William had never told her about it, never suggested they walk there at the weekend.

A path ran close to the river. In the direction of Frenchay, Tisdall had said, going north. Kristen glanced over her shoulder at a man with a thick grey ponytail, but he had crouched down to undo the padlock on his bike and had no interest in where she was going. On her left she could see the trickle of river. On her right, the ground rose steeply to a thickly wooded area, just the kind of place where a pickpocket could claim his dog had got stuck in a hole. She was prepared for a long walk but less than five minutes later she rounded a bend and drew in breath, recognising Tisdall's description immediately: the stone bridge, the overhanging tree, the pile of boulders.

She could be wrong. There could be another bridge, more or less the same, but something told her she had found the right place and when she saw the patch of earth near the water she could visualise the police tape that had sealed it off. The picture swam in front of her eyes then returned, clear, ordinary, as if every trace of the tragedy had been erased by passing time.

Halfway across the bridge, she stopped to gaze over the side. Surely it would be possible to survive such a fall, but not if you hit something hard, not if even before you fell you had the imprint of half a brick on the side of her head.

Something was wrong. If all you wanted was a wallet, why attack someone so badly that you risked being charged with murder? When Vi told her about the man called Cameron, who sold antique toys in the market, she had thought it unimportant. Suddenly, she knew she had to speak to him.

9

The market was in an old warehouse but some of the stalls, including one selling bacon rolls, had spilled out into the open air. A table covered in bric-a-brac – brass vases, carved wooden boxes, china bedpans – stood next to a ramshackle van where a dog sat motionless in the driving seat, following Kristen with its eyes.

Next to the van, an old man with a black beret pulled well down was inspecting a display of garden tools, picking up a rake and testing its weight, moving on to the trowels and hand forks and secateurs. Kristen watched him for a few moments, running over in her head what she was going to say to Cameron Lyle when she found him. *If* she found him.

As far as she could remember, the place had only been open since the spring but news must have spread. Inside it was packed, and the clientele looked more up market than she had expected. A middle aged woman with bronze hair and tight-stretch jeans was carrying a small inlaid table, lifted high above the crowds, calling out apologies as she made her way through the entrance doors. Kristen stood back to let her pass, stepped inside, and started along the first aisle, looking for a stall that sold antique toys.

Since the windows in the roof were covered in grime, the place was artificially lit. The floor was stone with areas of cracked lino and the occasional strip of carpet. A quivering spaniel had been tied to the leg of a table that held a display of homemade jewellery. Kristen considered asking its owner if she knew someone called Cameron Lyle, but the woman had such a sour expression she decided against it, moving on past stalls selling knitted hats, fireguards, golf balls, cigarette cards, brown sticky tape, old cameras, and polished pebbles.

Theo would have loved the pebbles, with their streaks of colour and their smooth shininess. Kristen had his letter in her pocket, the letter Ros had dictated rather than allowing him to write what he wanted. As she left the flat, she had crept up the steps from the basement, determined to avoid another encounter with Mrs Letts, another conversation about Theo. When William was alive, the woman had barely acknowledged their existence, now she was desperate to involve herself in what was left of Kristen's life. *I'm a widow myself, dear, if there's anything I can do ...*

Kristen had hoped Tisdall's investigations would make introducing herself to Cameron Lyle unnecessary, but his only contact with her since the day after she received the anonymous letter had been a brief phone call to ask if she had received any more. He would, of course, keep her informed. Would he, or was it just something the police said automatically, an exit line like a doctor assuring a patient he could return if the symptoms recurred?

Struggling past racks of Turkish trousers, she reached a less crowded area at the back of the warehouse and climbed onto a large wooden box to allow herself something approaching a bird's eye view of the stalls.

'Looking for anything in particular?' The voice at her elbow came from a man with a shaved head and tinted glasses.

Kristen jumped down. 'A friend of mine told me there's someone who deals in antique toys.'

The man gave a mocking laugh. 'Depends what you call antiques.' He pointed in the direction of the far corner. 'Next to the exit on the left.'

'Thanks.' She knew the kind of person Cameron Lyle was likely to be, an ex-actor who had started buying and selling pine furniture as a way of supplementing his income, and abandoned his non-existent acting career when the furniture took off. Either that or he would have been to art school, worked in a gallery, then decided he could make a better living as a middle man.

When she reached the stall no one was looking after it.

'Gone for a cup of tea,' said an enormous woman, stuffing herself with a chocolate muffin.

'Do you know him?' Kristen studied the glass case of old Dinky cars, along with a few lead soldiers and a wind-up clown.

'What was it you were hoping to find?'

'Mainly mechanical toys.'

'Cost a fortune, they do. Won't find much here but if you have a word with Cameron he may be able to help.'

'He's not here today?'

The woman shrugged. 'Might be. Kenny's been looking after the stall, he could tell you. Over there by the caff, long streak of piss with a shirt that makes your eyes water.'

When Kristen approached the caff, the man called Kenny had finished whatever he had been drinking and was looking for somewhere to dispose of his plastic cup. He turned, scrunching the cup in his fist, and started talking to another man with a square, craggy face and curly hair.

'That's him.' The fat woman had followed Kristen. 'That's Cameron.'

'Thanks.' Kristen waited for the woman to walk away but she was buying a cup of coffee and a second muffin.

'Someone to see you, Cameron,' she called. 'Lady's interested in mechanical toys. Yes, that's the one.' She pointed at Kristen. 'And it's your turn to mind my bits and pieces, Kenny.'

Kristen thought fast. She could pretend she really was a collector or she could come straight out and ask Lyle if he had known William. In the end she decided to tell him she was a friend of Vi Pitt's.

'Friend of Vi's?' Lyle had a cold, or the remains of one that had turned into a wheezy cough. He gestured to Kenny to get back to the stall. 'How can I help?'

'Vi said I might find you here.'

'Did she now?' He was looking all around him but something in his manner made her think he had been expecting her.

'My name's Kristen Olsen. I lived with William Frith. Vi said you knew him.'

Lyle's expression was impossible to interpret. 'If you wait a couple of minutes we can go outside, talk in my car.'

As it turned out, it was nearer to a quarter of an hour before he joined her at the entrance to the market. 'I'm parked over there.' He pointed towards a black van. 'Look, I'd better tell you straight off, William and I barely knew each other. I'm very sorry about what happened but I'm not sure if…'

'Where did you meet him?'

He rubbed his forehead and she noticed that his eyes were a very dark blue, set wide apart, giving the impression his nose was broader than it actually was.

'I used to go to a pub halfway up Whiteladies Road.' He unlocked the door to the passenger seat and she climbed in. 'There was this shop in Cotham Hill that took some of the stuff I'd picked up as part of a job lot but didn't want. It's closed down now, more's the pity.'

'Did you see William after he came back from America?'

'America?' he said, sounding a fraction too surprised. 'So he decided to take the job after all. In that case, what was he doing back in Bristol?'

'It's complicated.' The windscreen had steamed up, making the van feel claustrophobic. 'It didn't turn out the way he hoped.'

'No?' He glanced at her, aware that his slightly mocking tone of voice didn't square with his claim that he hardly knew William. 'Do the cops still think it was a mugging?' And when she said nothing, 'I'm sorry, I don't know what to say. I'm really sorry about what happened but I'm not sure why Vi suggested you talk to me.'

The van with the dog was leaving. Its driver gave a hoot and Lyle raised a hand in acknowledgement, smiling when the dog's paws scrabbled against the window. It was clear he was well known to the other dealers. Who else did he know, and had he and William really met in a pub?

'How much did William tell you about himself?' Kristen asked.

'Just that he was working at the university.'

'Did he mention any enemies?'

'Enemies?' Lyle gave a short laugh. 'That's a strange thing to say. Oh, you're thinking ... Someone who disliked him enough to ... As I said...'

'You barely knew him.'

He reacted badly to the sarcasm in her voice. 'How long have you known Vi?'

'I've only met her once.'

'And she said William and I were friends.'

'No, her husband told me. I'm teaching on the course for gifted children.'

He nodded and it was clear he knew about the classes. 'Can *you* think of anyone who had a grudge against William? Presumably not or you'd have told the cops. What about his ex?'

Any moment now, Lyle would climb out of the van and apologise for not being more help. 'Theo, William's son, has gone back to his mother,' she said.

'That's rough.' His eyes met hers. 'Look, I'll ask around. This dog man theory the cops have concocted sounds like bollocks, something they cooked up to keep the press off their back. If I hear anything I'll get in touch.' He took out his phone and she told him her number. 'You know,' he said quietly, 'with your colouring – fair hair, brown eyes – you and William could have been brother and sister.'

On Saturday, Tisdall and Brake had spent a fruitless evening touring the pubs and clubs in the city centre then on Monday, when Julie had protested that Tisdall had left her on her own for the most of the previous week, Brake had offered to search farther afield. Presumably Brake's wife was more concerned with her husband's career than Julie was with his, but Tisdall's fleeting resentment was quickly replaced by the usual feeling of guilt. What had happened to him? What was he doing?

Thinking back to when he and Julie first met, all he could remember was the sex. Had there been anything more? Not at the beginning, although they'd grown fond of each other before they grew apart. Maybe it was just a case of not appreciating what you'd got until you'd lost it. Lost it? He'd chucked it away, been flattered by the attention of a woman fifteen years younger, or worse, he'd used Julie as a way of getting back at Grace for trying to make something of her life. Was he really that shallow?

Before he met up with Brake, he had called round at the house, but Serena was out at the Sports Centre. Grace had reproached him for forgetting Thursday was one of Serena's training afternoons but let him come inside for a couple of minutes. She'd been watching an old black and white movie. Anyone else would have started to explain, justify. *I wasn't actually watching it. I've been dusting or ironing. I just put it on to keep me company.* Not Grace. 'Joan Crawford and Jack Palance,' she told him. 'She knows someone's trying to kill her –'

'Don't let me interrupt. If Serena's not here…'

'Coffee?'

'If you're having one.'

'I wasn't but I will.'

The ritual complete, they had moved to the kitchen where he sat on his old chair, except now there were two chairs instead of three. Grace was wearing jeans, something she had never done in the past, and she had lost a few pounds, not that she had ever been overweight. When she asked what he was working on he had told her more than he intended, mainly as a way of concealing how agitated he was.

Because what had happened was so appalling that for weeks, months he had denied it to himself. Then Julie had said something about going on holiday in the autumn and he had known a holiday with her was more than he could stand. Julie every minute of the day and night, the two of them trailing round gift shops, going on coach outings, and eating, forever eating. Not that Julie enjoyed her meals but, as with all finicky eaters, food was a constant topic of conversation. Once he had

66

thought she might be suffering from anorexia but as far as he could tell she had never dropped below eight stone. Maybe you could have the psychology of an anorectic but it came out in faddiness rather than actually starving yourself.

'How's Julie?' Grace handed him a mug.

'All right.'

'You look tired. Liz Cowie been overworking you? Incidentally, what does this dog man look like?'

He described the anorak and flat cap, and the grey and black scarf one of the pickpocket's victims had managed to catch hold of and pass on to the police. DI Cowie and Superintendent Reid had based their belief that the dog man was responsible for the murder on the remarkable similarity between previous victims' reports of the man, and two descriptions of someone seen close to the scene of Frith's murder. Height, weight, hair colour, type of clothing – they all matched up, and one of the witnesses actually claimed to have seen the dog man talking to Frith and pointing at the roots of a tree.

Grace pulled in her chair and her knee brushed his, but it was an accident, then the phone started ringing and when she found out who it was her tone of voice sent a blast of fear through his body. No name was mentioned but it was someone he didn't know, someone who seemed to be paying her compliments, referring back to time spent together. When she returned she looked flushed.

'Nina's new boyfriend,' she explained in answer to the question in his eyes. 'You remember Nina, the friend I met at college. He wants to give her something special for her birthday, wondered if I had any ideas.'

She was lying.

10

'You know the way?'

'I'll find it.' Kristen remembered her last visit to Brigid's had been in the dark, with William. 'First left, second right, then down past the railway line?'

'Number twenty. Blue front door. I'll go on ahead of you and see to Rebecca. The childminder's sweet with her but a bit sluttish when it comes to hygiene.' Brigid gave a nervous laugh. 'You have to be so careful with young babies.'

'I'm sure.' Kristen and Brigid had never been friends, only acquaintances. Their relationship was a blank sheet but with the advantage that Brigid knew all about her and William. Kristen had decided to confide in her, tell her about Cameron Lyle, so she was not best pleased when she rang the bell ten minutes later and discovered Brigid's husband, Alex, had decided to spend the day working at home.

'Hello there.' Alex let her into the house and told her to go through to the kitchen, Brigid was upstairs but would be down in a moment.

She remembered the house from her one previous visit, but the kitchen had been refitted with Shaker-style cupboards, a split hob, concealed lighting and a grey tiled floor.

Alex pulled out two chairs, adjusted a pot plant until it was dead centre on the table, and waited for her to sit down. *He* looked different too, but that might be a new pair of glasses, and as she watched, he took them off and held them up to the light, scratching at a mark on one of the lenses. His pale, rather coarse skin contrasted with the darkness of his eyes and hair. He was good looking but not in the way William had been. Alex's nose was large and one of his eyebrows was fractionally higher than the other, giving him a slightly amused, quizzical look although for a brief moment, without his glasses, he had looked quite vulnerable.

'How's the teaching going?' He opened a cupboard and took out a bottle. 'Drink?'

'No thanks. Yes, it's not too bad.'

They sat in silence for a moment then Kristen asked if he knew Neville's wife.

'Vi?' His voice was loud with relief that they had found a topic to discuss that had no connection with William's death or Theo's return to London. 'Two of her pictures were reproduced in the local paper. Apparently she's had some success with a London gallery.'

Kristen could tell he had no interest in Vi Pitt but she ploughed on just the same. 'Neville said she had ideas that could be relevant to the thesis I'm writing.'

'Ah, the thesis.' He was back on safe ground. 'Inherited ability, am I right?'

'It's about children with exceptional gifts.'

Alex laughed. 'Same thing in my book.'

'Vi wouldn't agree with you.'

'What wouldn't Vi agree with?' Brigid came through the door, holding the baby, still warm and sleepy from her cot, and Kristen jumped up to see her.

'Oh, she's lovely. Sweet. I like the name Rebecca.'

At the sound of a strange voice, the baby turned her head and stared at Kristen with wary brown eyes.

Alex was still sitting with his legs sprawled out in front of him. Brigid gave him a look of good-natured exasperation. 'If you're having lunch with us can you get some stuff out of the fridge? Pastrami and salad. Bread rolls on top of the microwave.'

'Right you are.' Alex held out a finger for the baby to grab.

'Is that all we're having? No, leave it to me.'

Kristen ignored the slight tension between them, pushing away memories of her own resentment when William had done less than his fair share of looking after Theo, and concentrated her attention on Rebecca. She had Brigid's nose and her fair, fluffy hair, not that there was very much of it, and it would probably turn darker when she was older, just as Theo's had done. She was fat and cuddly and Kristen longed to hold her, but she could be at an age when a stranger would make her cry.

'You didn't wake her, did you?' Alex said. 'Wouldn't it have been better to leave her in her cot until after we've eaten?'

Brigid fastened Rebecca into her bouncy chair. 'Kristen wanted to see her.'

'Yes, I did,' Kristen said, a tone of apology in her voice. 'She's lovely. Beautiful.'

Were Alex and Brigid finding it hard to adjust to the responsibility of caring for a baby after all those years of freedom? For the last five years, Kristen's own life had been governed to a great extent by Theo's needs. Now she was "free". Glancing at the digital wall clock, she tried to imagine what he was doing. Shopping in Knightsbridge, eating out in an expensive restaurant, or lying on his bed, crying as silently as possible for fear that Ros or the childminder would hear? Kristen had been expecting him to phone even though part of her dreaded it, knowing the conversation would be stilted, artificial.

'So.' Alex was holding a limp looking lettuce under the tap, 'Neville wants you to teach the little brainboxes how to philosophize. The place pays peanuts but three mornings a week suits Brigid pretty well. Any chance of another job in a school? I suppose it's getting late for the autumn term unless someone suddenly drops dead or gets retired on medical grounds.'

'I haven't looked for one yet.' Kristen was thinking about the anonymous letter while watching Brigid clench and unclench her jaw. Because Alex had used the phrase "drop dead"? William had once described him as tactless. Still, William was a fine one to talk. 'I'm not sure I want to go back to what I was doing before,' she said, 'I expect I'll do supply teaching for a while.'

Alex nodded, searching in a drawer for a knife then placing it on the draining board and taking a tissue from his pocket to wipe away the juice the baby had brought up. Looking up at Kristen, as if the subject could be avoided no longer, he asked if she had heard from Theo.

'He wrote a letter but I think it had been dictated by Ros.'

'What makes you think that?'

Brigid frowned. 'For God's sake, Alex, Kristen knows the kind of thing Theo would have written.'

Alex left the room and Kristen heard him running up the stairs. While he was away, she decided to raise the subject of Shannon. 'She seems so tense. Her extra maths lessons … I wondered…'

Brigid frowned. 'What about them?'

'I thought she might be finding the work a strain, or …' She broke off, unwilling to take the conversation any further. But Brigid had picked up on what she was thinking.

'Neville admires her ability with figures and that's as far as it goes.'

'Yes, of course, I didn't mean –'

'I hope you haven't been talking to anyone else?'

'Of course not. I only mentioned it because…'

'Lots of these children have problems. Bright kids nearly always do.'

Alex had returned, bringing with him a brochure that he left on one of the worktops. 'Show it to you later, Kristen, might come in useful.'

During lunch, he returned to the subject of her thesis. 'It's impressive the way you're carrying on with your research. If there's anything I can do … William was a good friend, a valuable colleague, if he'd been prepared to knuckle down he'd have had a brilliant career ahead of him.'

'Alex!' The sharpness in Brigid's voice made the baby's mouth turn down and her lower lip tremble.

'I simply meant if William had stayed in the States.'

'But he didn't, and I expect he was thinking of Kristen and

Theo.'

'No, it wasn't that.' Kristen was afraid both she and the baby were both going to cry. 'The job didn't turn out the way he hoped. There was too much teaching, not enough time for research.'

Alex rubbed his hands together. 'You know, I don't think I've met anyone with such an independent mind, who was still capable of carrying out instructions to the letter.'

'You must have thought him very ungrateful.' Kristen hated apologising on William's behalf. 'After all the trouble you'd gone to, fixing up the job. I tried to persuade him we ought to stay at least until the end of the year.'

'But he didn't take a blind bit of notice. No, well ...' His voice trailed away and he glanced at Brigid, as if to say he had only been trying to help and had no intention of upsetting anyone.

Brigid stood up and opened the fridge. 'I'm going to feed Rebecca.'

Alex pushed back his chair. 'The police are still sticking to the same theory, are they, this dog man character they keep talking about?'

Slipping her hand into her pocket, Kristen felt for Theo's letter. 'Yes, but they're making some new inquiries too.'

'I can't think why we didn't hear about him before. A pickpocket with the nasty habit of pretending his dog had gone missing.'

'We did,' said Brigid, 'it was in the local paper after he'd carried out the first two thefts.' She turned to Kristen, making it clear the subject was at an end. 'It's become easier since Rebecca's been more settled. Or perhaps I've got more used to leaving her. Babies pick up on how you're feeling, that's why it's stupid to get worked up when they won't stop crying.'

Kristen smiled. 'I'm sure all mothers are the same.'

'With their first baby, you mean?' Alex cut himself a wedge of blue cheese. 'What's Ros like? Typical actress type? I remember William mentioning how she can't have any more children, a complication after Theo was born.'

Kristen stared at him. 'William said that?'

'Yes. I think so.' A small degree of doubt had entered his voice but only because Brigid was glaring at him. 'Maybe I got it wrong.'

'I was thinking, Kristen,' Brigid said, 'why not give the Adult Education people a ring, see if they can fix you up with a couple of evening classes in October?'

'Good idea,' Alex joined in enthusiastically. 'I could put in a word. No, you don't need me. You're sufficiently well qualified to teach in a number of areas, and make a very good job of it too. That's why I brought the brochure downstairs. Give you an idea what kind of classes they hold.'

During the evening, Ros phoned. 'Hi, Kristen, the reason I'm calling, I wondered if you could have Theo next weekend. Once he's started at his new school it may be a difficult, although there'll be half terms and so forth.'

'Yes, of course. Will you be bringing him here?'

'Either me or John.' The voice, that had sounded a little desperate, suddenly changed to studied nonchalance. 'Anyway, I'll ring again nearer the time.'

Sinking into a chair, Kristen closed her eyes. Next weekend. Theo must have gone on at her, begged, and eventually she had become tired of arguing and given in. No, she was wrong. Theo had pestered her but Ros had only needed a small amount of coaxing. Already she was finding his presence in the flat a strain. Letting him return to Bristol was her way of saying it had been a mistake re-claiming him so soon.

Ros would buy him expensive presents, the kind of toys and games that had novelty value for a day or two. He would tell Kristen what he really wanted. But already she was spoiling it, dreading the moment when it was time for him to leave. Supposing Ros took him abroad: she was always hoping for a part in an American television series. His memory of her and William would fade with only a few vague recollections, visits to Leigh Woods, Blaise Castle … Kristen had looked after him since he was four, but how many people could remember much that happened before the age of seven or eight?

Struggling to her feet, she moved across to the mantelpiece

and forced herself to look at the photographs properly, not just glimpse them and look away, as she usually did. William and Theo on the Downs. Theo on his sixth birthday. The three of them, taken a year ago by a man on the beach at Oxwich. They were starting to look like pictures from a long time ago.

She thought about the gifted children, then about Vi, and Cameron Lyle, the man who claimed to have known William but hardly at all. What did it matter who had killed him? But it did. Not for her sake, but for Theo's. Somehow she had to find out more, face up to the fact that there were people William had never told her about, people who had been important to him, part of a life he had kept secret, people – someone in particular – who had wanted to get rid of him.

11

'We've passed it,' Brake said, drawing up fifty yards beyond a
lighted sign. 'I suppose they got their licence because there
were no houses close by. Used to be three tower blocks but they
were knocked down and since then the land's been derelict.'
Tisdall took his jacket from the back seat and started walking
back towards the club. It was still stiflingly hot. A group of
kids, who should have been in bed, were kicking a deflated ball
on an area that was supposed to be grass but had been reduced
long since to dry impacted earth.

'See that one with ginger hair,' said Brake, 'can't be more
than nine.'

'Unless the government comes up with new legislation,
curfews on innocent kids are outside our remit.'

'Until one goes missing,' Brake said, 'then there's an outcry
about how there ought to be more foot patrols, bobbies on the
beat. Incidentally, the anonymous letter seems to have changed
Liz Cowie's mind. I mean, how many people would have
known where Kristen Olsen worked?'

Up to last week, persuading Liz Cowie there was more to the
case than met the eye had been a lost cause. Then, like an
answer to Tisdall's prayers, someone had sent the anonymous
letter. Cowie had pretended it had all the hallmarks of an
oddball but Tisdall knew her better than that, she was never as
rock solid certain as she made out. *All right, Ray, I know the*

trend as well as you do, less emphasis on bits of information fed into the computer and analysed – often not very effectively – and more on pairs of officers following up particular lines of inquiry.

When he left her office, he'd had a job not to laugh out loud. He'd be working more or less off his own bat and could fix it so on Mondays and Wednesdays, when Grace was home but Serena was still at the Sports Centre he could call round and …

Driving past the club, Tisdall had heard the usual loud beat. Now someone seemed to have lowered the volume and when they started down the stone steps to the entrance the sounds were more reminiscent of an Indian restaurant than a nightclub.

'Sure this was the place?'

'Certain.' From his sharp tone of voice, Brake was still thinking about the parents who should have made sure their kids were in bed. 'Right name, right area.'

'And how often was Frith supposed to have visited?'

'He was a regular.'

The man on the door had heard them coming. He held out a lethargic hand for their membership cards then looked up, squinting through thick steel-framed glasses. 'Old Bill?'

Tisdall gave a brief nod and the man fingered the large black stud in his ear. 'I'll take you to Mrs Ronane.'

Brake had looked up details of the place before they set out. A drinking club with the occasional floor show. *Bimbam's* was a bit of a crazy name but there was no record of any trouble and no complaints from anyone living nearby.

The doorman led them down a short, dark passage and knocked on a door, waiting with his eyes darting all around, until a hoarse voice ordered him to 'Come!'

'Two officers to see you.' The man's earlobe was giving him trouble again.

'Let them by then,' said the voice. 'Don't block their way.'

An ornate gold lamp on a low table provided the only lighting. At first glance the room looked sumptuously furnished but when their eyes became accustomed to the gloom it had more the appearance of a jackdaw's nest. Everything was shiny, but to Tisdall's inexpert eye it all looked like tat. Mrs Ronane sat behind a desk with a tumbler of whisky at her elbow. A heavy-breasted woman with jet black hair and a thickly made-up face, she was probably in her late fifties or early sixties, possibly Greek or Italian, although when she spoke again she couldn't have sounded more English.

'Detective Sergeant Tisdall.' She checked his warrant card. 'To what do we owe the pleasure? Stan does tend to turn the music up a little too loud but –'

'We've had no complaints.' Tisdall accepted the offered chair, the only one in the room apart from Mrs Ronane's, leaving Brake standing.

'I won't get up.' Mrs Ronane adjusted her position. 'I'm recovering from a hip replacement, need to rest, but if you don't keep close tabs on your staff things soon get out of hand.'

Tisdall noticed that a fan had been switched on, although it seemed to have very little effect on the temperature. The curtains had a design of elongated dancing girls, and the same material had been used to cover a large floor cushion. Tisdall wondered what would have happened if it had been offered to Brake, and Mrs Ronane noticed his fleeting smile and asked if she had made a mistake and it was a social call.

'I'm afraid not,' he said. 'we're making inquiries about a murder and my colleague's under the impression the victim, William Frith, was a member of your club.'

'Ah, poor William.' A hand with several heavy rings moved up to pat her hair. 'Tragic. A mugging, they say. Is it true Bristol's becoming one of the most violent cities?'

'Did he come here every week?' Brake gave her an encouraging smile, displaying the straight white teeth that always made Tisdall draw his lips over his own.

Mrs Ronane closed her eyes. 'I'll introduce you to Glen, he could tell you more than I can. At the time of the murder … if we'd known anything … naturally we'd have been in touch. Quiet, not a big drinker, came here to relax more than anything else. He and Glen used to have a drink together.' She pressed a buzzer and a stoat-faced man appeared so fast he must have been listening outside the door. 'Reg, would you fetch Glen, these two gentlemen would like a word.'

Tisdall glanced at Brake then regretted it when Brake took the look to mean he was to ask more questions.

'You say Frith was the quiet type but if he came here regularly he must had made plenty of friends. Anyone in particular?'

Mrs Ronane sighed. 'If you're implying some kind of liaison, as I said –'

'You didn't know him well.' Brake finished the sentence for her. 'When was the last time you saw him? We need a precise date.'

She looked at Tisdall as if to say she knew Brake meant well so she would overlook his brashness. 'Glen will check the book. This is a membership only club.'

A man had appeared in the doorway and was standing, with one hand clasping the fingers of the other. His spiky blond hair contrasted with his eyelashes and eyebrows, which were exceptionally dark.

'Detective Sergeant Tisdall, Glen.' Mrs Ronane seemed to enjoy the introduction. 'And …' She turned to Brake. 'I'm so sorry, I've forgotten…'

'DC Brake.'

'Of course.' She and Glen exchanged glances as if they found the name slightly comical. 'They're making inquiries into the murder.'

'Murder?' Glen's face flushed. 'You mean Will?'

Mrs Ronane was making an effort to rise from her chair. Glen moved forward to help but she waved him aside, refusing her stick. 'If you want me I'll be in the bar. Tell them everything they need to know.'

Once she had closed the door behind her, Glen's manner changed dramatically.

'I thought you'd got the sod that did it. Some kind of mugging, it said, but Will would never have let himself get mugged.'

Tisdall suggested Glen sit in Mrs Ronane's chair but he declined the offer, pulling out two hard backed ones stacked in a corner and giving one to Brake.

'He was here the week before it happened.' Glen had been

speaking almost in a whisper. Now his voice was loud and clear. 'I checked. He'd only been back from America a short while. What was he doing down by the river? Had his wallet been nicked?'

'What did you talk about?' Brake's tone was deliberately intimidating.

'Talk about?' A slow smile spread over the man's face. 'Birds crawled round Will like flies. Not that he encouraged them, just the opposite.' He noticed Tisdall's expression. 'No, I don't mean he was gay. Had a boy, I forget his name. The kid liked football so I used to give Will the stickers from the stuff I eat for breakfast.' He was stumbling over his words. 'Will thought the world of him. Poor kid, what's happened to him?' He was sweating profusely, wiping his face every so often with the cuffs of his shirt. 'Pascale. You should talk to Pascale.'

Tisdall had started walking round the room. 'She works here.'

'Only on Saturdays. She's a singer – thinks she is. Mrs R gave her a chance but I reckon she needs more training, voice lessons. Will had all kinds of ideas, thought she hadn't made the most of herself.'

'Do you know where she lives?'

'Lives?' Glen repeated as though Tisdall had asked the impossible. 'Haven't a clue, but she'll be in on Saturday. Been staying with a friend. Bloke that repairs musical instruments.'

Tisdall turned to Brake. 'Can't be too many of those in the city. What kind of musical instruments?' But Glen was thinking about something else, licking his lips.

'There was a bit of trouble,' he said.

'What kind of trouble?'

'Will was one of those types that gets easily bored, likes a bit of action.'

Tisdall was losing patience. 'What kind of action?'

'Anything a bit risky, anything that made him laugh.' Glen warmed to the subject. 'Walk down the street, any street, you'd never believe –'

'What goes on behind closed curtains,' Brake said coldly. 'Why don't you stop talking in riddles and get to the point.'

'There isn't any more.' Glen's face turned sulky. 'You'll have to find Pascale.'

Kristen had moved Theo's single divan into the living room, and pushed it against the wall so she could lie with her head on the pillow and flick through the channels till she found something to send her to sleep.

The cheap wine had made her head throb but since tomorrow was Saturday it didn't matter if she woke feeling rough. William had disapproved of painkillers, refusing to have any in the house unless one of them had flu and insisting that drinking several pints of water was just as effective. Now she could buy whatever tablets she chose and the thought of her new found freedom caused her so much pain she spoke his name out loud in an anguished gasp.

Reaching for the remote control, she knocked her glass with her elbow and watched the remains of the red wine spread over the rug William had brought back from Morocco, years ago, before she knew him. How annoyed he would have been. Yes, he would. The real William – not the idealised version that had been with her since his death – returned like a blow. But she had loved him just as he was, moody, impulsive, funny, intolerant. Now every aspect of him, every experience, every piece of information that had been stored in his brain, had been wiped out, died along with the rest of his body.

If, instead of waiting until he had a permanent job, they had gone ahead and had the baby they longed for, part of him would still be with her. No, that was disloyal to Theo. But having William's child would have made no difference. She would have loved Theo just as much. She was drifting off. The mornings at the college were exhausting but she preferred to be exhausted. On Tuesdays and Thursdays, and at the weekends, she stuck to a strict regime, getting up at the same time each day, working on her thesis and eating proper food. She ought to be looking for a cheaper flat but not yet, not until the autumn. When Theo came to stay … when he came back…

By the end of the month, Ros would be having serious reservations, looking for a face-saving way of returning him to

Bristol. *I've been thinking, Kristen, losing his father and then moving here and losing all his friends ... It's only an idea but do you think if he did one more year at his old school ... Only a thought, Kristen, and naturally he could spend all his holidays with me, as long as I wasn't too tied up with work.*

The wine had soaked in, leaving a shape like a cliff and a shoreline. Cliff. Shaun. The names jogged her memory and she thought about a particular evening, nearly a year ago, when William had come home after working at the hostel for the homeless, incensed by someone called Shaun. No, not Shaun, that was someone else. Stan? Steve? When she asked what had happened he had changed the subject, told her the guy was an idiot, not worth a second thought. Steve. It could have been Steve. If she told Tisdall ... But was there any point? The police already had their suspect, the one they called the dog man. A blurry image, half Doberman, half devil, rose into her consciousness then the alcohol did its work and she slept, only to be woken three hours later by a crescendo of music from the television as two people, a man and a woman, let go of their surfboards and sank to their knees on the Californian sand. Twenty past one. The night still stretched ahead and she would have to start the whole agonising process of getting to sleep all over again.

12

One of the children had a headache. Kristen had taken her to the main office, found her some painkillers and left her lying on a couch in the tiny waiting room close to the front door. By the time she reached the coffee room, the A level teachers had returned to their classrooms but Brigid and Neville were still there, talking animatedly but in low voices. When Kristen appeared they broke off, smiling too much.

'Just discussing the selection of new applicants for the courses,' Neville said. 'Some of the present children, the older ones, will be stopping at the end of this term. As you know, we like to restrict attendance to nine and ten-year-olds, mainly because numbers need to be limited.'

Kristen nodded. Being a temporary member of staff she had no say in decisions about the coming year. Brigid had turned away and was gazing through the window at the small strip of grass between the back of the building and the high boundary wall.

'Jolly good.' Neville touched Brigid's arm, then Kristen's, like a sheepdog rounding up its flock. 'Should be some coffee left, Kristen, although I can't vouch for how hot it'll be.' He pointed at a plate with two custard creams. 'Finish them up, you're not looking after yourself properly – at least, that's my wife's opinion, but she always has a mission to fatten people up.'

After he left, Kristen turned her attention to Brigid, who had moved away from the window and had a tissue pressed to her face.

'Are you all right?' It was no use pretending she had failed to notice Brigid's reddened eyes.

Brigid managed a wan smile. 'Just got myself in a bit of a state. Jordan Hickman's father's been teaching him all kinds of stuff I'm unfamiliar with and I'm beginning to think I'm not really up to the job.'

'Of course you are.' Kristen knew a little about modern Maths and it was hard to believe Brigid could feel threatened by a nine-year-old boy. 'Did Jordan say something? I've always found him quite shy.'

Brigid removed the clips in her hair then replaced them, making sure there were no loose ends. 'You must come round to the house again, in the evening, for dinner.'

'Thanks. Or perhaps you could persuade Alex to babysit and the two of us could go out somewhere.'

'Yes.' Brigid sounded less than enthusiastic. 'In a week or two when Rebecca's more settled. I think she's cutting her first tooth. She woke three times last night. I expect that's why I've let the classes get me down.'

Shannon was waiting by the bus stop, talking to a woman with one baby in a buggy and another in a sling. Kristen drove slowly past, and Shannon saw her and waved. Earlier in the day there had been a slightly unpleasant incident that had started during a discussion about computers.

Hugo had insisted one day there would be nothing a human being could do that couldn't be done better by a computer. Computers would rule the world, he said, and only the cleverest people would be able to stop them. Hugo talked too much, everyone knew that, but the children's usual way of stopping him was to start laughing. This morning however, while he was in full flow, Shannon had pushed back her chair and shouted, 'You think you're so bloody brilliant but you don't know anything.' Shocked and upset, Hugo had struggled not to cry and for the rest of the time up to the morning break the whole group had been uncharacteristically subdued.

Kristen reached the end of the road and, acting on a sudden impulse, turned left then left again and started back towards the bus stop. If Shannon was still there, she would pretend she had to go in the direction of Downend and would be passing close to where she lived. If the bus had come and gone, she would take it as a sign that it was better to leave the girl to sort out her problems with her parents.

Shannon, and the woman with two babies, had been joined by a small, wiry man who appeared to be asking Shannon something. He had a hand on her sleeve and looked as if he might be up to no good. Kristen drew up at the kerb a few yards beyond where Shannon was standing and opened the passenger door.

'Jump in, I'll give you a lift. I'm going up Fishponds Road today – to visit a friend.'

Shannon hesitated, glancing at the baby in the buggy, almost as if leaving the others waiting at the bus stop would be unfair, then said an apologetic goodbye to the woman and climbed into the car.

'Bus late?' Kristen asked.

'Actually I'm not sure when they're supposed to come.'

Kristen leaned across to check Shannon's seat belt but it was clicked in place. 'That man at the bus stop, what did he want?'

'He asked about the classes.'

'At the college? How did he know –'

'He said he had a friend whose son went to them.'

'Anything else?'

Shannon hesitated. 'He asked if my teacher was called Mrs Frith.'

'Have you seen him before?'

'Never.'

'Let me know if he speaks to you again.'

Who was he? He must have seen Shannon leaving the college. Mrs Frith? He could be the man who had sent the letter. *The dog man.*

They had reached the mini-roundabout. 'Is the best way to go through the centre, Shannon?'

She nodded, holding her breath and letting it out in a sigh.

'I'm sorry about Hugo. I just felt so … I know you think it's because of the classes but it's not, I promise it's not.'

So there *was* something bothering her. 'You've a sister haven't you? Older or younger?'

'I've got two.' Shannon seemed surprised there was something Kristen didn't know about her. 'Jackie's twelve, she's at the school I'll be going to, and Danielle's seven.'

'How do they feel about you coming to the college?'

'Jackie's sorry for me, she thinks, like, if you're clever you have to do more work. Danielle doesn't really understand, only she's *really* good at reading for her age, better than Jackie, except Jackie doesn't try.'

Kristen could imagine the relationship between Shannon and Jackie might be tricky. They were close enough in age for comparisons to be inevitable. How did the parents deal with Shannon's gift for maths? Presumably she was far ahead of her older sister in most other subjects too.

Traffic was heavy and neither of them spoke again until after the turning at Trinity Road. Shannon kept yawning and rubbing her eyes but when Kristen glanced at her she smiled and folded her hands on her lap.

'Hay fever,' she explained, 'they call it hay fever but really it's an allergy. I'm allergic to dust mites and to dogs and cats. Have you got one? We've got a poodle but they don't moult. He's called Benji.'

'You think it's something in the car?' Kristen remembered giving a lift to one of Theo's friends and his border collie. Weeks ago it had been, not long after they returned from Ohio, but perhaps there were still hairs on the back seat.

'It's funny,' Shannon said, 'because, like, sometimes I'm all right for ages then it starts up again. You could meet my mum and dad, or would you rather drop me off at the end of the road? Dad's on holiday but we're not going away. Jackie may be out but Danielle will be there.'

Kristen was flattered. 'I'd love to meet them, Shannon.'

The house was on the edge of an estate, opposite a small industrial park. Some of the houses – the ones with modern front doors and replacement windows – looked owner-occupied, others still belonged to the council.

'Number fifty-seven,' Shannon said, 'you can stop anywhere along here.'

A child was peering through a downstairs window. She saw Shannon and waved wildly, and a moment later the front door came open and a large, bearded man, with a paintbrush in his hand, appeared.

'This is my teacher, Dad.' Shannon jumped from the car and ran towards him. 'She gave me a lift.'

'Good of you.' Mr Wilkins held out his free hand. 'Which would you be then, Brigid or Kristen? I'm afraid Shannon never tells us your surnames.'

'Kristen. I've only been teaching at the college for a couple of weeks. I came to fill in when Sarah Pearson had to go into hospital.'

'So you're the one who's showing them how to think straight. Hang on, I'll fetch my wife. Take your teacher in the front, Shannon.' He turned to his youngest daughter, who was dancing about and holding an ice lolly. 'And watch out, Danielle, there's drips going all over.'

Danielle pulled a face. 'My teacher's called Mrs Dixon,' she said, following Kristen into the front room and sitting down next to her. 'We did a collage last term. It was a supermarket.'

'That sounds fun. Which part did you paint?'

'Not painting.' Danielle looked as if she thought Kristen should have known better. 'It was cutting out and sticking. I did the fish counter, prawns and a lobster, only they've got whiskers and some of them broke.'

The room was small, with a pink fitted carpet, a large television, a maroon four-piece suite and a glass-topped coffee table with an African violet in a green pot and a copy of the *TV Times*.

Danielle was still talking about her collage, and how a boy called Sam had been sent to the head teacher for spoiling Ruby's oranges and bananas and being rude to Mrs Dixon, when the poodle ran in and jumped onto Kristen's lap.

'It's all right. I like dogs. Benji – is that right?'

'Benji with an "i" at the end,' Danielle said, 'and it's not short for Benjamin. I thought of his name. I did, didn't I, Shannon?'

Shannon gave her sister a look. 'She's nearly as bad as Hugo, talking all the time I mean, only Hugo hasn't got any brothers and sisters so I expect he's spoilt.'

Kristen gave her a non-committal smile. She was thinking about Theo and wondering if Alex had been right about Ros being unable to have more children.

'What's spoilt?' Danielle had finished her lolly but still had the stick in her mouth. 'Jackie talks more than me.' She jumped up, ran to the door, and shouted up the stairs. 'Jackie! Shannon's teacher's come, d'you want to see her?'

There was no reply, but a moment later Mr and Mrs Wilkins entered the room together with Shannon's older sister. Mrs Wilkins had the same dark colouring as Shannon but Jackie took after her father. On a man, his features looked rather nondescript but on Jackie they were extremely attractive. Shannon was a pleasant-looking girl but Jackie was going to be stunning. She was dressed in shorts and an emerald green top that brought out the unusual colour of her eyes, and she had her mother's curly brown hair.

'You see,' Shannon said, grinning, 'I've got the brains but Jackie's got the beauty.'

Mrs Wilkins turned to Kristen. 'She once heard her uncle say it and it's stuck in her head. You're both beautiful and you've both got brains so let's hear no more of that nonsense.'

'What have I got?' said Danielle, pressing up close to Kristen. 'Shannon says you make them do drawings. I can draw horses, would you like to see?' She jumped up and ran out of the door and as soon as she left the atmosphere seemed to change.

'How are you?' Mrs Wilkins took one of Kristen's hands in both of her own. 'I'd hate to speak out of turn but I just wanted to say how terribly sorry we are. Shannon told us what had happened and we think it's wonderful the way you're carrying on with your work.'

So Shannon knew about William. That meant all the children must know. Had Neville told them or had one of them found out and told the rest?

'Thank you.' Kristen saw Shannon's worried face and gave her a reassuring smile. Then Danielle appeared with her drawing and everyone relaxed.

When Kristen left the house a short time later, Mrs Wilkins accompanied her to the car, saying she needed some stamps from the post office on the corner. As soon as they were out of earshot, she asked if Kristen had noticed how sensitive Shannon was, and wanted to know if it was normal for clever children to be like that.

'It can be.' Kristen wondered where the question was leading. Had Shannon said something about the classes? About Hugo?

'Only the last couple of months ...' Mrs Wilkins looked flustered, as if she regretted raising the subject. 'Little things seem to upset her, programmes on the telly.'

'What kind of programmes?'

'Sad ones, even when it's only one of those silly soaps. She told me she thought it was wrong, people enjoying watching children in hospital and real-life crime. Then another time, Jackie was watching *Neighbours* and Shannon tried to switch it off, just because a couple were having an argument.'

As she drove away, Kristen felt convinced that any problem Shannon might have was unlikely to be the result of tensions at home. Jackie had complained how mean her father was, not letting Shannon help her with her homework, but Kristen could tell it was something they discussed openly and there was no real resentment.

In spite of the family being so friendly, Kristen felt uneasy. The car in front – a two-litre Golf GTI – was being driven at a little over ten miles an hour. Why buy such a powerful car? Slow drivers caused almost as many accidents as boy racers did – or was that one of those urban myths people trotted out as an excuse for dangerous overtaking? The sun had come out again and she considered driving to the coast – Clevedon or Portishead – as a way of raising her spirits, but it would only bring back memories. Better to spend the afternoon working on her thesis. Part of her had been unwilling to exchange the noise and good-natured banter of Shannon's house for the silence of her flat. And relief that Shannon's moodiness appeared to have nothing to do with the family was starting to give way to concern that the cause must have something to do with the college.

Today was Friday, one of the days Shannon had extra maths with Neville. Did that account for her outburst against Hugo? Kristen decided to talk to Brigid again although she would need to tread carefully. Brigid had known Neville for several years, since before the classes began. A week ago, Brigid couldn't have been friendlier, but these past few days she had been a little distant. How much help did Alex give her? Had putting off having a baby until they were in their late thirties and early forties been a joint decision, or had Alex had no wish for children and only given in after Brigid persuaded him how much she wanted one?

Ahead of her on the road, a crow had discovered the remains of a flattened animal. Unwilling to relinquish it, the bird flew up at the last possible moment so that Kristen thought it inevitable it would smash against her windscreen. Braking hard, without looking in her driving mirror, she heard the angry hoot of the driver behind and pulled into a lay-by with her heart thumping and tears pricking her eyelids. Accepting the job at the college had been a mistake. It was too soon. She was too raw. But what was the alternative? Sitting alone in the flat, drinking endless cups of coffee, pretending to work on her thesis? In any case she needed the money.

Since William's death she had been kept going by the routine of looking after Theo. William had been killed on a Friday evening. Theo had stayed at home until the following Wednesday then insisted on returning to school, and the pattern of their life, at least as far as their outward behaviour was concerned, had returned to normal. Without Theo for company, Kristen had spent her days reading, making notes, watching morning television with its addictive stories about babies who had survived against the odds or middle-aged women reunited with long-lost siblings. Then more desultory work on her thesis, followed by lunch – a biscuit or a piece of toast – followed by more work until half past two when it was time to buy something for supper and join the other mothers outside the school gate.

Re-joining the traffic, she forced herself to stop all the useless speculating about Brigid, about Shannon, about her brief conversation with Cameron Lyle. Only seven more days and Theo would be coming to stay.

13

A week had passed since Kristen's visit to the bungalow in Westbury-on-Trym. She phoned Vi but there was no reply and it occurred to her that she should have let it ring longer since Vi could be in her studio. The second time it was answered at once and Vi sounded out of breath.

'Was it you before? I was in the bog. How are you?'

'I'm fine,' Kristen said automatically. 'Look, I don't expect it's a good time but I wondered if it would be possible to record an interview about your views on artistic talent.'

'Now? You mean this afternoon?'

'You're painting.'

'I don't know if there's much I could tell you that I haven't said before.'

Kristen hesitated. The coolness in Vi's voice felt like snub. 'It was only a thought.'

She expected Vi to contradict her, apologise even, but she merely repeated how she was afraid she wouldn't be able to add much to her previous comments. 'Another day perhaps. Are you still there? Call round whenever you feel like a chat.'

As soon as Kristen put the phone down it started ringing.

'Kristen, is that you? Has Theo been in touch?'

'Theo?' Her heart began to race.

'He and Kimberly went to Hamleys. The toy shop. She thought he'd wandered off, gone up to another floor, would meet her by the door to the street.'

'Have you called the police?'

'Do you think I should?' Ros had picked up the panic in Kristen's voice. 'I wouldn't have bothered you only...'

'How long has he been missing?'

'Less than an hour but I thought he might have phoned you – I bought him a smartphone – but it's in his bedroom, he left it behind. He's been perfectly fine but you know how unpredictable children that age can be, and we had a slight disagreement.'

'What about?' Kristen realised she was shouting. 'I'll stay here in case he phones. You'll let me know if you find him. Where are you?'

'In the flat.'

Then why the hell couldn't you have taken Theo to the shop yourself? 'I'll ring off now in case he's trying to get through.'

He was on his way to Bristol. Did he have enough money for the train? Did he know which station to go to? Of course he did. He would have planned the whole thing. He was nearly nine. Nine was much older than eight. When he turned up what would she do? No use thinking about it, not until she'd talked to him. She could go to Temple Meads, wait on the platform. No, better to stay put, make absolutely sure there was no way they could miss each other.

Unable to relax, Kristen picked up an article about the parents of gifted children and stopped trying to work out exactly how far Theo's train had travelled. One of the children described in the article had been reading since he was two but by the age of five had begun to demand excessive attention and become violently disruptive if it was withheld. None of the children at the college appeared to have behaviour problems but perhaps that was because only a small sub-group could be described as having exceptional ability.

The phone rang and Kristen snatched it up.

'Kristen Olsen?' The voice was unfamiliar and she felt a stab of fear. Someone Theo had gone off with? Someone he had met at the station?

'Cameron Lyle,' the voice said, 'we met at the market. I

wondered if we could meet up. I've been talking to a guy called Steve. William may have mentioned him.'

'I don't think so.'

'Really?'

Lyle's surprise angered her. 'What did he say?'

There was a short pause. 'Why don't we get together so I can tell you properly? Tomorrow evening?' And when she hesitated. 'Later in the week if you prefer.'

'Tomorrow evening,' she said, thinking how she could easily cancel it if Theo was with her, 'but you'd better give me your number just in case.'

'Of course.' His voice was making it clear she had no right to sound so reluctant since she was the one who had contacted him in the first place. 'Eight thirty?' He suggested a pub in Kingsdown.

'Yes, all right.'

Her mobile was bleeping. 'Yes?' Her voice came out as a breathy croak.

'Panic over,' Ros drawled. 'I'm sorry I had to involve you in the little drama. The silly boy went to the wrong exit, waited half an hour then made his way back to the flat on his own, on the bus. I've ticked off Kimberly for not making sure there was no possibility of a mix-up, but really I don't think it was anyone's fault, just one of those things. I'd put him on the line but he's in the shower, washing off the London grime. Be in touch again soon. Bye for now.'

The pub was small and uninvitingly bare and unless there was another bar, not visible from the door, Cameron Lyle was late. Kristen ordered a pint and sat on a stool looking round at the flowered brocade wall seat, the Dickensian-style prints, stone jars, and brown gloss paint. The barman had close-cropped hair and looked about seventeen.

'Is that the right time?' She jerked her head in the direction of a wall clock with a brewer's logo painted on a speckled mirror and two racing cars for hands.

'Could be,' he muttered, coming round from behind the bar to collect some glasses and stamp a pile of ash into the black and green carpet.

The wall lights in the shape of fans were so hideous they were probably sought-after by collectors. On a raised section, three girls sat with their heads together, talking in hushed voices and every so often letting out a collective shriek of laughter.

Out of the corner of her eye, Kristen watched Lyle come in from the street and stop to have a word with two old men sitting at a table near the window. She had recognised him immediately because of his distinctive curly hair but in other ways he looked different from the first time they met. One of the old men gestured wildly with his arms and Lyle's eyes closed up with laughter, and she noticed the faint lines radiating towards his high cheekbones. She had estimated his age as roughly the same as her own. Now she was not so sure. Late thirties? His clothes were casual but smarter than hers and for a fleeting moment she wished she had taken more trouble with her appearance.

He had noticed where she was sitting but was in no hurry to join her and, by the time he had prised himself away from the old men and bought himself a drink, she had moved to a wooden bench in the corner and was pretending to take an interest in the competition on the back of a beer mat.

'Sorry.' His face had the feigned apologetic expression of someone who makes a habit of keeping people waiting. 'You haven't been here long? Did you have any trouble parking?'

She shook her head, hoping he would get to the point of their meeting as quickly as possible.

'This Steve I told you about.' He looked down at his glass. 'You say you've never heard of him? Apparently he and William had a shared interest in rock climbing then William had a fall.'

'He injured himself quite badly.'

'How long have you been living in Bristol?'

'We came here from London about three years ago. You say you just happened to bump into this Steve.'

'Sorry?' He gave her a long, questioning look. 'At the market. His girlfriend's interested in old cameras, binoculars, all that kind of crap.'

Why did she thinking he was making it up as he went along? It was all perfectly plausible but if there was anything he thought she ought to know he could have told her over the phone.

'Anyway,' he said, 'it's not important where the two of them met. It's what Steve told me about him.'

Her hand was steady on her glass but her head had started to throb. Lyle paused then, noticing her drink was almost finished, jumped in with an offer to buy her another.

'No thanks.' She kept her eyes on his face, trying to assess every transitory expression.

'Steve's a … how can I describe him? Cautious, set in his ways. If you ask me that could account for the way he described William.'

'How did he describe him?'

'Said he was a bit of a tearaway.'

'Is that how you saw him?'

'Me? No, but I told you –'

'You hardly knew him.' Kristen made a move to stand up. 'That's it then, is it?'

'Of course not. The reason I wanted to talk to you, Steve had an idea William could have been dragged into some kind of trouble.'

'Drugs?'

'It's crossed your mind already.' He looked relieved.

'No.' She was angry. 'If this Steve's so sure why didn't he get in touch with the police after William died?'

Lyle raised his eyebrows. 'You'd have liked him to?'

'If it helped to find who killed him. Anything's better than not knowing.'

He thought about his for a moment, as if he was weighing up how much to tell her, then he picked up his glass and asked how long she and Vi had known each other. 'No, sorry, you said before. You're working with Neville, only met her recently. What did you think of her?'

'I like her.'

He nodded. 'Most people do. So you'll be seeing her again.'

Kristen thought about her phone call the previous day and

Vi's unexpectedly off-putting response. 'I'm writing a thesis on children with exceptional ability. Vi doesn't believe in inherited talent, she thinks it's all a matter of motivation and hard work. I'm hoping to interview her, record some of her ideas.'

He laughed. 'I assume you favour the opposite view. This thesis of yours, how would you go about collecting evidence? I mean, who's going to be able to disentangle the effect of someone's childhood, who they met, their teachers ... it must begin at birth. And kids with bright parents start with a huge advantage.' He noticed her expression and broke off, smiling to himself. 'You're thinking I don't know what I'm talking about.'

'I'm hoping to do a pilot study. I started one in Ohio.'

'But you had to give it up when William decided to come back to Bristol. Why did you agree to it? No, sorry, don't answer that. I know I'm coming across as an insensitive bastard but it's only because...'

Kristen had stopped listening. She was remembering how William had said if they stayed on in America they'd have to get married or she'd be illegal. Had that contributed to his decision to leave? No, that was ridiculous. What difference would it have made, it would only have been a formality ... But supposing William had been lying when he said he wanted them to have their own baby, only not until he found himself a permanent job.

'Talking of exceptional ability.' Lyle could hardly keep a straight face. 'How come there are so few women geniuses? People claim it's because women have to spend so much time looking after kids but what about the ones who don't have any?'

'The most likely reason is that males, on average, score twice as highly as females on psychoticism, a trait that's closely related to creativity.'

'Say that again. No, I get it. The mad professor syndrome. There's nothing crazy about Vi, must be one of the sanest people I've come across. Still, she's hardly a genius.'

'You've known her quite a time?'

He counted on his fingers. 'Three years. We met when one of her paintings won a prize at an amateur art society exhibition. I could see she had potential, just needed someone to tell her how to market the stuff.'

'What about her teacher? She mentioned someone called Brian.'

'Oh, him,' he said scornfully, 'I daresay he's a reasonable enough teacher but he knows about as much about the London art scene as ...' He broke off, standing up and crossing to the bar, and she watched with annoyance as he chatted with the landlady for a couple of minutes before returning with replacement drinks.

When he sat down again his face was serious. 'On the few occasions I talked to William I got the impression you spent most of your spare time looking after his son. Before he decided to go to the States you had a job at the university too, did you?'

'I was teaching at a comprehensive.'

He nodded. 'So you could pick Theo up from school, and look after him during the holidays and half terms. I don't know how to say this, but obviously it's important to you, finding out what happened, whether he really was the victim of a mugging that went wrong.'

His eyes were partially closed, as if he was finding the whole conversation tedious. In that case, why had he bothered to get in touch? He was under no obligation and appeared to have taken very little interest in the murder until she contacted him. Under the table her fists had clenched.

'If you want the truth,' he said, speaking too loudly then lowering his voice when he noticed how people had turned to stare. 'Steve couldn't stand the guy, said he was a troublemaker, caused havoc wherever he went. The reason I'm telling you, the reason I'm here now, is I don't want you finding things out from other people, least of all from the cops. I won't bore you with the details but I could introduce you to a fair number of people who...'

Kristen never heard the rest. She reached the heavy glass door, dragged it open, and the noise of passing traffic blotted out every other sound.

14

Someone was leaning on Kristen's doorbell then a face peered through the window and, dragging the cover over her unmade bed, she hurried to let him in.

'Good.' The quietness of Tisdall's voice alarmed her. 'I hoped I'd catch you.'

'Theo went missing, but he's turned up.'

'Missing?'

'No, I don't mean ... A mix-up, outside a shop. He's coming here at the weekend.'

'Good.' He followed her, talking all the time and irritating her as he always did with the way he alternated between sounding almost like a friend, then reverting to polite formality. 'This hostel where Mr Frith did voluntary work – how many evenings a week did you say it was?'

'I told you. Tuesdays and Fridays.'

'Until you went to America.' He had the sympathetic expression of someone who was going to tell you something you wouldn't want to hear. 'I've spoken to Daniel Joseph, who runs the hostel, and he says Mr Frith gave up working there on Fridays three or four months before you left.'

'Why didn't you find this out before?'

Tisdall frowned. 'Sloppy checking, I'm afraid, although that might be a little unfair. At the time of the first inquiries, Joseph was on holiday and the man standing in for him had never met

Mr Frith, just looked up an old duty roster and assumed the hours had remained unchanged. After you returned to Bristol he was in most evenings, was he?'

Kristen struggled to keep calm. 'He was trying to find a job, had to see people who might be able to help.'

He nodded and they sat in silence for several moments, with Kristen wondering if he was hoping to force her into admitting she had known about the hostel all along. But when he spoke it was to ask why William had been unable to return to his job at the university.

'You can't leave and expect to be taken back a few months later. I don't imagine Alex Howell was very pleased he'd thrown in the job in Ohio. What you're trying to say – William pretended he was working at the hostel but really he was having an affair?'

'There are reasons why he might have wanted to keep you in the dark. Perhaps he was moonlighting, wanted to make some extra cash.'

'Or doing something outside the law, have you thought of that?'

Tisdall looked over her shoulder at the crumpled bed. 'There's probably a simple explanation. It made sense to ask you first. You might have forgotten he'd cut it from two nights to one.'

'Either I've been lying to you or I've told you the truth as far as I know it and William went out every Friday, pretending he was going to the hostel.'

Tisdall stood up. 'If you think of anything…'

'I've told you everything.' But she knew what he was saying. The information he had given her might trigger off a memory, a stray remark William had made, an evening when he had come back even later than he usually did.

Tisdall was hardly out of the flat before the phone started ringing.

It was Ros.

'Me again, Kristen. About next weekend, would it be terribly inconvenient if we changed it to the one after? My father has decided to pay us a visit – I expect William told you he lives in the south of France – and it would a shame if he and Theo missed each other.'

'Yes, all right.' She had barely taken in the news about William's nights out. Now another blow.

'Theo was disappointed when I told him but I've shown him the new date on the calendar and he's counting the days. Oh, hang on, here he is.' Ros's voice faded but Kristen could still hear what she was saying. 'Darling, it's Kristen, come and talk to her, tell her what you've been doing.'

'Hello.' Theo sounded as if he had a cold.

'Theo, it's lovely to hear your voice, how are you? Have you been visiting lots of interesting places?

'We went to the seaside but there wasn't any sand, only stones.'

'Oh, Theo,' Ros shrieked, 'you had a wonderful time.'

'Did you get my letter?' Kristen asked.

'I was going to write one back but Mum said I could stay the night with you, only now Grandpa's coming.'

'But it won't be long till you come here.'

Ros came back on the line. 'He's had a bit of a snuffle, nothing serious and he's over the worst. We had a day trip to Brighton. John drove us down. Marvellous sea air and all those fascinating little shops. Anyway, I won't keep you. Bye for now, and nearer the date I'll let you know the exact time we'll be arriving. Oh, by the way, you remember I told you about the filming in Yorkshire? Looks as if it may actually come off. Only be two or three days and fortunately Kimberly's agreed to sleep here.'

After Ros rang off, Kristen ate a Mars bar in three bites, and washed it down with a glass of red wine. Agonising questions piled up in her head. Where had William gone those Friday nights? He had told her the hostel was understaffed, which was why he was often back so late. Had he ever spoken the truth? All the time they were together, had he been sleeping around while pretending they had such a perfect relationship? During the months before they left for America, they had both been working hard and often gone to bed exhausted. Then, in Ohio, the apartment had been cramped and Theo had found it hard adjusting to a new school. How often had they made love? Once a fortnight? Less? When things were easier, when they felt more settled … but they never had. Lately, it had even crossed her mind that William had asked her to live with him because he thought it would make it more likely the judge awarded him custody of Theo. Or perhaps she was simply a useful person to look after his child. But it hadn't been like that, they had loved each other and no one, not even William, could have pretended that convincingly.

Bimbam's was more crowded than last time. Tisdall showed his identification to the same man as before and was escorted to Mrs Ronane's office only to discover someone else sitting in her chair, a fat man with hair so greasy Tisdall half expected drops to slither onto the collar of his jacket.

'DS Tisdall,' he said, 'I spoke to Mrs Ronane last Tuesday.'

In spite of his weight, the man had leapt out of his chair as if he had received an electric shock. 'Mrs Ronane won't be back until next week. If it's about the new licence.'

'I'm looking for Pascale.'

'Oh, is that all?' The man's chins sank onto his chest with relief. 'What's she done?'

'Nothing. I need to ask her a few questions, nothing to do with the club. One of your staff suggested she might be able to help with some inquiries we're making.'

The man made no comment, asked no questions, and escorted Tisdall to the bar where he had a word with a bloke, busy polishing glasses, and disappeared back into his room.

'Over there.' The barman jerked his head towards two women dressed in the usual get-up of short skirts, low-cut tops, and high-heeled shoes. They were watching him, as if they had been waiting for him and as he approached the spot where they were standing one of them moved away.

'You wanted me?' The remaining woman was younger than her companion, probably in her mid-thirties, and better-looking, quite classy. Her hair was a reddish-brown mass of curls, with a fringe that covered her eyebrows, and a light covering of freckles on her nose. Looking at her reminded Tisdall of how he had once been obsessed with getting Julie into bed. Was that all life was about? Males picking up as many females as they could get their hands on. And then what? Did he want Grace back because she no longer wanted him? No, Grace was different.

'You're Pascale?' he asked, 'I'm sorry, I don't know your other name. I spoke to someone called Glen earlier in the week and he told me you might be able to help.'

She gave him a warm smile. 'Shall we sit down, my feet are killing me. If it's about Will, I've a theory or two you might be interested in. Or there again you might not.'

Tisdall followed her to a table in a dark corner. 'If you know something you should have contacted us weeks ago.'

'There's knowing and knowing. I can't tell you anything definite but if you're having doubts about this dog man person I reckon it's about bloody time.'

'What makes you say that?' Her perfume smelled expensive although, as Julie often pointed out, Tisdall was no expert on such matters. He felt sleepy. Maybe it was the lack of air-conditioning. He'd been hoping to talk to the woman well away from other customers but having their conversation blocked out by the noise around was preferable to having it overheard by the fat slob in the office.

'To explain that I'd have to tell you about Will.' She placed a hand on the table and her fingers kept time with the rhythm of the music. 'Good friends we were, but nothing more and you can believe it or not, makes no difference to me. Most men, I won't say they only want one thing since there's plenty not satisfied with that. They like a good listener, someone to make them feel cared for, like when they were kids and their mum kissed them goodnight and tucked them up in bed.'

'That's what Frith was like?'

'No! What I'm trying to explain, he wasn't the little boy type. In fact, I can't imagine him wanting his mummy even when he was a kid.' She turned her head and Tisdall saw Glen come into the bar, glance in their direction, and pretend not to have noticed them. 'And don't call him Frith,' Pascale said, 'like he wasn't a person, like he's just part of a murder investigation. Some loved him, some hated him, but me … If I knew the person who did it I'd pay someone to shoot the fucker in the back.'

'These people who disliked him, I don't suppose you'd be prepared to give me a list.'

She gave a short, humourless laugh. 'What I mean, people took notice of him. He wasn't the kind who gets overlooked.'

She had whetted his appetite. Now he was in danger of leaving the place with nothing more than the opinion of one of Frith's obvious admirers.

'What happened to the kid?' she asked suddenly. 'I heard he'd gone back to his mother, only that's not what Will would have wanted. He loved that boy, and he was fond of her and all.'

'You mean Kristen Olsen.'

She nodded. 'I never met her. Well, I suppose that goes without saying. Felt sorry for her, stuck at home with the boy while Will was out enjoying himself but I daresay it made him nicer to her when he got back home.'

The club was so crowded Tisdall's groin was being pushed against the table. He decided to drop the subject of Frith for the time being and ask Pascale what went on at the club apart from the usual after-hours drinking.

'You only come here on Saturdays?' he said, 'is that right?'

'Glen told you. I'm not on the game if that's what you're thinking, it's just somewhere to go. Will and I used to have these discussions – about what makes people tick, about life and that.'

The woman she had been talking to when he came into the bar had edged closer. Pascale looked up and gave her a wink.

'Lisa,' she told Tisdall, 'she's on her own like me. There's three of us shacked up together.'

'I see.' He was thinking about Brake's vain attempts to find out where she lived. 'Glen mentioned a man who repairs musical instruments.'

She burst out laughing. 'Ned's old enough to be my grandfather, only don't have a go at Glen. Poor kid, he picks up bits and pieces then makes out people like to confide in him. No, I don't mean he's simple, just a vivid imagination and no one to keep him on the straight and narrow.'

Lisa had pulled up another chair. 'We take it in turn to look after the kids,' she explained. 'Dotty's with them tonight. Better than being stuck on your own in some high-rise dump.'

Tisdall was irritated by her presence. On the other hand she must have known Frith too. 'Sounds like a sensible arrangement.'

'Sounds like a sensible arrangement,' Pascale imitated, patting the back of Tisdall's hand to show she meant no offence. 'I've told you all I know. If I think of anything else I'll give you a call. Write your name and number on my wrist and I won't wash it off for a week.' She tried to stand up but the table had wedged her into the corner.

'I haven't quite finished.' Tisdall made it clear he was including Lisa in the conversation. 'You're aware of the time and place where William Frith was killed?'

Pascale shrugged. 'Only what we read in the paper.'

He looked at her closely and decided he had underestimated her age, she was nearer forty. 'People must have talked about it. Incidentally, when was the last time you saw him?'

'Saw him or talked to him?'

'Either. Both.'

She paused, deliberately keeping him waiting. 'To talk to, that would be just after he came back from the States, although he only called in for an hour or so.'

'The day he was killed he'd gone out to meet someone he thought might give him a job.'

Lisa looked puzzled. 'Why would he want to do that? He was going back to his old job in the autumn.'

'Who told you that?' Tisdall asked.

'He did, of course.'

'So you've no idea who he might have been meeting? And you say you both saw him again only not to speak to?'

'Two days before …' Pascale broke off and the expression in her eyes convinced Tisdall she had been genuinely fond of Frith. 'I saw him at the shopping centre. He was with this woman.'

'It could have been Kristen Olsen.'

Pascale shook her head. 'He told me how Kristen looked, described her in detail. This one … no, sorry, I can't help, there was nothing about her that stuck in your mind.'

'Oh, come on. Tall? Short? Fat? Thin? What age would you say she was?'

'Couldn't tell you, not specially young but definitely not old. Anyway, she could have been a stranger wanting directions. They were standing on the corner near the Odeon, where the bus comes. Then they split up and went in different directions.'

'And you never saw him again?'

'I told you.' She spoke quietly. 'What would be the point in keeping something back?'

Tisdall said nothing. He was thinking about Kristen Olsen, wondering if she had known all along that Frith left her looking after the boy so he could go out and enjoy himself. Hardly grounds for murder, but he was beginning to doubt most of what he had been told about Frith.

15

In spite of Kristen driving her home and meeting her family, Shannon still had the same strained expression as before, although when she caught Kristen looking at her she tried to conceal it. If there was something about the classes that was worrying her, Kristen had hoped the visit to her home would give her the confidence to tell her what was wrong, but several days had past and nothing had been said, and the other children were beginning to notice how subdued she had become.

One morning, Kristen had given them some ambiguous pictures and asked them to describe what was going on. Shannon kept putting up her hand and asking how to spell a particular word and, when Kristen suggested she look it up in the dictionary, she complained that dictionaries were no good unless you knew the first few letters of the word.

'Shakespeare was useless at spelling,' said Hugo, 'anyway I've heard you can get computers you speak into and they do the writing for you.'

Shannon bit her lip and attention soon turned towards Jack who wanted to know how to spell 'psycho' and whether psychopaths always killed people.

'Why would they want to do that?' said Hugo. 'My dad says the clever ones go into business or politics. They don't care what anyone thinks of them so they can do what they like.' He looked at Kristen and for once his self-assurance was a little shaky. 'That's right, isn't it?'

At the end of the morning, Kristen wanted to catch Brigid before she left and, since Brigid was usually in a hurry, she finished her own class a few minutes early and was waiting in the corridor when Brigid came out of the other room, noticed her, and frowned.

'You're in a rush,' Kristen said, 'perhaps I could walk with you to the end of the road.'

'Not really.' Brigid's frown was replaced by a cheerful smile. 'My childminder's had to go to the dentist so Alex is looking after Rebecca. Quite an achievement persuading him. When she was born I thought we'd share the childcare. Some hope!'

'If you need a break I'd be happy to help. I haven't much experience of small babies but I'm sure I could manage for an hour or two.'

'What was it you wanted to talk about?'

'I met Shannon's parents.'

Brigid's eyebrows shot up. 'Does Neville know?'

'I gave her a lift home. I was going in her direction anyway. They seem a very nice family. Nothing wrong there.'

'Good. Not long until you see Theo.' Brigid was halfway through the outside door. 'When's he arriving, on Friday evening?'

'Ros's father is coming to London.' Kristen was oddly reluctant to explain how the visit had been put off. 'He's coming the following weekend instead.'

'I'm sorry. Sorry for Theo too. Still, it's only one more week. Look, I'll have to go, Neville's asked me to buy some books for the classes. Oh, by the way, did Vi Pitt give you any good ideas for your thesis?'

'Not yet, but I'm hoping to see her again.'

'I thought the two of you would hit it off.' Brigid sounded almost resentful. 'Have a word with Neville about Shannon. It'll put your mind at rest.'

What would put her mind at rest? Passing on the responsibility to someone else? When she knocked on Neville's door there was no answer, but before she could walk away it

112

came open and he stood there with a sheaf of papers in his hand.

'You're busy,' she said.

'Expecting a phone call that hasn't materialised. Come along in.'

Kristen closed the door behind her. 'It's about Shannon Wilkins.'

'Oh yes.' He had his back turned, sorting through the papers. 'Brigid said you found her rather quiet.' His hand shook a little – or had she imagined it?

'I gave her a lift home on Friday.'

He spun round. 'You told her mother you were worried about her?'

'No, of course not. Both her parents were at home, and her two sisters. I only stayed a short time and I certainly didn't gain the impression there was anything wrong there.'

'Interesting how such ordinary parents produced such a gifted child. You know there used to be a theory, rather an unpleasant one I've always thought, that a child with a markedly different IQ from its siblings almost certainly had a different father.' He gave a short laugh. 'Yes, I agree, far too many theories about with very little evidence to back them up.'

He was still smiling but it was a fixed smile, designed to conceal his real feelings. 'Incidentally, don't forget to make a date to interview Vi. She's always keen to talk about her work and the famous Brian, the teacher who got her started in the first place.'

Instead of returning straight home after the classes, Kristen decided to walk on the Downs. The sun was shining but there was almost always a breeze because it was so high up. Leaving her car near the metal railings, she stared down the sheer drop to the bottom of the Gorge. The tide was out, leaving a narrow channel of river running between great slabs of mud. Once or twice since the Suspension Bridge had been built, someone had jumped and landed in the mud, surviving with only minor injuries, but they were the lucky ones – or perhaps the unlucky exceptions, since most of the suicide victims achieved their purpose.

The first signs of vertigo, a shivery sensation at the back of her knees, forced her to turn her back on the Gorge and start watching two boys who were attempting to fly a kite. One held the string and the other ran flat out, letting go then spinning round only to see the red and white bird drop to the grass. Beyond them a man was wheeling a pram, bending towards the baby, probably making sure it was not being bumped about too much, and as he drew closer Kristen was surprised to see it was Alex Howell. Why surprised? Brigid had told her he was looking after Rebecca but somehow she had never imagined him pushing a pram, let alone taking the trouble to walk all the way to the Downs. When he saw her he raised his hand in greeting, waiting for a cyclist to pass, and crossing the road to join her.

'Didn't expect to see you here.' He fixed the brake on the pram. 'Childminder's away so I've been left in charge.'

'You walked all this way?'

He laughed. 'Afraid not. This contraption folds up, fits into the boot. Until we had Rebecca I was almost completely unaware of the number of consumer durables the baby goods trade had dreamed up. Slings, seats, bouncy chairs, how on earth do people on low incomes manage?'

Kristen bent over the pram and Rebecca gazed back at her. 'She's looks as though she's grown,' she said, 'even in the short time since I last saw her.'

Alex smiled. 'She eats well enough. Not so hot on sleep. I saw you looking down at the river. Amazing the way the water rises and falls with the tide. Back in the thirteenth century, the lower park of the River Frome was diverted to join the Avon and provide a harbour, nothing like the size of our floating harbour now but quite a feat of construction for the time.'

'I didn't realise you were interested in history.'

'Dry scientist, dry historian, what's the difference?' He was looking into the distance. 'Brigid's been tired lately. Yes, I know she's bound to be, it's perfectly normal. All the same I wondered … Has she said anything? I try to help as much as possible but…'

'She wanted to go back to work, didn't she?' Kristen had no

intention of becoming a go-between in any dispute they might be having about who got up in the night to see to the baby.

'Good for her to get out of the house,' he said. 'Trouble is, she worries.'

'About Rebecca?'

He touched the baby's cheek. 'She was three weeks premature, had mild breathing difficulties, but only for a couple of days and the doctors and nurses were wonderful. I expect all parents say the same, especially if there's some concern about their child. That's what I'd like to be if I could start all over again.'

'A doctor?' Alex, the successful academic, had some regrets about his chosen career.

'Sounds corny, I know, but I'd like to think I was doing something worthwhile.'

'What about your work at the university?'

He shrugged. 'Progress tends to be slow. My research assistants are bright enough but ever since you and William went to America …'

'Do you know why he wanted to go?' she said, surprising herself. 'Surely he could have got a lectureship over here.'

'The grass was greener.' Alex pulled at the light blanket that had caught on one of Rebecca's feet. 'There's more cash in the States, at least there used to be. I was going to ask after Theo but it must be painful talking about him. Do you have any family living nearby?'

'Family? Oh. No. My mother died when I was sixteen and my father … He's living in Indonesia at the moment. With a girl called Wangi. It means "fragrant". She's having a baby.'

'He knows what's happened?'

'I'm going to tell him when the police –'

'He might want to come back here. See you.'

'What would be the point?'

He put a hand on her shoulder. 'Life must go on. When disaster strikes, some people fall apart. Others summon up all their strength. I admire the way you're handling things. So does Brigid. No, we really do.'

The baby was making sucking noises and Kristen wondered

if Alex had remembered to bring her bottle or if he would have to drive her home, yelling all the way.

'No doubt the children on your courses have got parents who'll go to any lengths to get them into the best schools,' he said, 'move house, convert to Catholicism. Although when the time comes I wouldn't hesitate to do the same for Rebecca.'

Kristen made no comment and he took it as a criticism. 'Take away the window dressing and are we really different from any other species? Tell me about the girl, Shannon. Would you say the more imaginative ones have a tendency to indulge in flights of fancy so whatever they told you would need to be taken with a pinch of salt?'

'What makes you say that?' Had Brigid said something about Shannon?

'I'm interested in your thesis. There's a visiting academic in the Education Department who's written a book about genius. Perhaps you'd like to meet him. Find out a few details, shall I?'

'Thanks.' Having a child seemed to have had a good effect on him. He was softer, gentler than she remembered. Maybe this trip to the Downs was a one-off. If not, Kristen wondered what Brigid had to complain about. He seemed besotted with the baby.

'Oh, by the way.' Alex made it clear from his change of tone that he was moving to a more mundane topic. 'What do you think of Vi and Neville's bungalow? An offence to someone with an artistic eye, I'd have thought.'

'I assumed it was where Neville lived before he and Vi got together.'

'Good heavens, no. Vi had a tiny flat in Southmead, so I suppose from her point of view the bungalow's a palace, but when Neville's sister was alive he had a Georgian place. Brigid told you about Jane, the accident.'

'Jane was Neville's sister?'

He nodded. 'Apparently she'd taken it into her head to go up into the roof space, then coming down ...' He broke off, twisting the ring on his wedding finger. 'A verdict of accidental death was never in doubt but ... Vi gave evidence, said she'd caught Jane once before trying to climb up to the loft, and of course there was no one to contradict or corroborate this. At the first opportunity, Neville sold the house.'

What was Alex trying to say? That Neville should have allowed a longer period to elapse before he and Vi lived together? Jane had been his sister, not his wife. Or was his remark more accusatory? Was he implying Jane had become such a burden…

Rebecca was making hiccupping noises. Alex began pushing the pram backwards and forwards. 'It was all pretty grim for Neville and Vi, but it brought them together. Tragedy has that effect.'

The baby's hiccups turned into full-scale crying and in an instant, Alex had lifted her out of the pram and was holding her against his sweater.

'She's not hungry,' he said, 'I fed her before we came out. And it's unlikely to be wind. They get lonely, need the comfort and warmth of another human being. Have you seen how much hair she's got? She's lovely, isn't she? I'd no idea such a small baby could be so beautiful.'

'Alex, I wanted to ask you, did William tell you about his voluntary work? Only I thought he worked at this hostel two evenings a week and it turns out –'

'Don't believe he mentioned it. Some problem, is there?'

'No, not really. The police seem set on blackening his name, making out he wasn't at the hostel when he said he was. Anyway, what difference does it make?'

Alex put an arm round her shoulder. 'I'm so sorry. If there was anything I could do. If they're right about this dog man character it's high time they arrested him. Still, there must be any number of pickpockets in the city.'

'But not ones that pretend to have lost their dog.'

He gave her a rueful smile. 'No, I suppose not. And as far as I could tell, the description of him was vague, could have applied to any number of down and outs. Come round to the house again. Fix it up with Brigid. We're always pleased to see you. Oh, and about this hostel business. If I were you I wouldn't give it another thought. If you want my opinion, the police are clutching at straws.'

So many people who wanted to reassure her, but none of them knew the truth. And what *was* the truth? That a pickpocket had got into a fight with William and he had fallen and hit his head? But the man at the bus stop, talking to Shannon, wouldn't have had a hope in hell of overpowering William in a struggle.

A short distance away, she could see Alex fastening Rebecca into her car seat. Would Rebecca cry all the way home, or would the movement of the car send her to sleep?

Alex's kindness had upset her, weakened her defences. Getting up each morning was so hard, but she had to keep going – if only for Theo's sake. Besides, what was the alternative? Soon, she would have to start looking for a full-time job. In Bristol? If she was in London she would be able to see Theo more often. Except … would that be what he wanted?

If she knew who had killed William perhaps she would be able to move on. *Move on*: an expression endlessly repeated in television programmes about missing people and unsolved crimes. Was it true? Did the people left behind move on?

Turning back to the Gorge, Kristen watched the cars crawling along the Portway. A large bird flew out of the woods on the other side of the river. One of the peregrine falcons that nested there? William would have known. So would Theo. For the first time, she thought about all the things William would miss out on now his life had been cut short. Birdwatching, rock climbing, swimming in the sea, watching Theo grow up. Growing old – but that was something he would have hated.

The sun felt warm on her face and, for a fleeting moment, she felt a small twinge of hope. One day, things would change.

She might even get Theo back.

16

On his way to see Alex Howell at the university, Tisdall stopped off at the shopping centre to buy a birthday present for Julie. During breakfast he had asked her what she wanted and struggled to contain his irritation when she put on a silly, little girl's voice and said 'A surprise.' Surprise … if she wanted a surprise …

The store had air conditioning but the area where he was standing was chokingly stuffy with a mass of conflicting perfumes. Women, whose faces had grown hard with the effort of achieving the required perfection of appearance, re-arranged their bottles and pots and exchanged pieces of gossip as they waited for a customer to approach. Tisdall picked a saleswoman 'of more mature years' than the rest, asked how much the box of skin preparations that entitled him to a complimentary purse would set him back and took his card from his wallet without even listening to her answer.

'Would you like me to gift-wrap it, sir?'

'Sorry? Oh, yes, please.'

The woman was much as he would expect Ros Richards to look in ten years' time. Dark hair, probably dyed, but then most women did a bit of touching up these days. Even Julie did something she called "bringing out the highlights".

With his mission accomplished, he returned to the multi-storey car park and set off, more or less on automatic pilot, on a route that would take him past the house he had bought twelve years ago when Serena was still a toddler. Grace would be at work so there was no risk of her seeing his car. During the week he had called round twice, once when he knew Serena would be home and again when she was out. The first time Grace had seemed pleased to see him, talked about old times, said complimentary things about him in front of Serena, but the second visit had been different. Why had he called round *again*, Grace kept asking, adding that even if Serena had been in it would only have confused her, let her think he was going to make a habit of it. In any case she was going out.

Changing his mind about driving past the house, he turned right at the lights and accelerated up the steep hill that led to the Downs. Liz Cowie wanted to be brought up to date on how he and Brake had been spending their time. Lately he had been finding it hard to keep Brake occupied then he'd hit on the idea of asking him to get hold of a print out of the dog man cases that had been reported to the police and start searching for a pattern. Times of day, types of victim, precise spots where the thefts had taken place. Brake, in the politest way possible, had suggested all that must have been done before, but Tisdall had brushed aside his objections telling him it never did any harm to take a fresh look, pick out a few victims that could be re-interviewed.

The traffic at the top of Whiteladies Road had come to a standstill. A van that could never have passed a reputable MOT test had broken down and two people, a man and a woman, were attempting to push it towards the kerb. Tisdall decided he had better help although, on second thoughts, turning up at the university covered in oil and grime might not be such a good idea. For reasons that would not require the insight of a trained psychologist, he disliked all places of further and higher education, and Grace's announcement a couple of years back that she had enrolled for a course in computing and business studies had knocked him off balance, stirring up prejudices he had never known he had.

From his father's point of view, the world consisted of 'people like us' and 'snobs'. The rich were either crooks, or people who had inherited cash, and his father had a fixation about blokes who had been to university – and as far as women were concerned … It was absurd, decades out of date, but somewhere along the line Tisdall must have picked up something of his father's attitude and Grace going to college had felt like the beginning of the end.

The department where Alex Howell worked was in a large purpose-built building with steps leading up to double swing doors. Tisdall entered the foyer and came face to face with a glass-fronted display with the names of each member of staff, along with a coloured photograph. Howell's glasses obscured most of his face but it was still possible to see how he had wanted to portray himself; serious, important, but able to produce a faint, quizzical smile.

As he gave his name to the uniformed man on the desk, Tisdall began going over in his head the best way to encourage Howell to talk openly about William Frith, his character, general attitude to life, and above all any extra-marital activities he might have hinted about to his employer. Strictly speaking, the university had employed Frith, but it was Howell's research money that paid his salary. Was that how everything worked these days?

Howell was expecting him but still managed to keep him waiting seven minutes. One of Tisdall's wisdom teeth ached and exploring it with his tongue did nothing to relieve the discomfort. To take his mind off the twinges, he read the fire instructions twice, then a list of publications that must have dropped out of a student's bag; either that or it had been discarded as not worth keeping.

When a message finally came through that he could go up to Howell's room he took the lift, emerging on the third floor to find Howell waiting in the corridor, wiping his hands on a cloth.

'So sorry, Sergeant. Lucky you caught me. Been looking after my daughter while my wife was at work.'

Tisdall noted with a faint smile that the fingers of Howell's left hand were black, presumably from a marker pen. 'As I said on the phone, I wanted to have a few words about William Frith.'

Howell showed him into his room and pulled forward a metal chair with a padded seat. 'Whatever you need to know. Are you still working on the same theory or have some new lines of inquiry been set up?'

'We're keeping an open mind.' Tisdall pushed back his chair to increase the distance between them. 'I realise another officer spoke to you at the time of the murder, but that was to ask if you knew what Frith could have been doing down by the river that particular evening.'

Howell removed his glasses then replaced them when a letter in his in-tray caught his eyes. 'Afraid I couldn't be any help. As far as I can tell, the Avon Forest, as they like to call it, is not specially noted for its interesting flora and fauna. Like everyone else, no doubt, I could hazard a guess William had been going on one of his runs. He was a fitness fanatic, took as much exercise as he could fit into his busy schedule.'

'And this person he was meeting later, the one he thought might be able to help him find a job, you've no idea who it could have been?'

'I've thought about that, gone over snippets of conversation, a talk I had with him shortly after he returned from the States. No, I'm sorry.' Howell pulled at a loose thread on the cuff of his olive green shirt. 'If anyone else at the university was interested in employing him I imagine I'd have heard about it. Must have been some other kind of work he was after. I've an idea he'd become a little disillusioned with academic life, found it too painstakingly routine.'

Howell's office was smaller than Tisdall had expected but most of his work was probably carried out in a laboratory. He was flicking through a desk diary and Tisdall wondered if something useful had occurred to him. But when he came to the end he closed it without further comment.

Tisdall tried again. 'And the brief conversation you referred to, that was the last time you spoke to him?'

'We were hoping to have him and Kristen round for a meal but our baby was only a few weeks old so we'd put it off for a while.'

'What did you talk about – the last time you met?'

'Why he hadn't been able to settle in Ohio. Oh, and I made a few suggestions about a career change, but he seemed unsure what he wanted to do. Universities are market-orientated these days, there's pressure to carry out research that guarantees a substantial grant rather than spend time on something that might or might not achieve an important result.'

'That's what Frith objected to?' Tisdall was thinking about Grace's course and how Howell would despise anything that had a purely practical application. 'That's the case in your field too?'

Howell gave a bitter laugh. 'My field's no different from any other.'

Consulting his notes, although everything he wanted to ask was in his head, Tisdall inquired if Howell had felt Frith owed him an apology. 'After he returned from the States.'

Farther down the corridor a door squeaked open and a group of students who must have come out from a lecture passed by, laughing and talking. Howell appeared oblivious to the racket. 'For not sticking it out, giving the post a chance? Perhaps he thought I'd take him back but that was out of the question, we'd started work on another project and I'd taken on two new research assistants.'

He was angry with Frith, Tisdall thought, but he was not going to admit it for fear of losing face. All the effort he had put into helping him onto the first rung of a promising career, and Frith had returned to Bristol within the year and more or less told him he could stuff the academic world.

'I felt sorry for Kristen,' Howell said, 'she'd given up her teaching to go to America. Jobs in decent schools are not easy to come by.'

'So she wasn't too pleased about what happened either.'

'As far as Kristen was concerned, William could do no wrong. I daresay she worried about uprooting Theo twice within the space of a year but kids his age are pretty adaptable.'

Did Howell include adapting to living in London with a mother he had only seen for the odd weekend since the age of four? 'One last thing, Dr Howell, would you say you knew Frith well – as a person, I mean?'

Howell yawned. 'There's a question. If I had to give a thumbnail sketch I'd say he was highly intelligent and amusing company, but a bit of a maverick. Didn't like being told what to do but that's true of most creative people. I liked him. He could drive you insane, frequently did, but it was more than compensated for by the intellectual stimulation he provided. Do you have children, Sergeant?'

'One daughter.'

'Then you'll understand how Kristen must be feeling. Ros Richards is the legal parent, no one can dispute that, but surely the first concern ought to be what's best for the boy. My wife sometimes accuses me of being too logical, too rational, but as far as Kristen and the boy are concerned I'd be inclined to bypass the letter of the law and settle for some kind of rough justice. If I could think of anything that would stand up in court I wouldn't be sitting here now.'

17

During the evening, Vi phoned to ask if Kristen would like to accompany her to an exhibition.

'Not my stuff,' she explained, 'I haven't nearly enough.'

'That's because it sells so well.' Kristen was pleased that the slight coolness the last time they spoke had been replaced by a friendly invitation.

'The exhibition,' Vi said, 'it's children's work. The winners of a competition organised by a Sunday paper. The first time I met Cameron was at an exhibition. What they used to call psychotic art. Horrible name for it, I expect they use something different these days, but wonderful work, so powerful, so original.'

The first time she met Cameron. Hadn't he said the first time had been at an amateur art show where Vi had won third prize?

'I'd love to go with you,' Kristen said.

'Good. And perhaps we could have some lunch together afterwards. We'd better make our own way to the exhibition.' She gave Kristen the time and place. 'See you soon then. Take care.'

Just before she put the phone down, Kristen thought she heard a man coughing. Neville? Home already, telling Vi how Kristen had spoken to him about Shannon Wilkins and seemed intent on stirring up trouble? Was the invitation to the exhibition a way of providing an opportunity to sound her out?

On the other hand, if Neville had anything to do with Shannon's behaviour he was hardly likely to mention her name to Vi.

Of course, the man in the background, the one with a cough, could have been Cameron Lyle. Had he told Vi about their meeting at the pub and the way Kristen had walked out on him? Since then she had spent sleepless nights going over his exact words – and her own – trying to work out why he had thought it a good idea to pass on someone else's criticism of William. To prevent her hearing it from the police, that was what he had said, or was it because Lyle himself had an axe to grind?

Theo's latest letter was propped up on the mantelpiece. Kristen re-read it and her spirits lifted a little.

Dear Kristen, it's very hot here. We saw a dead rat floating in the river. Kimberly had to go and see her mother so John took me to the park. He's not very good at football and he hurt his toe. We had spaghetti rings for tea.

So Ros had talked John into looking after Theo while she attended an audition, or more likely met up with friends. The novelty of having her son living with her seemed to be wearing off faster than even Kristen could have imagined. What a bloody stupid situation. Ros either paid or cajoled people into staying with Theo while she, Kristen, sat alone in her flat with one thing uppermost in her mind: how to find a way to convince Ros he would be better off living with the person who had cared for him virtually every night and day since he was four and a quarter years old.

The exhibition of child art had been touring the country for several weeks before it reached Bristol. Kristen vaguely remembered reading about it. Different classes for different age groups, an overall winner who was only six, but people always liked the younger children's work best.

She reached the gallery early and found Vi in the foyer, looking as if she had been waiting for some time.

'I'm not late, am I?'

'Shouldn't think so.' Vi was wearing a brown cotton jacket and a pair of trousers that stopped well above her ankles. Her beige sandals had thick, shiny straps that spread across her knobbly toes and as Kristen watched she reached down to adjust one of them and straightened up, breathing hard.

'How are you?' She took Kristen's arm and guided her into the first gallery. 'Last time I was here it was an exhibition of Miro's. Wonderful! Left me torn between wanting to give up altogether and feeling I ought to rush home and start on something completely new.'

The room they were in had the entries for "Twelve years and above". Vi scanned the walls, then turned to Kristen. 'That time you phoned, about wanting to interview me for your thesis…'

'Oh, that.' Kristen brushed aside the apology but Vi refused to be put off.

'I was feeling low, sometimes do, days when the hormones are playing up. Anyway, enough of that, how's it going, your thesis? I meant to ask you before but as I recall I spent most of the time talking about myself. Have you found a full-time job for the autumn?'

'Not yet.' What was Vi leading up to? Something about the college, about Shannon Wilkins?

They had stopped in front of a picture of an old woman, so beautifully drawn that Kristen was surprised it had failed to win first prize.

'I agree.' Vi had read her thoughts. 'Who do you supposed does the judging? "Highly commended", I ask you. A panel no doubt that includes a half-witted celebrity and a journalist.'

Vi was peering into her face. 'Don't look so cross,' she said. 'No, I'm sorry, you look however you want. We'll have some lunch later. I bet you never bother to cook yourself a decent meal. This is the same gallery where they had the exhibition of psychotic art I told you about.'

'Where you met Cameron Lyle.'

Vi looked at her curiously. 'Actually, the first time was at an art society do. They'd hung my painting in a dark corner but amazingly the judges spotted it and gave me third prize.'

So there was no mystery about how she and Cameron had met. Vi had temporarily forgotten. 'Quite a time ago, was it?'

'Two years. No, it was when …' She broke off, raising her hand in a wave as a dark, exotic-looking woman, wearing an

127

embroidered jacket, entered the gallery. And was followed a few moments later by Cameron Lyle.

Vi rubbed her eye with her fist. 'There's the blighter. The two of you've met, haven't you? Yes, of course, you've been to the antique market. We're starting with the older children, Cameron, and working backwards. Kristen doesn't have too high an opinion of the judges and I'm inclined to agree.' Vi turned her attention to Lyle's companion. 'How are you, Naomi?

'I'm good, thank you, Vi. Just returned from a trip to Rome. Only got off the plane late last night but Cameron persuaded me I ought to see the kiddiewinkies' pictures.'

Vi introduced Kristen, explaining how she was doing some teaching at the college where Neville worked, and the woman called Naomi smiled politely and started talking about the exhibition where Cameron had 'discovered' Vi.

Cameron turned to Kristen but avoided her eyes. 'Vi had done this tiny painting of a frog, a million miles better than anything else.'

Kristen said nothing. A week had passed since their meeting in the pub. Reporting the words of the mythical 'Steve' was supposed to be a way of sparing her the humiliation of finding out from the police what William was really like. But the more she thought about it, the less she believed his explanation.

Turning away, Lyle held an inhaler to his mouth and administered two quick puffs. Then he whispered something in Vi's ear, making Kristen feel excluded. The two of them were roughly the same height although Vi probably weighed about three stone more, and they had the slightly flirtatious way of talking to each other that Kristen had noticed before between people of different generations. Moving on, Kristen pretended to be absorbed, looking at a drawing of a bicycle that was brilliantly executed but totally lifeless, although when you thought about it how could a bicycle be anything else?

'Cameron's all right when you get to know him.' Vi's hand was on Kristen's shoulder. 'Can be a little thoughtless but doesn't mean any harm. I'm afraid we all use our own particular problems as an excuse for bad behaviour.'

So what problems did Cameron Lyle have?

'Nev's ever so pleased with your work at the college,' Vi continued. 'He tells me a little about the children, especially the one called Shannon. Come on, let's skip the rest of this room and go and see the stuff the little ones produce before they become self-conscious and lose their spontaneity.'

Cameron Lyle spoke to them once before they left but only to make sure they hadn't missed a family portrait by a five-year-old boy called Aaron. Mummy, Daddy, and Aaron were each the size of a small doll but "my sister Ellen" was enormous, dressed in scarlet and black, and with outsize boxing gloves for hands.

'I can just imagine her, can't you,' Vi laughed, and Kristen joined in, although secretly she felt sorry for Ellen whose life must have been torn apart by the birth of her baby brother. Would Theo have enjoyed the exhibition or would he have found it boring? Boring was a word he had started using a lot after they returned from America, until one day William had lost his temper. *For Christ's sake, Theo, if you're bored when you're only eight, heaven help you when ...* He never finished the sentence. There was no need. *When you're my age.*

'Right.' Vi steered her towards the exit. 'Enough of that. There's me criticising Cameron for being insensitive and all I've done is make you feel worse, although I hope you'll believe me when I tell you I had no idea Cameron was going to be here.' So he had told Vi about their conversation in the pub.

The row of terraced houses had front doors that opened directly onto the street. Tisdall noticed a dog looking through one of the windows, but on closer inspection it turned out to be a soft toy with glass eyes.

'Marrakech,' said Brake, lifting a length of wisteria to read the painted nameplate. 'D'you suppose in Marrakech they call their houses Stow-on-the-Wold?'

Tisdall laughed, mainly out of surprise at Brake's attempt at a joke. When they first started working together, he had found Brake's presence a strain, but recently the man had started to ease up a bit. Not that his level of interest in Frith's murder had abated. Most of the dog man's victims had been re-interviewed during the last few days but, hard as Brake had tried, nothing of any interest had come up. Malcolm Wisdom was the last on the list and Tisdall, who had heard about Wisdom from Dave Wood, who was now doing a spell in uniform, had decided it was best if he accompanied Brake for this particular interview.

Wisdom was an academic, like Alex Howell, but worked at a different university and lectured in computing. Dave Wood had said he was the sort that went on Gay Pride marches dressed in nothing but a pair of cycling shorts and with his arm round another bloke's neck.

'Lives alone, does he.' Brake smiled to himself. 'What d'you suppose he was doing down by the river?'

'I believe he has a partner.' Tisdall deliberately allowed a short pause. 'I imagine he was going for a walk, getting some fresh air, or maybe he's a fitness freak like William Frith.'

Brake inspected the back of his hand. 'Maybe Frith was on the turn and only lived with a woman so there was someone to look after his kid.'

They had left the car down the road. People disliked the neighbours seeing a policeman call at their house, even a plain clothes one, and if the vehicles in the road were anything to go by the area was more upmarket than Tisdall had expected. Of course you met the odd person who was more interested in his car than his house, saw it as an extension of himself, a kind of suit of armour and lethal weapon rolled into one. Tisdall had no strong feelings about where he lived, nor about the car he drove as long as it kept going on the motorway and didn't refuse to start on icy January mornings.

Today made winter seem like another place. Sweat gathered on his neck and he wiped it with the sleeve of his jacket. The suit he normally wore had been dropped off at the cleaners by Julie in the mistaken belief that the smarter his appearance, the more likely he was to be promoted. The fact that he had no interest in promotion, couldn't stand the thought of being stuck in an office, was seen by her as a way of cushioning himself against feelings of failure.

Ever since she started borrowing popular psychology books

from the library, she had been blathering on about self-esteem and the evils of categorising individuals according to their sex – she called it gender – age or social class. Oh, and "human aggression", that was another of her interests. Are we born bad or does a sick society turn us violent? Grace's course had included some psychology but she'd taken it with a pinch of salt, hung on to her critical faculties.

The terrace on the other side of the road had given way to a small stretch of grass.

'Just think,' Brake said, 'the dog man could be living in this street.'

'What makes you say that?'

Brake shrugged. 'It's a well-known fact most petty criminals do their thieving within a mile of their own home.'

Tisdall checked the statement Wisdom had given. His wallet had been taken from the jacket he had removed when he crawled through some bushes searching for the pickpocket's dog, but he had taken the incident philosophically, even blamed himself for being such a mug. In his early thirties, with a PhD in Computer Science, and – according to Dave Wood – an expensive taste in clothes, he was just the type the dog man favoured: younger rather than older, reasonably well to do. If Tisdall had not known better, he could have seen the dog man as a bit of a Robin Hood character, robbing the rich to give to the poor. A more likely explanation was that victims were selected because they looked the helpful kind rather than types who'd tell you to sod off.

The block of flats where Wisdom lived was purpose built with concrete steps leading to the first and second floors. Brake rang the bell and the door came open at once, revealing a slightly built man in the process of drying his hair with a purple towel.

'Sorry, have you been waiting long? I had the water running.' He led them into a small study with a desk and a swivel chair then realised there would be nowhere to sit and continued on into a larger room, sparsely furnished with three steel-framed chairs, a bookcase and a bamboo table. Everything was so spotlessly clean and tidy, Tisdall would not have been surprised to find the books were in alphabetical order.

'As a matter of fact,' Wisdom folded his towel and roughed up his short, brown hair, 'I was more upset about the wallet than the money. It was a present from my sister, had sentimental value. Only contained a small amount of cash. And my credit cards, of course, but I cancelled them before I called the police.'

'Very wise,' said Tisdall. 'As I mentioned on the phone, the reason we wanted to talk to you again was because of the exceptionally detailed description you provided.'

Wisdom leaned back in his chair, with both hands supporting the back of his head. 'And you still think the same person could have killed William Frith? The guy who nicked my wallet didn't look the violent type. I'd have thought Frith would have had very little trouble overpowering him.'

'You knew Frith then?' Brake had adopted his most inquisitorial expression.

Wisdom shook his head. 'Knew of him. He'd been one of Alex Howell's research assistants.'

'You know Dr Howell,' Tisdall said.

'Only by name. So you still haven't discovered where the guy lives?'

'I'm afraid not.' Tisdall focussed on a Japanese print. At least he assumed it must be Japanese because the picture was of tall reeds and a dragonfly. 'It would be a help if we could go through your description once more. Sometimes after a gap of a few weeks…'

Wisdom started to protest but Tisdall held up a hand. 'Yes, I'm sure you'd have been in touch, but going over it with a third party –'

'An anorak.' Wisdom stifled a yawn. 'Fawn, beige, you know the kind of thing. Flat cap. I didn't notice the trousers or shoes. Age anything between late twenties and early forties. Impossible to tell with the way he had his collar turned up and a scarf over his chin.'

'I believe you thought the cap could have been two shades of brown,' said Brake, 'would that be a check pattern?'

Wisdom closed his eyes. 'More like lines crossing each

other, and the scarf was woollen, thick for the time of year. It was April. April the twenty-second, the day before my mother's birthday. I'd forgotten to post her card.' He sat up straight with his hands on his knees. 'I'm not sure if I mentioned this before but he was wearing gloves, not leather, more the kind a woman might wear, and I remember noticing what exceptionally small hands he had for a man.'

Small hands. Tisdall thought about the print on the anonymous letter Kristen Olsen had received. Brake had made the connection too. Did Wisdom know Howell better than he was letting on? Was it likely he would have heard of him since he worked in a different university? Still, what did he know about university departments? Academics were a cliquey bunch, thought themselves a cut above.

Leaning well back, Wisdom seemed almost to be enjoying their company. 'Read me back what I told you before,' he said, 'the part about his face. You get an impression. Very pink skin, although I suppose that might have been because he'd climbed up the bank, pretending to have lost his dog. He was wheezing badly, that's why I agreed to help.'

'And the dog,' Tisdall said, 'you thought it was a terrier.'

'Although after you phoned it occurred to me I wasn't certain I'd seen an actual dog, just its eyes, and I'm not even a hundred percent certain about that. People tend to see what they expect to see. One thing occurred to me.' Wisdom shifted on his chair and Brake leaned towards him in the "attentive" pose he had perfected. 'If you knew about this guy's technique – pretending he'd lost his dog or it had got stuck in a hole – why didn't you publicise it, save the rest of us from falling for the same ploy?'

Brake jumped in fast. 'If we publicised all the crazy tricks people come up with…'

'Yes, sure, I get it, copycat crimes.'

'Just one last thing,' Tisdall said. 'Bimbam's. Name mean anything to you?'

'You mean the club?' Wisdom's feet had started to tap.

'Frith used to go there,' Brake said.

Wisdom glanced at each of them in turn. 'I've heard of the

place but I've never been there. Nor has my partner. If you've checked your notes you'll know his name is Chris Silvester. He's away at present. His mother's been unwell.'

'I believe he was away last time someone called round,' Brake said.

Wisdom pushed his hands in the pockets of his white jeans. 'That was when his mother was first taken ill. She had a heart attack.'

Driving back to the city centre, Tisdall listened with half an ear as Brake gave a blow-by-blow account of his impression of Wisdom, but the rest of him was thinking how he was running out of ideas and would have to admit as much to Liz Cowie. The visit to the hostel off Fishponds Road, together with a few remarks made by Ros Richards, had led to investigations that had shown Frith to be a liar and probably a womaniser, but they had come no nearer to finding a new suspect.

'Now what?' Brake said, 'Inspector Cowie mentioned something about putting me on another case but if you have a word with her, tell her you still need me.'

'For what?'

Brake looked disappointed. 'So you think we've been wasting our time.'

'Looks that way.'

'So where is this dog man character? You'd have thought by now someone would have…'

Tisdall was watching the car in front. From the back of her head, the driver could have been Grace. Same hair pushed behind her ears, same long neck, strong shoulders, except Grace would never have been seen dead in a jacket that colour.

'If the so-called dog man's an amateur we haven't a hope.' Brake sounded thoroughly pissed off. 'Mind you, whether he killed Frith or not he must have been shitting himself these past eight or nine weeks.'

Tisdall was thinking about Kristen Olsen. If he introduced them both which would she hit it off with best, Julie or Grace? No contest.

'Don't worry,' he said, trying to keep Brake's spirits up. 'I reckon Liz Cowie will give us another four or five days.'

18

Before she drove to the college, Kristen walked on the Downs.
It was not yet nine o'clock but plenty of people were out and
about, exercising their dogs. A golden retriever bounded up to
her then swerved away at the last moment, continuing on into
the bushes with its nose to the ground, sniffing from side to
side. Theo had wanted a dog. Not much chance of it now, living
in a flat in Putney, although Ros was the type to see an
appealing little puppy and make an impulse buy she regretted
almost at once.

Was Ros really like that or was she cool, calculating?
Kristen had been thinking about Alex Howell's remark that Ros
was unable to have more children. He must have made a
mistake. It was unlikely William would have forgotten to
mention something so important. He had talked enough about
the five years he had lived with Ros, mostly complaints,
although occasionally Kristen had sensed that his life at that
time had not been quite as fraught as he liked to make out.

An old man was walking towards her, a stick in one hand
and a brown vinyl shopping bag over his arm. He looked a little
unsteady on his feet and when he drew closer she noticed how
frail he looked.

'Can you give me a hand?' he whispered, 'I shouldn't have
gone so far but it was such a lovely morning.'

Kristen slipped her arm in his. 'Where do you live?'

'Over there.' He nodded in the direction of the large houses adjoining the Downs. 'But if you could take me to those bushes, I need to spend a penny.'

Walking, half running back to where she had left the car, she glanced over her shoulder and saw the man stagger out from behind a tree. Was it something he tried on several times a week? How did his other "victims" respond? Tell him to get lost or give him the benefit of the doubt, and walk away feeling a mixture of anger and disgust?

He was like the dog man. Only worse. The world was a horrible place. Everything good turned rotten, everyone you loved was taken away. She thought about William, lying in the mortuary freezer. What happened after the post-mortem? Was the body put back together again or were the organs kept in separate bags, pending a possible second post-mortem while the defence counsel was preparing its case?

She could ask Tisdall. He would tell her the truth, at least as far as such technicalities were concerned. In every other way he liked to keep her guessing, even allowed her to think she was one of the suspects. *Why had Theo been staying the night with a friend? Was it something he did fairly often? No? In that case wasn't it rather a coincidence ...*

Switching on the engine, she checked the driving mirror but without registering whether or not a car was coming up behind her, and accelerated in the direction of the Gorge. Once, because Theo had begged her to, she had walked the whole length of the Suspension Bridge, from Sion Hill to Leigh Wood, and back again. Sensing her fear, he had been scathing, then understanding. *You can't fall, nobody could, not unless they climbed the railing.*

Kristen had laid out scraps of paper that covered most of the carpet. The notes for her thesis that she had made over the last few months and not yet had time to transfer to her computer. She was trying to assemble them in some kind of order when the doorbell rang. What did Mrs Letts want this time? To tell her again how the woman on the first floor kept coughing and did Kristen think she had TB since it was a notifiable disease these days? Or perhaps she wanted to tell her the Betterware man had left a brochure and the window cleaning spray was really good value. In answer to Mrs Letts' veiled inquiries, Kristen had explained why she would be out three mornings a week, even told her a little about the classes, not that the old woman had been satisfied. She always wanted to know more.

It was nearly nine o'clock and getting dark. When she opened the door a crack there was no sign of Mrs Letts, or anyone else, then a voice spoke her name and Cameron Lyle stepped out of the shadowy area behind the steps going up to the street.

'Sorry.' His voice had the apologetic tone that irritated her so much. 'Didn't mean to give you a fright. The exhibition, I wanted to talk but there wasn't a chance. Then Vi dragged you off for lunch.'

'What did you want to tell me?'

He jerked his head towards the open door. 'Is someone with you?'

'Vi told you to come round?' She led him into the room where she now ate, slept, and worked, and left him to pick his way between the scraps of paper. 'How did you know where I lived? Vi told you that too?'

'I've interrupted your work,' he said. 'Still, it looks like you could do with a break. Why all the paper, why not put stuff straight onto the computer? I'm sorry about the pub, I wanted to help but ended up –'

'It doesn't matter.' She had no wish to cover the same ground again. 'You haven't answered my question. How did you know where I lived?'

'Subterfuge.' He picked up a note at random and started to read. '"Francis Galton on genius. Academic achievement is not sufficient; success in the real world is just as important." Why genius? Your thesis, why did you choose … William's idea, was it?'

'I read a book by Eysenck.'

'The personality test guy. Introverts and extraverts. So your background's psychology.'

'My degree was in Psychology and Philosophy.'

'Really? Anyway, this quote from Galton – I thought your thesis was about kids.'

'It is.'

He nodded, replacing the slip of paper exactly where he had found it. 'I've a friend who works for BT. I gave him your number and he ... No, not true. I rang Neville at the college, said I was on my way to Bishopston to deliver a print you'd had framed, knew the number of your house and that your flat was in the basement but couldn't read the name of the street. Hilldown? Millhouse? He soon put me right.'

He selected another piece of paper. '"Adult intelligence, combined with childish emotions, leads to certain difficulties." Yes, well, I should think that's fairly obvious. You won't say anything to Neville? He's a nice guy, would feel bad if he thought he'd let you down.'

She took the paper from his hand. 'Exceptional children with an IQ above one hundred and eighty.'

He reached the sofa and sat down with a thump. 'The kids you teach are in that bracket?'

'Most of them are probably around a hundred and twenty or thirty.'

'How do their teachers pick them out? Choose the ones with nice neat hair and posh accents?'

'There are ways of guessing, not very scientific, but based on experience. The classic signs of a high-ability child ...' She broke off, annoyed by his bored expression.

'No, go on. The classic signs?'

'Very good general knowledge, learn fast, sensitive, magnanimous, hate being told something hasn't been done right, always look bored, bone idle.'

He laughed. 'Did Vi show you her painting of a little girl called Daisy, a neighbour? Neville had an idea she might be gifted but –'

'Vi said it was one of her first.'

'The family moved to another part of Bristol. I just wondered if Vi had said anything.'

Did he know something? That Neville had a taste for young girls? But if there had been an unpleasant incident it seemed highly unlikely Vi would have shown Kristen the portrait.

Cameron knelt by one of the bookcases and began reading out the titles. *Brazzaville Beach, The Tortilla Curtain.* Ah, *Tony and Susan.* What did you think?'

'It gave me nightmares.'

'Brilliant. D'you want me to go?'

She could have said yes. Instead, she offered him a drink. If he knew more about William it was better to get it over with, better to find out here and now.

He looked surprised at the offer but not in the smug, self-satisfied way she had expected. 'A beer would be good.' He had returned to the sofa and was feeling under where he was sitting, making contact with the broken spring. 'Actually, I'd prefer a cup of tea. Then before I leave you could tell me some more about your thesis. Would you say intelligence is one generalised attribute or could a person be brilliant in one particular area and useless at everything else?'

She started moving towards the kitchen, knowing he would follow and probably remark on the mess. 'The majority of very clever people do well at most of the things that interest them.'

'How about getting on with other people? Has anyone tested the streetwise characters who never did anything at school but make their fortune in the outside world. Incidentally, where did William go to school? Some private place, was it? Isn't it a fact that all geniuses are a little crazy? Maybe William inadvertently stepped on someone's toes.'

She turned the tap on too hard and water splashed on the floor. 'Someone who decided to teach him a lesson, you mean. Someone who lured him down to the river and smashed his head in with half a brick.'

'I'll wash some mugs,' he said. 'If you ask me the cops have run out of ideas, just stick with the same old theory to make it look like they haven't been sitting on their arses doing bugger all. The reason I came round, it was partly to apologise but there's something else.'

'Go on.' Cameron had Theo's mug in his hand, the one with a picture of a hippo, and she was terrified he was going to drop it.

'Steve wanted to know if William played any musical instruments.'

'Musical instruments,' she repeated. 'Why would he want to know that? He learned the piano when he was a child but never kept it up. Oh, and he had a concertina but it needed repairing.'

'Have you still got it?'

'I gave it to Theo.'

He nodded. 'You must miss him like hell. I noticed the photos, looks just like his father, and quite like you as a matter of fact but they say adopted kids get to look like their parents. If you'd adopted him…'

'That wouldn't have been possible, not as long as Ros was alive. She'd never have agreed to it.'

'Look, I'm really sorry, not just about the pub. Everything. Has your doctor given you something?'

'Some happy pills, you mean. William believed the best cure was vigorous exercise.'

He looked away. 'Being unhappy is not the same as suffering from clinical depression.'

She shrugged. 'He thought depression was a weakness, an inability to pull yourself together. Exercise stimulates the hormones, gets the right chemicals coursing through your blood.'

'Chemicals!' He spat out the word. 'How bloody fucking moronic.' He started coughing then managed to control it, holding his chest as if it hurt him to breathe.

Kristen said nothing. His reaction was much the same as her own had been when William told her how an acquaintance of his had topped herself but it need never have happened, not if she'd looked after her body instead of concentrating on what was going on in her head.

19

Kristen's car needed servicing and now she was paying for it. As she struggled to start the engine, a man was watching her, aware no doubt that it was a lost cause. Why was he so interested? Was he going to offer to help? Dressed in a beige anorak that was too large for him, and badly fitting jeans, he looked faintly familiar although she was probably imagining it. Was she imagining it? Not a stalker, please God not a stalker. She was becoming paranoid. He had no interest in her and, on second thoughts, he looked a little like the man Shannon had been talking to at the bus stop. Or did he? Hundreds, thousands of men looked like that. What was wrong with her? Why couldn't she get a grip on herself? Lack of sleep. Perhaps she should get some sleeping tablets, the chemicals Cameron despised so much.

'Trouble?'

Neville had appeared and was bending down until his face was level with Kristen's. 'The battery, I imagine; doesn't sound as if you're going to have much luck. Come on, I'll give you a lift home and you can ring up the garage, ask them to sort it out and run the car back to you later on.'

As soon as they were in the car, he started talking about the classes. 'When we began it was one small group, then news spread and for a time we were inundated with applicants, many of them quite unsuitable. Sarah Pearson will be back in

September, when the Saturday class resumes, but since the waiting list of children hoping to join us is starting to build up again I'm hoping to persuade the powers that be to let us have a third classroom in another part of the building. If it comes off I'd be more than happy to keep you on.'

'Thank you.' Kristen was uncertain if she wanted to tie up her weekends. 'I'll have to do supply teaching during the week until I can find something permanent. I've been asking around but the idea of full-time work…'

'Of course. Mustn't overdo things, not until you're back on your feet. How's your thesis progressing?'

'Slowly.' She thought about the notes laid out on her floor.

'That's the ticket,' Neville said brightly. 'Will it include work on people who can do one thing brilliantly, reciting the telephone book or playing the piano, although their general intelligence appears to be well below average?'

'Memorising strings of numbers seems to be a technique anyone can learn if they have enough patience.'

'Really?' Neville was sweating profusely. He put up a hand to ease his collar and Kristen noticed his tie was knotted so tightly that the loose skin on his neck overhung his collar. He began asking her opinion of the nature-nurture debate, how much of intelligence is innate, inherited, and how much depends on experience, environmental influences. She made a few comments but mostly he seemed happy to spell out his own ideas, together with information from recent journal articles he had read.

'I've a book you might like to borrow,' Kristen said, 'I could bring it on Wednesday.'

'Good. I'd like that.' He was silent for a minute or two then he started talking about Vi's paintings, asking what Kristen thought of them and, before she had time to answer, suggesting her taste was probably a little more esoteric. He seemed to know the quickest route to Bishopston without her giving him directions.

'This book,' he said. 'Perhaps when I drop you off I could take it with me, or are you still using it?'

'I borrowed it from the university library but it doesn't have

142

to be back till the end of the month.'

'So you've kept up your connections with people at the university.'

'Since I'm registered for my thesis, I'm allowed a library ticket.'

He passed the turning to her road and cursed under his breath. 'Sorry, wasn't thinking, we'll have to go on to the junction and round the other way.'

He had a sprinkling of dandruff on the shoulders of the jacket he wore whatever the weather, and his hands on the steering wheel were red with large veins standing out on the backs of them. Kristen wondered if he and Vi shared a double bed. It would have to be a large one! How had he felt, getting married so late in life, and after all those years looking after his sister?

As they swung round the next corner, Kristen put out a hand to steady herself and caught her nail on the seat belt fastening. Looking down at the rough edge, it reminded her of the deal she had made with Shannon. *Stop biting your nails and on the last day of the course I'll give you a reward.* Shannon had laughed – it was relief to see her looking cheerful – but Hugo had said it was unfair, like the story of the Prodigal Son.

'I gave Cameron Lyle your address,' Neville said suddenly, 'I hope that was what you wanted. He said he had a picture to drop off at your flat, one you'd had framed. He and Vi are thick as thieves but I hardly know him myself, although he was generous enough to give me a hand with one of my fundraising projects. Took a tin round the antique market, collected a fair bit. My sister suffered from a rare genetic disorder. So rare in fact that the medical profession has shown very little interest.'

'I'm sorry. I didn't know.'

'Since her death I've raised money for an organisation that helps provide breaks for the carers. I was fortunate myself. Vi helped enormously, as did various other friends. Some of the carers have a hell of a life. On her good days Jane could be left for a short while. Others need supervision more or less twenty-four hours a day.'

'Her death must have been a terrible shock.'

'Yes, well, there we are.' Neville cleared his throat noisily. 'She'd already outlived her life expectancy, but it's a mistake to imagine being prepared for a death makes it any less traumatic when it actually comes.'

Were all men so tactless? Or was it that she was so obsessed with William's death, she was incapable of putting herself in anyone else's shoes.

'Don't think I don't know how hard it is for you.' Neville glanced at her then back at the road. 'You'll tell me it's best to keep busy but in the circumstances I'm not sure I could have carried on.'

You would, she wanted to say, because you'd have had no choice. Instead, she told him he had reached her turning and he'd be welcome to come inside and collect the book.

The phone rang when Kristen was having a shower. Leaving wet footprints on the lino she raced into the other room, petrified in case it was Ros putting off Theo's visit again.

It was Cameron Lyle.

'Not in bed, were you?' His voice was only just audible above the background noise of clinking glasses and the loud thump of piped music.

'I was having a shower.'

A short pause followed and she thought she heard someone telling him to get a move on.

'Listen,' he said, 'Thursday evening, how are you fixed? I'm going round to Vi's to select some paintings to take to London, wondered if you like to join us.' He made a dry wheezing sound. 'Sorry, air in this place is unfit for human consumption. Actually, it was Vi's idea. Pick you up about seven thirty?'

For a moment she thought they had been cut off, but then he came back, his voice raised above the music. 'Are you still there?'

'Yes.'

'Have the police been in touch since I saw you last?'

'No.'

'Only I was thinking. Obviously the pickpocket guy knows he's suspect number one. The thing is, he could be afraid you might pass something on to them.'

'If I knew anything I would.'

There was another short pause. 'Yes, well, let's assume, just for moment, that the dog man, so-called, had nothing to do with it. That means someone else … and if whoever it is suspects the police have given up on their original line of inquiry … Yes, all right.' She had said nothing but he had responded to the silence. 'You can look after yourself, don't want me muscling in. So I'll see you Thursday, right?'

She returned to the shower and turned the water on hard. She was thinking about the man Mrs Letts claimed to have seen in her garden. She could hear something now. Only water dripping. The overflow pipe from upstairs. That meant it would splash into the yard for weeks before the landlord got round to asking someone to fix it.

Letting up the blind, she peered into the darkness and was surprised to discover for the first time for weeks that it was raining. She thought she could see a light. Mrs Letts? But the old woman had told her she was in bed by nine thirty. The light was moving about, flickering on and off, then it went out altogether and Kristen thought she heard someone mutter an expletive. She could go out and check but that would mean getting dressed.

Cameron's phone call and the light in Mrs Letts' garden might be too much of a coincidence to ignore. Was it some kind of joke? William had enjoyed planning practical jokes, some of them so elaborate they were bordering on the cruel.

During their brief stay in Ohio, he had become cynical, disparaging of everyone they met, and Theo had begun to copy him. When she asked if he regretted leaving Bristol he had shouted that he hadn't had much choice since Alex's research was going nowhere. Had Alex put pressure on him to leave? Because he found him so difficult to work with? *Steve couldn't stand the guy, said he was a troublemaker, caused havoc wherever he went.*

How much did Cameron Lyle really know about William? Perhaps they had been friends, gone drinking together in the evening William didn't work at the hostel. Next time she saw him she would question him more closely. What did he want from her? Did he know who had killed William? Was it even possible he had been involved in William's death himself?

20

Vi had propped up her paintings round the wall, about a dozen altogether, and two more, one on the easel, another on the mantelpiece. Cameron had inspected each in turn, without comment, and while it was going on Vi had kept glancing at Kristen and pulling a face as though to say "He doesn't think much of them and he's trying to think how to let me down lightly".

Ever since Cameron arrived, Vi had been chain-smoking and it had surprised Kristen how nervous she appeared. Her relaxed, comfortable expression had been replaced by a series of little facial twitches and every so often she pushed her cigarette to the corner of her mouth and started clasping and unclasping her hands. Kristen had expected Neville to be there but Vi explained how he spent Wednesday evenings with friends he had known since the days when he belonged to a sports club on the edge of the city. *Nice for both of us. Nev has a night out with his mates and I can watch the telly, whatever rubbish I fancy.*

'Good.' Cameron stepped back from the paintings and gave Vi a reassuring smile. 'The gallery won't take as many as this so either I could show them the lot and let them make their own selection or we could decide now which will go down best.'

'What do you think?' Vi lit another cigarette and balanced herself on the arm of the sofa. 'Is it better to choose ones that go together or pick as varied a selection as possible?'

He thought about this, jerking his head as he counted up the exact number of pictures on display. His hair had been cut and he was wearing new jeans and a white T-shirt with a reproduction of a Paul Klee drawing on the front. 'Normally galleries like each picture by a particular artist to be more or less a clone of the last one. But your gallery's more concerned with showing paintings people actually want to hang on their walls.'

Vi gave a snort. 'You mean they don't care two hoots as long as it matches the wallpaper.'

Cameron looked at Kristen and raised his eyes to the ceiling. 'See what I'm up against? Half the battle's believing in yourself.'

'No it's not,' Vi protested. 'That's why you get your cut so I won't have to do the humiliating part. You know, Kristen, painting's nothing compared with trying to sell the wretched stuff.'

Kristen smiled. 'I believe you. I'd be hopeless at it.'

'Whereas Cameron,' said Vi, 'was born to charm the birds off the trees or, put it another way, to pull the wool over everyone's eyes.'

The painting on the easel was of a garden with a summer house at the far end and a wooden seat where a man – Neville had been the model – sat reading a book, with a small grey terrier by his side. Kristen found it hard to imagine Neville staying still long enough – he always seemed to be in a rush, on the move – although the time he had come to her flat to borrow the book he had assured her he was in no hurry and accepted her offer of coffee and a sandwich.

Ever since her conversation with Alex Howell on the Downs, Kristen had been thinking about Neville's sister and the circumstances of her death. Alex had implied negligence, or even that someone had deliberately turned a blind eye when she climbed up into the loft. Carers sometimes lost control – who could blame them – but Neville had sounded as though his sister's death had been a shattering experience, and collecting for charity was the only way he knew of trying to come to terms

148

with what had happened.

Recently Kristen had started waking at four in the morning then every hour, more or less on the hour, until it was time to get up. Lying in bed, one question followed another. Who had William been planning to meet that evening? Had he made up the meeting as a way of stopping her accompanying him? But another much more worrying question kept returning. Why, in spite of his lack of a job, had William always had plenty of cash? No, not plenty, that was an exaggeration. Plenty for what he wanted to do; plenty for when he took it into his head he needed a new laptop or an electronic game for Theo.

Blackmail.

The word kept coming back into her head. Nothing too ambitious, nothing that anyone would be able to check. Just a word, a look, and the handing over of small but regular sums of money?

Vi and Cameron were watching her. Kristen opened her mouth to say something complimentary about one of the paintings but Vi got in first, asking when Theo was arriving.

'Saturday morning.' Kristen was surprised she knew about the visit. Brigid must have told Neville who had passed the information on to Vi. 'He's staying until Sunday afternoon.'

'Good.' Vi gave her a kiss on the cheek. 'He must be looking forward to it.'

'Right, I think they'll accept up to eight.' Cameron lifted the garden painting from the easel and exchanged it for one from the shelf. 'I suggest I take a dozen and we'll see what happens. That one's great.' He pointed to the picture of the Yorkshire terrier. 'What do you think, Kristen? It's the detail people go for, the hair on the ears, the shiny black nose.'

'Yes, I like that one too.' Kristen felt awkward, out of place, wondering why she was there, wondering if the two of them had been talking about her behind her back. Had the real reason for the invitation been because Vi had spoken to Cameron and the two of them wanted to question her about Shannon Wilkes? 'Painting something that's all fur must be difficult,' she said, 'and the eyes are wonderful.'

'Fluff,' Vi said, 'that's the name of the poor little bugger.

Got a mummy who dotes on him, feeds him chicken breast and lamb's liver.'

'Got a Burberry for the winter, has it?' Cameron asked. 'God, the way people anthropomorphise their pets, it makes you wonder what kind of a life their owners have, whether they've ever risked a relationship with a human being.'

'Don't be so cruel.' Vi gave him a shove in the back and the atmosphere in the studio relaxed. 'Fluff's owner's been happily married for thirty years or more. Love's not a finite commodity that has to be apportioned.'

'I'll take your word for it.' Cameron picked up another painting and turned to Kristen. 'Talking of dogs, it occurred to me this dog man character the police came up with may not even exist. How many crimes is he supposed to have committed? Supposing someone used the trick of pretending he'd lost his dog then a totally different person decided to do the same, and on the basis of a couple of incidents –'

'I don't think so.' Kristen had been hoping that for once the subject would be left alone. 'There were at least six cases.'

'Six cases before ...' He broke off, rubbing his chin. 'There haven't been any since?'

'Pick your paintings,' said Vi crossly, 'and I'll find us something to drink. When do you suppose you'll be going up to London, Cameron?'

'Next week.'

Vi ran a hand through her hair. 'And is the gallery likely to make a decision on the spot?'

'It won't take them long. In any case I reckon they'll want the lot. And don't keep giving me the evil eye. My intention was not to upset Kristen, just the opposite. Until William's killer's been charged, how can any of the people who knew him get on with the rest of their lives?'

'Now, we'd better find something to eat. Oh, I see, you've helped select Vi's paintings, now you'd prefer to go straight back to your flat.'

'I didn't say a word.'

Cameron laughed. 'No need to. Why don't I drive us to

150

Severn Beach and we can watch the sun set over the water?'

'You make it sound like Acapulco.'

'I've never been to Acapulco.' He switched on the engine.

'I used to take Theo to Severn Beach,' Kristen said. 'He liked to collect tiny pieces of coloured glass from the shingle on the beach and use them to make pictures.'

'So you'll come. It won't take long, we'll be there and back in forty minutes.'

'If you drive like a maniac.'

What was she doing? They were talking like two people in a play. A bad one. Before they left Vi had opened a bottle of wine to celebrate the fact that her studio was going to be cleared out and she could make a fresh start, as she put it. Kristen had said very little about the paintings, apart from a few comments that they all seemed very good to her, and if she had the money she would buy one herself.

'I'll give you one,' Vi had told her, 'No, not now, another day when you're feeling better…'

Cameron was whistling through his teeth. 'So,' he said, turning on a blast of loud music then switching it off again, 'time Vi branched out a bit, tried something new?'

'Is that what you think?'

'Not me, wouldn't want to kill the goose that lays the golden eggs. Problem is, people like Vi have a tendency to become increasingly more skilful and start to lose the particular style the gallery wants.'

They were passing under the motorway. Cameron had one hand on the steering wheel and with the other he was searching for something in the pocket by his door.

'Selling paintings is a tricky business,' he said, 'things go in fashions, gallery owners can't afford to make mistakes.'

'I don't see how they can lose. If the stuff doesn't sell –'

'Yes, but it takes up precious space. Incidentally, those prints in your flat, where did they come from?'

'William found them.'

'You don't remember where?' He passed her a street map. 'Have a look at page twelve. I've been thinking, if William had wanted some exercise he would have done better to run across the playing fields rather than down to the river.'

She took the map but didn't bother to find the page. 'There's a steep path, the kind that would make you out of breath, just the sort of place he liked.'

'You've been there have you? With William?'

'I went there the week before last.'

'On your own?'

She nodded.

He was silent for a moment then he started asking about her flat. Did she like living in a basement? Was the back of it at ground level? Had she got locks on the windows? Was there a garden?

'Yes, but it belongs to the ground floor flat. We – I don't own the place, it's on a lease that runs out in November. When we came back from Ohio we'd used up most of our spare cash.'

'What's Theo like?' he said. 'He's eight, am I right?'

'Nearly nine.'

'Would you say he takes after his father?'

She sighed. 'What is it you're trying to say?'

'Nothing. Nothing at all.'

'He's quieter than William. Sensitive but fairly confident for a boy of his age. Very perceptive. Very intelligent.'

They drove through Easter Compton and on past the dark outline of a row of pylons stretching towards the lights of Avonmouth.

'What went wrong in the States?' Cameron asked.

'Didn't William tell you?' Her voice was light, artificial, and bore no relation to how she was feeling.

'As I said, I only met him a couple of times. The job didn't turn out the way he'd hoped?'

Kristen stared at the road ahead and Cameron gave a short laugh. 'Right, don't want to talk about. Fair enough. What now then? I know, do you have any brothers and sisters?'

'No, What about you?'

'One sister. Lives in Kent. Three kids and a surveyor husband. Nice enough guy but a bit boring.'

'My father was a surveyor.'

'Really?'

'Three years after my mother died, he gave up his job so he could travel round the world. Sold his car and cashed in an insurance policy or something. Later, he wrote a book about Vietnam and Cambodia and it did rather well. Actually, he's written several others since then.'

'Really?'

'Yes, really.'

Cameron laughed, and she joined in, stopping abruptly when he asked if her father had met William. 'I imagine the two of them would've got on pretty well. Two of a kind, or am I wrong?'

'You say you went to Manchester University?'

'Got a crap degree in Politics.'

'And then?' They were passing an estate of new houses, built in a semi-circle round a kind of village green. 'After you got your bad degree?'

'Messed about, worked for a trade journal until the tedium became too much, bought and sold what people call "collectables".'

'In Bristol?'

'No, London. I moved to Bristol five years ago when –'

As they rounded a corner a cat darted across the road. Cameron swerved but it doubled back and there was no way he could avoid it.

'Shit.' He pulled over to the side and sat, gripping the wheel, then climbed out and started walking back to where the dark shape lay close to the gutter.

Kristen wanted to stay in the van, have nothing to do with it. Instead she forced herself to join him and together they crouched over the limp body, jumping when the cat moved its leg.

'It's alive.' His voice was shaky. 'Could be stunned, although without a proper examination … We can't just leave it.' He picked up the cat and carried it to the nearest lamppost where he began inspecting it very gently, first its head, then its back, then each leg in turn. 'Unless there are internal injuries I reckon it's going to be OK. What do you think?'

Kristen squatted beside him. The cat was grey with green

153

eyes that shone in the dark. She reached out to stroke the soft fur but as her hand made contact with its head it scrabbled free, scratching Cameron's hand in the process, and darted towards a house, disappearing over a low wall.

'Let's tell ourselves it's all right,' he said.

'It *is* all right.'

He put his arms round her and held her against his chest. 'I'm sorry, it gave you a shock. Look, shall we go on to Severn Beach or would you prefer –'

'Let's go on.'

'If you're sure.'

Back in the van, she fastened her seat belt and sat, staring out of the side window, trying to calm herself.

'I didn't think you'd come,' Cameron said, 'to Vi's I mean. It was a cop-out inviting you there instead of arranging something for just the two of us.'

'I thought it was Vi's idea.'

'No, you didn't.' He leaned towards her and she felt the roughness of his cheek. 'You've got me down as an arrogant, unfeeling bastard, and who could blame you. Now it's up to me to prove you wrong.'

21

The call from Malcolm Wisdom had come while Tisdall was visiting his daughter. Back at the station, Martin Brake conveyed the message as if he personally had been responsible for Wisdom getting in touch.

'I had a feeling he might. Something about the expression on his face as we were leaving.'

'So what did he want?' Tisdall was in no mood for games. Grace had left the house almost as soon as he arrived, saying it would be nice for him and Serena to spend time alone together. When it was time for him to leave she still hadn't returned, even though her excuse had been feeble in the extreme. They were short of milk. She would buy some at the local shop.

'It was about the club,' Brake was saying.

'Which club is that?' As if he didn't know. 'Wisdom lied to us, did he? It didn't look the kind of place gays frequent, apart from that Glen bloke.'

'Gays don't have to go to gay clubs,' Brake said priggishly.

'What?' Tisdall was trying to decide if Grace had been avoiding him deliberately. And if so, why? What was it Julie had once said? *If you love someone enough it makes you think they must love you back.*

'Anyway,' said Brake, 'Wisdom wants us to believe it was only after we'd left he remembered how he and his partner had called in at Bimbam's one evening about a year ago, only they'd never gone back because someone had joined them and started an argument.'

'Who joined them? What argument? Get to the point, Martin, I want to go home.'

'He didn't know his name but he thought he was some kind of dealer.'

Tisdall yawned. 'Dealer in what? Stocks and shares, scrap metal?'

The investigation was going nowhere. They had re-interviewed all the dog man's victims, and talked to all the witnesses who claimed to have seen a man answering his description close to the scene of the murder. For a time Tisdall had thought the hostel for the homeless, or the club, would come up with something they could get their teeth into. Frith had skeletons in the cupboard – that much was clear – but who didn't, and none of them seemed likely to provide a motive for smashing his head in with a brick. Asking round the pubs, in the Fishponds area and near to where he had lived, had come up with nothing of any importance. A handful of people admitted to being on nodding terms but none of them had known much about him. Surely if Frith had been involved in anything dodgy an informant would have come forward weeks ago.

'I could call round on my way home,' Brake said. 'See if Wisdom's partner's returned, try to find out a bit more about them.

'Yes, you do that.' Tisdall was so tired he could hardly keep his head upright. 'Tell me in the morning, only don't take too long over it, don't want your Kelly feeling neglected. No case is so important it's worth wrecking your home life.'

'Matthew's father came round on Wednesday.' Mrs Letts licked her lips in anticipation. 'He was asking after you.'

'Matthew's father? Oh, you mean Mr Reynolds.'

Mrs Letts put down the damp cloth she had been using to wipe the tiles outside the front door and folded her arms to indicate she was in no hurry, wouldn't mind providing more details if required. She had been to the hairdresser's and her white curls were even tighter than before.

'Did he come round specially or was he just passing?' Kristen asked.

Mrs Letts pressed a hand against her flat chest. 'Indigestion. Had a kipper for my tea. He was parked in a van across the road, old wreck of a thing. There quite a while he were.'

'Matthew's father was driving an old van?'

She nodded, happy now she had aroused Kristen's curiosity. 'Now if people was more neighbourly, kept their eyes open … You heard about Mr Parsons' cat?'

'No.' Not another cat knocked down, crushed under somebody's wheels.

'Disappeared.' Mrs Letts spoke the word as dramatically as possible and waited for Kristen's follow up questions.

'How long has it been gone? Cats often go off for a few days.'

The old woman's tongue moved round her lips. 'I reckon they took it for one of those laboratories where they test face cream. He's looked all over, stuck notices on lamp posts, and he's going to put notes through all the doors in the road.'

'I'll watch out for it.' So the light in the garden earlier in the week had been Mr Parsons. 'When did it go missing?'

'Theo was fond of that cat, used to try and stroke it but it was never the friendly kind. Bite you soon as look at you. What time's he arriving? You'll be ever so pleased to see him. Wait, I almost forgot – little treat I promised him.' She took a paper bag from her pocket that Kristen assumed contained sweets or a bar of chocolate. But after she had thanked Mrs Letts and the older woman had returned to her flat, she looked inside the bag and was surprised, and rather touched, to see a packet of football stickers and two one-pound coins.

When Ros arrived she looked thinner, or perhaps it was the effect of her black trousers and dark green jacket. Theo was wearing red Kickers boots, black designer trousers, and a T-shirt with a caricature of Einstein on the front. His hair was longer and parted on one side and he looked like a miniature adult, not a child who would be celebrating his ninth birthday in a month's time.

Kristen had no idea how to greet him, nor he her. It was only four weeks since he left but it could have been months.

'Theo.' She moved awkwardly towards him. 'It's lovely … so lovely to see you.'

He gave her a slightly self-conscious hug then craned his neck, looking past her at the door to his old room.

'It's just as you left it,' she said, 'ready for you to come whenever you like.'

He glanced at Ros and frowned, chewing the inside of his cheek.

'Oh, no,' Ros said, 'did I forget to ring you? How stupid of me. John brought us down – he's in the car – but after he's seen this man he's meeting I'm afraid we'll have to drive straight back so he can take his children to the zoo in the morning.'

Kristen took a tight grip on herself. 'You still haven't got your licence back?'

'No. Yes.' Ros pulled a face. 'You have to apply and I've been so busy I haven't got round to it. If it's all right I think I'd better rush off or John will be late for his appointment.' She ruffled Theo's hair. 'All right if I pick him up about six?'

Five hours and twenty-five minutes. 'Six will be fine.' Kristen looked straight into Ros's heavily made up eyes. 'Has your father returned to France? Did he enjoy his visit?'

'Had to put it off, I'm afraid.' Ros gave an apologetic smile. 'Chest infection, nothing serious but since he's getting on in years … I'd have let you know but it was all rather last minute, then John said he had to see someone in Bath this weekend so…'

She broke off, moving quickly towards the door. 'Have a lovely time, darling, and don't eat too much junk food.' She turned back to Kristen. 'What a struggle, providing them with a decent diet. Oh, heavens above, I'm not blaming you, they're all the same! Theo has made a little friend in the Close, a boy called Marcus who goes to his new school. Nice little chap but I've never seen a child eat so many bags of crisps.' She glanced at Theo, who had wandered to the other end of the room. 'Anyway, I'll love you and leave you. Oh by the way, no news from the …' She silently mouthed the word 'police'. 'I told

158

you, didn't I, how I'd had another visitation? I know what they say about the police but personally I've always found them very well-mannered.'

22

As soon as Ros left, Kristen told Theo about her plan to drive to Cardiff.

'Yes, all right.' She was disappointed at his lack of enthusiasm, wondered if he would have preferred to stay in the flat, even wondered if he had wanted to come and see her at all.

'If you don't want ... No, silly of me, you must be sick of sitting in the car.'

'I'm not.' He screwed up his face. 'I told her I could stay the night and go back on the train but she wouldn't let me, she thinks I'm a baby.'

He was fiddling with the smartphone Ros had given him. William had always refused to buy him one, not because he thought he was too young, he just "hated the things".

Driving through Bristol, Kristen asked a few questions about the flat in Putney and the places Ros had taken him to, but each time he changed the subject, wanting to know what she had been doing, wanting to hear about the gifted children. What were their names? What kind of lessons did they have? Could they do long division in their heads?

'How can you work out which five consecutive numbers add up to ninety?' He was staring straight ahead and his voice was very serious.

'I've no idea.'

'Do you promise? You're not just saying it? Divide ninety

by five and that makes eighteen. Then you take the two numbers that come before and the two that come after. Sixteen, seventeen, eighteen, nineteen and twenty. That makes ninety. I read it in a book.'

'Very good.' She wanted to ask which book. One Ros had bought him or had he asked Kimberly to take him to the local library? Instead she told him about Vi and the exhibition of children's paintings. Then about Mr Parsons' cat and how it had gone missing but would probably turn up in a day or two. And the money Mrs Letts had given her for him. And the football stickers.

He listened attentively – the smartphone was switched off and in his pocket – but his responses were formal, polite, and it was only when they were approaching the Severn Crossing that she sensed he was starting to relax.

'Mum's not like you.' He shaded his eyes to look upstream at the other bridge.

'Well, no.' Kristen wondered what was coming next. 'Things are bound to be a bit different but you seem to be having a good holiday.'

'Has the policeman been to see you? Mum thinks I can't hear what she says. She thinks I'm thick.'

'I'm sure she doesn't. Yes, he came round not long ago.'

He leaned forward, hugging his knees. 'They haven't found the man though, have they? Did you know Dad was younger than Mum? She's thirty-six next birthday.'

'Is she?' Kristen knew exactly how old Ros was.

'When I was a baby.' His voice was so quiet, she only just heard. 'When I was a baby, I mean when I was four … why did she leave? Dad told me she had to travel about, only why didn't she take me with her like Marcus's mother does?'

It was a question she and William had expected years ago but when it came she was unprepared. 'Marcus's parents are divorced?'

'No, separated, but when it goes to court his father's not going to make a fuss because he only lives just round the corner so he can see Marcus whenever he likes.'

'That's good.' She wanted to ask if Theo would have felt

162

better if she lived just round the corner, but she was afraid of the answer, afraid it was William he missed, not her.

'Why did I stay with Dad?' he asked again. 'It's all right, you don't have to pretend. I just want to know the truth.'

'Sometimes people who live together stop loving each other.' She was falling back on the usual mindless platitudes because she couldn't think of anything better. 'But that doesn't mean your mum stopped loving *you*. I expect she thought you'd be more settled with Dad, because of her work, because she's an actress.'

'She doesn't like the word "actress".' He had a sneer in his voice. 'She says ladies are called actors these days. I thought she was going to marry John but I don't think she is. He's all right but he doesn't know anything about football and he calls me "Sonny Jim".' He began to giggle, then the giggling turned to laughter that brought tears to his eyes. 'Sometimes John stays the night,' he squealed, 'but in the morning he's so horrible Mum says she doesn't want to see him any more, only she always does. He eats lots and lots of pills, not drugs, I don't mean drugs. He gets them from the health food shop and he wants her to have them too. What a prick!'

Determined not to make a single adverse comment that could be reported back to Ros, Kristen said nothing, just turned her head to smile at him. But his mood had changed again and he was breathing hard.

'If I ask you something,' he opened the glove compartment and clicked it shut again, fiddling with the catch on his seat belt, 'will you promise not to tell her?'

'Yes, of course.' It was never possible to make such an absolute promise to a child but if it was humanly possible …

'I heard her talking to some of her friends,' he said. 'She thought I wasn't listening. She thought I was watching a programme about newts. They were laughing and drinking wine and stuff and she said Dad was a bit of a headcase.'

How could Ros be so stupid, talking about William in front of him, imagining he would fail to pick up such a comment, thinking it was all right to make jokes, even though Theo had been devastated by his father's death?

'I don't suppose she meant anything, Theo. When people have been married and they've split up, they often say things about each other.'

He shook his head. 'Headcase means mad.'

'I expect she just meant Dad liked to enjoy himself, have fun. Rock climbing, and that time he did a bungee jump. What he'd really have liked was a round the world trip in a balloon.'

'Is that why someone murdered him?'

'No, of course not.' She was shocked. Had Ros said something else? 'It was an accident, a terrible accident. The man who did it …' But he wouldn't let her finish.

'Mum doesn't think it was an accident.'

'Yes she does. She'd been drinking. You know what people are like when they've had a few drinks. Listen, I forgot to tell you, Matthew's father came round. Matthew's been missing you a lot. Next time you come down I'll arrange for the two of you to have a kickabout on the Downs.'

'When?' He sounded puzzled. 'When did Matthew's father come?'

'I wasn't there. A few days ago. Mrs Letts told me.'

'That's funny.' He was silent for a few moments, glancing at her then looking away. 'I had a postcard from Matt yesterday. He and his mum and dad and his sister are on holiday in a place called Menorca. They're not coming back till the end of next week.'

Not Matt's father? So who was it? Don't think about it, not now. Later she would ask Mrs Letts what he looked like, although the woman was unlikely to remember accurately and might even make it up.

When they reached Cardiff, the car park Kristen remembered was full and they had to search for a space then walk back to the shops. She had decided to buy Theo whatever game or toy caught his eye, regardless of what Ros might think. But was that how he wanted to spend the afternoon? How much did Ros allow him to talk about William? *Don't think about it, darling, it'll only upset you. Think about something nice instead.* They passed McDonald's but Theo said he wasn't hungry, and muttered something under his breath.

'Sorry,' Kristen said, 'I missed that.'

He sighed. 'I said I have to make a new life for myself.'

'Oh, Theo.' She could feel a tight, hard knot in her chest. 'Is that what Ros … Is that what Mum said?'

'No, I read it in a book. A girl's mother and father died, like in *The Secret Garden* except she didn't live in India, it was a place called Inverness.'

'Let's go in here.' Kristen steered him into a coffee shop. 'Even if you're not hungry you can have a drink.'

As soon as they sat down, he noticed a mark on his new trousers and licked his finger, rubbing at it then swearing under his breath when the rubbing had no effect. 'There was a girl at my old school whose mother and father got divorced. After that she only saw her father on Sundays and she couldn't think of anything to say to him.'

'Is that how you're feeling now?'

'No!' He was shouting, 'I can think of masses of things, only there won't be enough time so what's the good?'

Kristen ordered coffee, cola, and a plate of cakes. 'Tell me about all the places you've been to in London.'

He began reeling off the names of the various museums and parks, first in a deliberately flat voice as if he was afraid she might think he had enjoyed himself, although when he reached the Science Museum his face lit up as he described the exhibits.

'I wish you lived in London,' he said at last. 'Mum's out a lot and I have to stay with Kimberly.'

'Don't you like her?'

He shrugged. 'She's only seventeen. Mum pays her. Well, she wouldn't do it for nothing, would she, except she's always taking stuff from the fridge so I suppose she might come round to get food. If you lived in London I could see you *and* Mum. That would be fairer, wouldn't it, don't you think it would?'

Kristen leaned across to give him a hug and he didn't protest or pull away as he might have done a few months ago. 'It'll be all right,' she said, 'you'll see. Now tell me about your new school. You've been to visit it, have you? Is it close to where you live?'

He wasn't listening. The plate of cakes arrived but he took

no notice, keeping his head down. 'Dad used to phone her,' he said.

Kristen felt a twinge of fear. 'Phone your mum? Yes, of course he did, to arrange for you to visit.'

'No, other times, nothing to do with me. Sometimes they went out to dinner.'

'That's what she told you?' Her thoughts were rushing ahead, remembering the times William had gone up to London in connection with his work then phoned to explain how he had been unable to get everything sorted in a day so had decided to stay the night with a friend.

The coffee shop was filling up. A woman with a double buggy struggled through the swing door, searched for somewhere to leave it, then gave up and struggled out again with one of the children shrieking its head off. Theo selected a chocolate éclair, turning it over, and returning it to the plate, wiping his fingers on a paper napkin.

'I thought by now the police would have found the man who did it,' he said. 'Do you think there were things Dad didn't tell us about? Do you think he'd done something bad? Mum and John keep whispering. I don't think John ever met Dad but he knows all about him. He called him a selfish bastard. He said he had it coming.'

The rest of the afternoon was spent searching for a present. Theo wanted a radio-controlled car but it had to be a particular kind. Kristen knew it would have been easier to give him the money and let him buy it in London but it became a point of honour that he take the present back with him, and Theo seemed equally determined. Finally, after consulting with a group of teenage boys, they had located the right car in a small arcade away from the main shopping centre.

Back in Bristol, she had suggested they to go to the park and try it out, but Theo had insisted it must be kept in its box to take back to London. Neither of them mentioned the fact that Kristen would miss seeing it in action, and when he climbed into John's car at half past six his face was expressionless. As they started down the hill he turned his head and waved but didn't smile. He had been pleased to see her but the small hope she had clung to – that he would deliberately "fail to thrive" as a way of forcing Ros to return him to Bristol – had faded. Like any child his age he had accepted the inevitable and had only complained about Ros because he thought that was what Kristen would want to hear. Once the car was out of sight he would cheer up immediately, give them a brief description of the trip to Cardiff, and push her out of his mind until Ros suggested he write a letter, or it was time for another visit.

During the two hours since he left, Kristen had packed William's clothes into bin bags, ready to take to the charity shop, and put the rest of his stuff in boxes under the bed. There were one or two things Theo might want one day – a Swiss army penknife, a chess set, a pair of binoculars – but not yet. Or was she thinking of herself rather than Theo? Did keeping some of William's possessions make her feel she had more of a hold on him, on Theo? Quite soon she would have to start looking for somewhere cheaper to live. When they went to America she had left eighteen hundred pounds in her building society, money she had saved over the past year or so, something William had not known about. Why had she done it? Had she doubted all along that he would be able to settle in Ohio? Had William been so irresponsible that she had felt it necessary to provide herself with a small 'insurance policy'?

Someone was coming down the basement steps then a face appeared at the window. It was Cameron.

'Don't worry,' he said, almost before she had pulled open the door, 'I know you're busy, just came to give you this, it's a present from Vi.'

Kristen took the unframed drawing of a rabbit in a hutch. 'You've been back to her studio?'

'To pack things up to take to London. By the way, I forgot to ask before, what's the problem with that girl you've been teaching?'

She had to think for a moment what he was talking about. 'Oh, you mean Shannon. Neville gives her extra tuition, she's exceptionally good at maths.'

'So what's a problem?'

'No problem. She missed her bus so I gave her a lift home.

She lives off Fishponds Road.'

He looked at her as if he thought she was being evasive. 'Anyway, I just thought I'd drop by with the drawing. If you like I could have it framed. No, don't decide now, you've got Theo with you.'

'He's gone.'

'Gone?'

'They had to get back to London. His mother's boyfriend drove them down. He has to see his children tomorrow morning.'

Cameron looked over her shoulder into the empty flat. 'How was he?'

'Fine.'

'But you're feeling pissed off. Don't blame you. Want to go out for a drink?'

She shook her head. 'Not just now.'

'I had an idea for your thesis.' And when she made no comment, 'You know the trouble with you, you think you've a monopoly on…'

'On what?' But she was weakening, could do with some company. 'If you've had an idea for my thesis I suppose you'd better come in.'

He reacted with exaggerated surprise and she managed a weak smile. Then suddenly, without warning, she started to cry. Silent tears ran down her face and neck, and turned into choking sobs.

'Oh God.' Cameron followed her into the flat. 'What can I say?' He put his hands on her shoulders and pulled her towards him. 'How long was Theo here for? What did you do?'

'Drove to Cardiff, walked round the shops. He wanted a radio-controlled car.'

He let her go. 'You could have bought one here in Bristol.'

'I know. Theo always enjoys crossing the bridge. What was your idea for my thesis?'

'I forget. It'll come to me in a minute. Something about the effect on the other kids in the family of having a gifted brother or sister. I knew someone once who was the only academic one in her family, and her two brothers gave her hell, and even her mother seemed to resent her.'

I knew someone once. Why did she feel so certain he was talking about someone he still knew, someone who was important to him?

'What's Theo's mother like?' He sat down on the broken sofa. 'Do you hate her?'

'She's tall, good-looking, worries about getting old. No, that's something William once told me. Apparently she once threatened to commit suicide rather than reach forty.'

'Sounds like a fucking moron.'

The degree of venom in his voice surprised her. 'I don't suppose she meant it. Actresses are always terrified of losing their looks. She's obsessed with keeping her metabolism in balance. Something like that.'

'Sounds half-witted.' He patted the space next to him but kept his eyes focussed on William's print on the opposite wall. 'Jugglers with poker faces. I like the little dog leaping up to catch the ball. That print and the one above the mantelpiece are worth a bit.'

She joined him on the sofa and they sat together in silence, pretending to study the print.

'I'd better go,' he said but neither of them moved. 'Oh, Kristen.' His voice was so full of anguish she instinctively put out a hand to touch him, and he responded by drawing her close.

Out in the street a car had drawn up. Doors slammed and the occupants started talking in loud voices, discussing who was going to pick someone up from a house in Bedminster. Cameron's eyes were closed. He could have been asleep. She was sharply aware of what was going on, every sensation, every sound, the way her body, for the first time in months, had lost its tension but at the same time come back to life. She could smell his skin, his hair, then he murmured something she couldn't hear and the two of them slid to the ground, speaking each other's names. He fumbled in his pocket and she thought: you've come prepared, or more likely you're always prepared, and she didn't care because it didn't matter, nothing mattered. She wasn't drunk. Later, it would be no use pretending she had

169

been. Silently, urgently, they moved against each other, too fast, but barely fast enough…

When it was over she sat with her back against a chair.

'Shit.' Cameron hauled himself onto the sofa. 'I'm sorry, that was a stupid thing to do. Now you'll think I deliberately took advantage of the way you were feeling.'

'Oh, for God's sake.' How dare he make out the decision had been his, and she had gone along with it because she was feeling so weak and sorry for herself.

He stood up and smoothed back his hair. 'No, don't say anything. Not now.' He paused and she thought he was going to apologise again but already his hand was reaching for the door. And a moment later she heard him running up the steps to the street.

23

The children had left and Kristen was alone in the classroom. She had been surprised when Brigid put her head round the door, and alarmed when she raised the subject of Shannon. Had Neville said something?

'She's a bit young by our standards,' Brigid was saying, 'but not these days. If it's not boyfriend trouble, perhaps it's a best friend who's let her down. In any case, we're not counsellors. I always think it's best to stick to teaching.'

'I'm sure you're right.'

'Good.' Brigid gave her a reassuring smile. 'By the way, bit short notice but can you come to dinner tonight – to meet the man Alex told you about?'

'The academic who's written a book on "genius"?'

'That's the one. Any time after half seven, earlier if you like although you might have to watch Rebecca having her bath.'

'Thanks.'

'Good. Now tell me about your day with Theo. It was very unfair of Ros, telling you he could come for the weekend then not letting him stay the night. Still, she'll probably feel bad about it and he'll come down again in a week or two.'

Kristen was thinking about the conversation Theo had overheard. Ros and John discussing his father, making derogatory remarks. Theo's remark about William and Ros meeting each other in London. Brigid was being so sympathetic she was tempted to confide in her, but not now, not when Brigid would have to rush off home in time for Rebecca's feed.

After Brigid left, Kristen began tidying up the mess the children had left behind. Because there was only one more morning to go she had let them choose what they wanted to do, but it had led to an argument and in the end she had been obliged to find a different task for each child, creating more work for herself rather than less.

Shannon had written a story set on a farm, the kind that no longer exists, with two cows, two sheep, and a pig. The story had nothing in particular to commend it and Kristen suspected she had deliberately made as little effort as possible. Certainly Theo could have done better, but then Shannon had an analytical brain. Theo's was more imaginative.

The previous evening, Ros had phoned to say how much Theo had enjoyed his trip to Cardiff. There was no need. All the call had achieved was to underline the fact that Ros was his mother and she, Kristen … Or was she being paranoid? Ros was only trying to be as co-operative as possible, although before she rang off she couldn't resist mentioning Theo's birthday in September and how John, who had a friend who made television documentaries, had arranged for Theo to go behind the scenes at London Zoo. Lucky Theo, Kristen said, and Ros had given one of her tinkly laughs. *I know it's a huge change for him, coming to live in Putney but we're doing our best and he really seems to have taken to John, although I wouldn't want him to get too attached if you know what I mean.*

While she was unlocking her car, Kristen paused for a moment, looking back at the building. It only took a few seconds and the man was by her side, a skinny, scruffy creature, sweating profusely.

'Excuse me.'

'Yes. What do you want?'

He pushed the folded scrap of paper into her hand and waited while she smoothed it out.

'What is this?' she said. 'Who are you?'

He was shaking so much he could hardly speak. 'This evening.' His voice was husky and he had to clear his throat.

'Go there this evening, see for yourself.'

She glared at him. 'I've no idea what you're talking about.' Then her expression changed. He was the man at the bus stop, the one who had asked Shannon about the classes. 'You? Was it you who sent the letter?'

'Letter?' He started backing away. 'He didn't have nothing … The dog man, he never done it. I only wanted …' He never finished the sentence. Neville had come into the car park. The man gave Kristen one last beseeching look. 'Go there this evening, see for yourself.' And he started to run.

The address she had been given was a short distance from the road where Shannon lived. Kristen drove to an adjacent street and sat in the car for several minutes, studying the map. It was already seven thirty and she was due at Brigid and Alex's at eight but as soon as she had checked the address she could drive straight to Redland and with any luck would be only a few minutes late.

After the man gave her the slip of paper she had considered contacting Tisdall, then decided against it. She was almost certain he was the one who had been talking to Shannon at the bus stop so this could be something to do with Shannon and quite unconnected with William's murder.

Two boys, aged about ten or eleven and dressed in England kits, were heading the ball between them. They paused, then resumed with practised skill and timing after the car had passed by. Since Theo's visit the feeling of loss had become almost unbearable. The best she could hope for was that Ros would remain in England and allow Theo to visit Bristol several times a year. But would he want to? After a time it might seem like a chore. *No, I can't play in Saturday's match, I have to go and see a friend,* or *my aunt,* or *this woman my father used to know.*

She was letting herself become morbid, self-pitying. Theo would never think of her like that, but the only way to keep in touch was to make sure she never put any pressure on him, never encouraged him to behave as a go-between, passing on gossip about Ros.

The boys had given up their football game and were sitting

on a low wall, sharing a bag of crisps. Kristen climbed out of her car and started walking back towards the main road. The noise of the traffic sounded further away than it actually was, but in her present state all sights and sounds appeared slightly distorted. Four days had passed since Cameron had called round at the flat. She had expected a phone call but by now he would be up in London, taking Vi's paintings to the gallery and doing whatever else he did. Where did he stay while he was up there? With the woman called Naomi who had come to the exhibition of child art?

Turning into the next road she found a house with a number on the gate and realised she was at the wrong end and would have done better to have continued on, past the place where she had left her car, then turned left and left again. Why had she come? Was it really because of Shannon, or was it because someone at the house just might turn out to know something about William? During the last few weeks she had even started to wonder if it might be better if the murder remained unsolved. Once the police had arrested someone all kinds of stuff could come out, stories in the newspaper that could ruin Theo's memory of his dead father.

Number thirty-three. Now she had reached it what was she supposed to do? Watch it from a safe distance? Go round the back and peer through a window? In the end she decided to ring the bell and tell whoever answered the door that she had lost her cat and was hoping someone might have spotted it. Of course, it was possible she was walking into some kind of trap, but if the man outside the college had some reason for wanting to harm her he was unlikely to have gone about it in such an amateurish way, and shown himself so openly. Her main impression of him was that something was making him very afraid.

The house was red brick, attached to another identical one. A short paved path led up to a porch that was really just a sheet of Perspex held up by two lengths of wood attached to the wall. Someone had trained a wisteria over it in an attempt to make it look more attractive. The ground floor window was open at the top and Kristen could hear the buzz of conversation, enough voices to make it sound like a party was going on, although there was no music.

She pressed the bell and the voices stopped for a moment. Then she heard laughter and saw a figure appear, just visible through the fluted glass in the front door.

'Yes?' The woman was middle-aged, wearing a blue, belted dress and with a string of glass beads round her neck.

'I'm sorry to disturb you.' Kristen looked beyond the woman, hoping to see into the house. 'I've lost my cat, it's black with two white paws.'

The woman smiled. 'I don't live here, dear, but I'll ask the owner. Hang on, shan't be a minute.'

Several people had come out of the room at the back, women dressed in calf-length skirts and silk blouses, with exotically coloured hair and high-heeled shoes. One of them had a cigarette and was waving away the smoke that was drifting towards her face. She approached the front door while still looking at someone over her shoulder.

'Can I help?'

'My cat,' Kristen repeated, 'he went missing the day before yesterday and I was wondering…'

'Were you indeed,' said a familiar voice, and a third woman appeared from the shadows. 'I haven't a clue who gave you this address but since you've taken so much trouble to find us the least we can do is invite you inside.'

It was Neville Unwin.

24

The man who had written a book about genius was called Jed Croner. He was short, slightly built, with small indeterminate features and pockmarked skin. He came from Toronto, and took himself very seriously.

Brigid had made an effort with the food. Spiced grapefruit with black grapes, followed, as Alex informed them, by something called Chicken Basque Style. Kristen had no appetite and had to struggle to finish what was on her plate. Her thoughts kept returning to the house in Fishponds, and on several occasions she was forced to guess what one of them had just said to her then watch Brigid and Alex exchange glances as though they were afraid she might be losing her grip.

The room smelled of carnations, although there were no flowers in sight and Brigid never wore perfume, disliking, as she had once told Kristen, the way it was exorbitantly priced and turned the people who bought it into idiots. Kristen had taken more trouble than usual with her appearance, but Brigid was wearing a skirt she often wore at the college, and a slightly crumpled top with a stain on one shoulder.

Alex was telling Jed Croner the history of the floating harbour and how Brunel had been responsible for a special lock, built to broaden the entrance.

'Two hundred and sixty feet long and fifty feet wide. Disused now of course, closed by a concrete wall, but still an interesting feature of the dock landscape.'

'Sounds worth seeing,' Croner said politely. 'So far I haven't had too much time to look around, although I'm aware the history of the city goes back to Roman times.'

'Tell me,' Alex said, steering the conversation round to Croner's book and Kristen's thesis, 'would an individual defined as a genius be in a special category or simply at the top of the intelligence ladder?'

Croner looked at Kristen then realised the question had been directed to him. 'Both views have their adherents.' He had a very small mouth that barely opened when he spoke. 'And then there's the question of being born at the right time.'

'How do you mean?' Alex drained his glass and pushed it across the table to be refilled by Brigid. 'Oh, you mean, if Einstein had lived a century earlier … but what about Mozart? If he was alive now surely he would still be a genius?'

It took Croner some time to finish chewing his mouthful. 'It's possible,' he said at last, 'I'd need to think about that for a while.'

Brigid frowned irritably. 'Surely deciding who is a genius must be fairly subjective.'

'Yes and no.' Croner had to think about that one too. 'Musicologists rating composers have been shown to be more or less in agreement, at least as far as the first few contenders are concerned.'

'Beethoven,' Alex interrupted, 'Bach. But what about those lower down the list?'

'That's where the problem lies.' Croner started to list some lesser composers, while providing figures for degrees of disagreement with regard to their status.

Kristen stifled a yawn. No doubt Croner's book was well-researched but he was one of the most boring men she had ever met. She thought about her conversation with Neville the day her car refused to start and he had given her a lift to the flat. Compared with the dry, cautious approach of most academics, Neville's interest in intelligence and personality, and the whole nature-nurture controversy had been in order to understand the practical outcomes of differing theories. At the time she had assumed he was thinking about the gifted children. Now she wasn't so sure. Why did men cross-dress? Because their mothers had wanted them to be girls, or because they were jealous of their sisters? Most things in life were far more complicated than that. Once she had got over the shock of recognising him, dressed as a woman, there was something endearing about the trouble he had taken with his appearance. But what did Vi think about it? Presumably, she didn't know. And the man who had told her to go to the address in Fishponds? If he was the dog man, why did he think she should know about Neville? He had been watching her when her car refused to start and Neville offered to give her a lift? Did he think Neville had something to do with the murder? What did he want? Was he following her, checking up on her?

'Would you agree with that, Kristen?' Brigid asked, and Kristen had to ask her to repeat what Croner had just said.

Alex laughed. 'Jed was quoting Francis Galton. How with two men of equal ability the one with a truth-loving mother would be more likely to become a scientist.'

'So it's not all in the genes.' Brigid began clearing away plates. 'Tell Jed about the work you've been doing at the college, Kristen.'

The baby had woken. Brigid made a move but Alex jumped up, assuring her he would deal with it while she carried on serving the next course.

'Not time for a feed, is it?' he asked.

Brigid shook her head. 'If she won't settle bring her down and give her some milk.'

The rest of the evening dragged. Kristen drank very little and her head remained clear. Too clear. The shock of seeing Neville was wearing off and she was left with a depressing awareness that nothing she said would convince him she had been tricked into turning up at the house rather than taken it into her head to spy on him. Naturally she had no intention of telling Vi what she had seen, but Neville had no way of knowing that. As far as he was concerned he would want her to stay well clear of Vi – and of the college when the term ended in two days' time.

'Oh, by the way,' Kristen tried to sound as if what she was

going to say had only just come to her, 'I meant to ask you before, Brigid, there's been a rather odd-looking man hanging about near the college.'

'Odd in what way?'

'He was talking to Shannon at the bus stop but at the time I assumed he was asking about the times of the buses.'

'And now?' Alex stood in the doorway, minus the baby who must have gone back to sleep. 'You've seen him again? What does he look like?'

'Thin. Losing his hair.'

'Age?' Alex sounded like a policeman.

'I'm not sure. Late twenties, early thirties. I thought Brigid might have noticed him too. I expect he's harmless, probably unemployed, bored.'

'All the same,' Brigid said, 'I think you should tell Neville, don't you, Alex?'

Alex sat down again and took a sip of wine. 'Better safe than sorry. Anyone hanging about where children go in and out…'

'I couldn't agree more.' For the first time Jed Croner looked quite elated. 'We had a case back home. Kid raped and strangled less than a hundred yards from her friend's home. My two are eleven and nine but Beth and I never let them out on their own. Just isn't worth the risk.'

Brigid stared at Alex, willing him not to start an argument. Kristen agreed – Jed Croner wasn't worth it – and something far more important had jumped into her head. The scruffy man had looked mystified when she asked if he was responsible for the anonymous letter, but it was an act, he had sent the letter and he had no wish to harm her, he wanted to help. And to help himself too by finding out who was responsible for William's death, the real killer. He *was* the dog man so he knew he was innocent. The police had got it all wrong.

Tisdall was not looking forward to talking to Kristen Olsen. The day had started badly and would finish even worse. Julie wanted to fix up a holiday for the two weeks leave he had due at the end of September. Unable to raise any enthusiasm for a fortnight in the Algarve, he had told her he would think about it, then groaned inwardly as she pushed aside her breakfast and burst into tears.

Grace had never cried, not when she found out about Julie, not when Serena had told him she never wanted to speak to him again, not when he had packed a couple of suitcases and moved out. Even then there had been doubts in his mind. But it was no good blaming Julie. She had put the maximum pressure on him to move in with her, but he could have used it as a way of ending things between them.

A fortnight in the Algarve. What would they do? Lie on the beach, trail round endless bars and clubs, take trips to local tourist attractions, eat too much, drink too much. He couldn't face it. As soon as Julie mentioned his leave in September he had realised, without thinking about it consciously, that he had set the end of September as a deadline. Grit his teeth and make a go of it, or leave.

Did Julie suspect what was going on in his mind? He doubted it. The arguments were becoming more frequent, more vitriolic, but she put it down to lack of space in the flat and the fact that he had to pay out so much of what he earned for Serena. When Serena left school … When they could afford a house … Lately she had started on again about babies. In the beginning she hadn't wanted children, couldn't stand the thought of being pregnant, getting fat. Now all that seemed to have been forgotten. He was forty-four, could leave the force in a few years' time, but not if he had a young kid. Him and Julie and 'the baby', years of nappies and interrupted nights, buggies, tantrums…

What was he doing? Trying to justify his decision, trying to convince himself he was being rational, that leaving would actually be in Julie's interest in the long run. If he put his foot down about the baby she might go. But that was the coward's way out, quite apart from the fact that it wouldn't work. And the real fear, the one that was with him all day, and most of the night, supposing Grace had found someone else.

When he knew he would have to talk to Kristen Olsen again, he had decided to take Brake along for moral support. It would have been sensible to phone her first but then she would have wanted to know what it was about. Now, they had reached the flat in Bishopston and rung the bell but there was no reply, just a shuffling sound as the old woman from the ground floor flat leaned over the railings to see who was there.

'She's out.' She finished whatever she had been eating and forced a fingernail between two of her teeth.

Tisdall managed a pleasant smile. 'You don't happen to know when she'll be back?'

'Oh, it's you.' The old woman started down the steps. 'Didn't recognise you in this light.'

Tisdall signalled to Brake to return to the car but Mrs Letts was blocking their way and had no intention of moving.

'She's said I expect, about the man who ...' She broke off, checking to make sure she had their full attention. 'Said he was the father of one of Theo's little friends from school. Only later I thought ... Didn't make sense see because –'

'When was this?' Brake asked. 'What man?'

She fixed her eyes on each of them in turn. 'He come in a van, see, parked it down there.' She pointed in the direction of the main road. 'Mrs Frith was out but I told her all about it, just in case. Mind you, at the time I believed him when he said he was Matthew's dad. Afterwards I wasn't so sure.'

'Matthew is Theo Frith's school friend?'

'Nice little boy, both lovely boys. Could be noisy, mind, but never rude, never cheeky. Theo was down last weekend, just for the day. He was going to stay the night but ...' She glanced at Tisdall and decided she had better get on with her story. 'Thing is, later I remembered it was me said he must be Matthew's father and he just agreed. D'you s'pose I could've put the idea into his head and...'

Tisdall nodded encouragingly.

'Had a feeling about him,' she continued, 'because of the van, I s'pose. Wreck of a thing it was and why was he here such a time?'

Brake asked if she had noticed the colour and make or, with any luck, the registration. She thought for a moment, scratching the back of her head, disappointed that she hadn't more clues to give them.

'Grey, I think, or it could've been blue. Couldn't tell you the kind of van, all look the same to me.'

'And the man?' Brake asked.

Her smile returned. 'Now that's easy. Thin, skinny type. Losing his hair here.' She touched the place where her own hair was scraped back from her forehead. 'What was he wearing? Jeans. One of them zip- up jackets, not leather.'

'Thank you,' Tisdall said, 'you've been very helpful.'

'So you think he was up to no good. Oh!' She clamped her hand over her mouth. 'You don't think he was the one, the one who…'

'One last thing,' Tisdall said, 'did you notice anything about his breathing?'

She wanted to say she had, wanted to tell them more. 'Spoke very quiet he did, and fast, I had a job to keep up with it. Tell you what, after you've gone I'll lie down, close my eyes, and see if any more comes back.'

'Good idea,' Tisdall told her, 'and if it does we'd be grateful if you could contact this number. Ask for Sergeant Tisdall, or leave a message for me to call you back.'

'I haven't a phone,' she said. 'Never need one normally. Still, I can always ask Mrs Frith if I can use hers.'

Back in the car, Brake asked if they would try Kristen Olsen's again later.

Tisdall nodded, although he had decided he would return on his own. 'In the meantime it might be a good idea if we paid one final visit to the hostel for the homeless. No, I tell you what, you go there without me, might notice something I missed.'

The more he found out about Frith the more questions it raised. But there were very few answers. No one knew who he had planned to see that day. The most likely explanation was that Frith had invented the meeting. Why? Because one evening out was no longer enough? Because he was having an affair and the woman involved had insisted they meet up? Somewhere in the back of his mind, Tisdall cherished the notion that solving the Frith case would lead to a resolution of his own problem. In one fell swoop the killer would be arrested, Julie would tell him she had met someone else, and Grace would welcome him back.

A more likely scenario was that Liz Cowie would tell him he and Brake were off the case, Grace would suggest he saw Serena away from the house, and Julie would want to 'try for a baby', an expression he disliked almost as much as the thought of her wish coming true.

25

Kristen had slept badly, waking before it was light then drifting off just before six. When the phone rang dead on nine o'clock she was still in bed.

'Kristen? Is that you?'

She recognised Vi's deep, gravelly voice and felt her stomach lurch, although nothing in Vi's tone had suggested she knew how Kristen had knocked on the door of the house in Fishponds.

In the event Vi's call had turned out be an invitation to 'pop round for coffee later in the morning', followed by a friendly inquiry about Kristen's health.

On her way to the bungalow, Kristen tried to re-live the incident outside the college when the man had given her the address of the house. She had been exchanging a few words with Brigid in the car park then Brigid had crossed the road, and suddenly the man had been by her side, breathing hard and with sweat standing out on his shiny forehead.

Why was he so determined she find out about Neville? And if it was the same person who had sent the anonymous letter, would he have shown up in person?

During the night it had occurred to her that the house in Fishponds was only a short distance from the hostel for the homeless where William had worked. Not that she had ever been there but she knew which road it was in. Could the man outside the college be someone William had met? Had William been blackmailing Neville and the man had found out about it and thought she ought to know? Surely he would have done better to go to the police. But not if he was in trouble himself.

Once, before they left for America, she had said something to William about the fact that he always seemed to have plenty of money. He had laughed then sworn her to silence, saying he earned it doing statistical analyses for PhD students who were hopeless at stats. She had believed him, but supposing he had been lying, supposing she was right about the blackmail. Neville had paid up then William had asked for more and, desperate to prevent Vi from finding out, Neville had decided to …

'There you are.' Vi had heard her car and come out to meet her. 'Been having a clear-out now a batch of paintings has gone. Let's hope the gallery accepts some of them or they'll be back to clutter up the place all over again.'

She was talking too much. Or was Kristen imagining it and she was just her usual self? She looked cheerful enough.

'I'm sure the gallery will want them.' Kristen followed her round the back where she noticed that two green and white canvas chairs had been positioned under the only tree in the garden, a magnolia that had dropped most of its creamy flower petals on the grass.

Vi pointed to the chair in the shade. 'I thought we'd sit out here but with fair skin like yours I expect you have to be careful.'

So far Kristen had avoided Vi's eyes. Now she looked straight into them and smiled. Vi's expression told her nothing.

In the distance, across towards the Brecon Beacons, clouds were building up that might bring rain later on. Vi was dressed in an old tennis shirt, pale blue cotton trousers with an elasticated waistband, and a pair of leather shoes with no laces.

Kicking off the shoes, she wiggled her toes then scratched the sole of one of her feet. 'I'm glad you've come,' she said, 'I'm not sure what I'd have done if I'd been you, but I think I might have made an excuse, stayed well clear.'

Kristen made a feeble attempt to feign incomprehension and

regretted it when Vi made an impatient noise with her tongue.

'Come on, Kristen, don't let's beat about the bush. Who told you and why did you take it upon yourself to go and check?'

Kristen moved her chair to make it steadier on the grass. 'I know what you must be thinking, but it wasn't like that. A man came up me when I was leaving the college. He pushed a piece of paper into my hand and told me I must go to the address he'd written down that same evening.'

'What man?'

'I'd never seen him before. At least, I might have done but I've no idea who he is.'

Vi stared at her impatiently, waiting to hear the rest. 'Didn't you ask who he was, what he wanted?'

'Never gave me a chance. No, he did say one more thing. He told me the dog man didn't do it. If it hadn't been for that I'd probably have taken no notice. I thought the address must be something to do with William.'

'So you've told the police.'

'Of course not.'

Vi bent down to pull a dandelion out of the lawn but the leaves broke off, leaving the root in the soil. 'You'll have to, though. So they can try to trace this man.'

'You believe me then.'

Vi was silent for a short time. 'Yes, I believe you. Whatever you think of Neville and his friends ... No, don't say anything. Only I can't see why this man, whoever he is, thought it could have anything to do with William.'

'He didn't look very bright.' Kristen was aware her explanation had sounded feeble in the extreme. 'I suppose he must have picked up some gossip and couldn't resist interfering, making trouble.'

'What's done's done,' Vi said firmly. 'Nev wasn't very happy about it. Not because you'd seen him and his friends but because he couldn't think what you were doing there, why you felt the need to spy on him.'

'I told you,' Kristen said angrily.

'Yes, so you did. I'll make some coffee. When I phoned, did you realise ... Yes, of course you did. Nev and I have no secrets. What on earth must you have thought when he came to the door?' She gave a short laugh. 'Must have been quite a shock. Of course, people assume cross-dressers are gay.'

'I don't.'

'No, well, they couldn't be more wrong. Nev told me about it ages ago, before his sister died, explained how it satisfied a need in him.' She pushed her feet into her shoes. 'I don't mind admitting it was a bit of a surprise but later, when we decided to live together … At our age you have different priorities, want an agreeable companion. Anyway, I'm not the easiest person to live with. For a start I'm a frightful cook. And I spend far too much time painting, time when I should be dusting and polishing or whatever it is people do.' She began to laugh a little hysterically. 'I'll tell you something that'll amuse you. Sometimes Nev asks my advice about make-up, clothes, what goes with what. Advice from *me*. Can you imagine!'

Kristen smiled but she was thinking about Nev's sister Jane, and how she had fallen from the loft. Who had found her? Neville himself, or had it been one of the days when Vi called round? 'Does anyone else know?' she asked. 'Only I was wondering how this man found out.'

'Only one other person. I suppose I needed someone to talk to, someone I knew wouldn't be shocked. You'd think I'd have chosen a female friend, wouldn't you, but the people I know wouldn't have understood. Cameron took it in his stride.'

'Good old Cameron,' Kristen said, watching Vi's head jerk up.

'Has something happened?'

'I was only wondering if he'd told William. You see, as far as the police are concerned William was a compulsive liar who led a double life.'

A magpie had landed on a strip of concrete near the garden shed. It strutted about for a few seconds then gave a squawk and flew up into the trees on the other side of the hedge. A cloud had covered the sun. Kristen shivered and Vi asked if she wanted to go inside the house, or borrow a cardigan except it would be about six sizes too big.

'I'm fine,' Kristen said. 'Has Cameron taken your pictures to

London?'

Vi stood up and rubbed the backs of her legs. 'It's never any good trying to pin him down to dates and times. Normally he spends four or five days in London, looks up friends, does a bit of buying and selling. All the same, if I haven't heard from him for several weeks I do start to worry in case he could have had one of his attacks.'

'Attacks?'

'He hasn't had one for well over a year. These new treatments seem to have done the trick. A couple of puffs from an inhaler first thing in the morning. How much has he told you about himself?'

'Just that he lives on his own in a flat in Kingsdown, sells antique toys. No, you told me that.'

'He hasn't mentioned Eve?'

'She's his girlfriend, is she?' Kristen said much too quickly. 'No, as I said we haven't talked that much, only about William and someone called Steve. I'm really sorry about what happened yesterday evening. If I'd had any idea…'

Vi waved her words aside. 'I'd hate to interfere but if he hasn't told you perhaps I ought to explain, it might help. Eve and Cameron lived together. For about four years, I think. She suffered from depression, but as long as she took her tablets she was all right. Although now and again the illness got out of control and she'd go on big spending sprees, buy all kinds of things she couldn't afford and didn't even want. Then she'd sink into a bad state, so low she couldn't get out of bed in the morning.'

'Bipolar?'

'Your William persuaded her the pills were doing more harm than good and she should stop taking them and start talking about herself, her childhood, all that kind of stuff.' Vi sat down again and hugged her knees, swaying from side to side. 'When Cameron found her she was still breathing. They rushed her to hospital, did everything they could, but it was a massive overdose, she never regained consciousness.'

Kristen was thinking about the last time she had seen Cameron. His words to her when she was so distraught about

Theo. *The trouble with you, you think you've a monopoly* ... He had never finished the sentence.

'When did it happen? When did she die?'

'Eighteen months ago? No, must be two years. And that wasn't all.' Vi was staring into the distance as if what she had to say next was so upsetting she was unable to meet Kristen's eyes. 'It was a double tragedy, something Cameron found almost impossible to come to terms with. He had no idea – I'm not sure if poor Eve knew – but when they did the post-mortem they discovered she'd been fourteen weeks pregnant.'

'I called round this morning,' Tisdall said. 'Thought I'd find you in on a Thursday. Mondays, Wednesdays, and Fridays, aren't those the days you work at the college?'

'I was with a friend.' Why did she feel the need to explain? Why was his presence so threatening?

'How's the boy?' Tisdall was strolling round the room, examining the prints on the wall, just as Cameron had done the first time he came inside the flat. 'Your neighbour said he'd been down to see you.'

'What else did she say?'

'Some man who might or might not be the father of one of Theo's friends. She told you about it I think.'

'Mrs Letts is not exactly a reliable witness.'

'You didn't bother to check?'

'Check?'

'Phone to see if it really had been him?'

She could feel her cheeks burn. 'I didn't see the point. It didn't sound anything like Matthew's father.'

Tisdall sat down. 'Ever heard of a club called Bimbam's?'

'No.'

'Apparently William used to call in there occasionally.'

So he was 'William' now, not 'Mr Frith'. She was thinking fast, trying to decide how much to tell him. Not about Neville, definitely not that. 'A man stopped me outside the college,' she said.

'And?'

'He said the dog man didn't do it.'

'You think it was the man who sent you the anonymous note? What did he look like?'

'Receding hair, thin, in his late twenties or early thirties.'

'Similar description to the one your neighbour gave us. On foot or in a car?'

'On foot when I saw him. Could have parked round the corner I suppose.'

Tisdall was making notes. 'Why didn't you get in touch? You must have known he could be the man we've been looking for.'

'Someone who'd committed a murder would hardly be stupid enough to walk up to me and –'

'Don't you believe it. Did anyone else see him?'

'You think I'm making it up. Like you did with the letter.'

He stared at her. 'Whatever makes you say that? Now, to return to the club William frequented.'

'I've never heard of the place.'

'No? Well, it's not important.' But his tone implied the exact opposite was true. 'I've talked to one or two people who met him there, the woman who runs the place, a few others.'

'What others? What you're saying is, you think he was seeing someone else. A married woman whose husband found out.'

'Steady on.' Tisdall held up a hand. 'Does the name Pascale mean anything to you?'

'No, why?'

'A friend of William's, or so I've heard.'

'French, is she?'

'Not as far as I know. If she is she's acquired a convincing Bristol accent. Anyway, she assures me she and William were just friends, and I'm inclined to believe her.'

Kristen sat on the edge of the bed. 'So what do you want me to say?'

'I don't want you to say anything. Unless there's something you think you ought to tell us. I'm only interested in facts, evidence I can corroborate. So far, nothing I've discovered leads me to believe William's death was anything other than a mugging that went tragically wrong.'

'I suppose he went to this club on Fridays when I thought he was at the hostel. Is this Pascale there every night? What is she, some kind of hostess?'

'As far as I can tell she goes there for an evening out, sings a little, although I got the impression that was in the past. She shares a house with two other women. They babysit for each other, take turns looking after the kids.'

'Is that it then?' Kristen was no longer capable of controlling her anger. 'Five weeks of new inquiries and the best you can come up with is some woman William was shagging. If there's more why not tell me now, get it over with? William's dead, does it really matter what comes out about him as long as it leads to his killer?'

Tisdall looked tired. Almost as tired as she was. 'Are you married?' she asked, and from the way he reacted she could have asked if he was a serial killer. 'Children?'

'One. A daughter. This business about the nightclub, I wouldn't want you to make too much of it. The only reason I mentioned it, I thought William might have said something.'

'No, you didn't. You thought if you came up with another humiliating revelation I might break down, start telling you all the secrets I've been keeping to myself. Except there are no secrets, or if there are I'm not the person you should be talking to.'

She was crying. Because of William. Because of Theo. Because of Neville, and Cameron, and Vi. Because she was so exhausted she didn't care about any of it, just wanted to curl up in a ball and sleep for a hundred years.

'I'll make some tea,' Tisdall said, 'or would you prefer it if I left?'

'Tell me about your daughter,' she said, using her sleeve to dab at her runny nose and watery eyes. He wouldn't of course because that would be unprofessional, but for a fleeting moment she saw the anguish in his face and suspected she wasn't the only one whose life was falling apart.

26

It was Kristen's last day at the college. After what had happened it was unlikely Neville would employ her again, but when she bumped into him in the corridor he acted as though nothing had changed, even repeated how he was hoping to expand the courses to all day Saturday in term time and possibly one evening a week. Three of the children in the first group had gone on holiday so it was down to two boys, Hugo and Jack, and four girls, Lynne, Becky, Amy, and Shannon. Kristen was explaining how easy it was to take two events, or two facts, put them together and make it appear as though one had caused the other.

'I don't get it,' said Becky, grinning at Shannon, 'do you, Shan?'

Shannon said nothing. She was very pale, looked as though she was sickening for something, and as Kristen watched she put her finger up to the corner of her left eye in an attempt to conceal the nervous tic Kristen had noticed earlier on.

'Hang on,' Kristen smiled at each girl in turn but got no response from Shannon, 'I'm going to give you some examples. How's this? Twenty children each write a story.'

'What about?' asked Jack.

Hugo pulled a face. 'Doesn't matter what it's about, twit face.'

Kristen began again. 'Twenty children each write a story.

The ones with large feet have better handwriting. So that means the bigger your feet, the better your writing.'

'No it doesn't,' said Jack, 'it could have been just luck.'

Shannon had her head thrown back and had closed her eyes. Kristen assumed she was thinking about what she had just said, but when she spoke her name the girl's eyes jerked open and she started apologising for not listening properly.

'Barnaby's got gigantic feet,' Hugo said, 'and terrible writing.'

'There are always exceptions.' Kristen was aware that she had explained badly, was confusing them, but just as she was about to provide a better example Shannon suggested, very quietly, that the ones with larger feet could be older and that was why their writing was better.

'Well done, Shannon.'

'It's a swindle,' Hugo complained, 'when you said twenty children I thought you meant they were in the same class.

'She never said they were.' Shannon made an angry sound with her tongue.

'I didn't say she did.' Hugo muttered something under his breath, and Shannon pushed back her chair and stood up, folding her arms.

Kristen sighed. 'Sit down, Shannon. I'm sorry, Hugo, I should have made it clear. Let's see if we can come up with some more examples. I'll give you five minutes to think.'

To her relief, Shannon sat down again and started sharpening her pencil. Hugo nudged Jack and they both made faces at her but Shannon had her back turned.

Sitting down at the end of the table, Kristen took some papers from her bag and pretended to be looking through them. Ever since she'd learned about Eve's suicide, she had been going over in her mind all the things she and Cameron had talked about. If he'd told her what had happened to him – but why should he? She was far too preoccupied with her own unhappiness to consider he could be suffering. Vi had said Eve died two years ago. Not very long, especially if Cameron blamed himself, felt he could have done something to prevent the tragedy. She had taken him at face value, treated him as if his cynical remarks were all there was to him. No, that wasn't quite right. If she had thought that would she have …

Hugo had started humming 'Why are we waiting?' Kristen glanced at her watch and asked if anyone had something they would like to try out on the rest of them.

Hugo nodded vigorously. 'I know one, except it's a different kind of mistake.'

'Let's hear it.'

He hesitated then took a deep breath. 'All dogs like biscuits. My dad likes biscuits. So my dad is a dog. My grandmother told me that. She died last year. She was only sixty-two.'

'I'm sorry.' Kristen had picked up the sadness in his voice.

'What did she die of?' asked Amy.

'Cancer. Everyone dies of cancer or a heart attack unless they get killed in a road accident, or murdered.' He broke off with a gulp. 'Hey, what's up with Shannon?'

The children turned to look. Shannon was breathing very fast, clutching at her neck as if she was about to be sick. Becky offered to fetch a glass of water but before she reached the door Shannon had beaten her to it.

Kristen caught up with them in the corridor. 'What is it? Calm down. Try to breathe more slowly. That's better. No, keep breathing.'

Hugo had joined them. Kristen asked him and Becky to go back to the classroom.

'Is she going to die?' Becky squeaked.

'No, of course not. I expect it's the heat. She'll be fine in a couple of minutes.'

The coffee room was empty. Kristen led Shannon through the door and carried two chairs to a space by the open window. A breeze blew in, lifting the tops of their hair and fluttering the timetable Neville had pinned to a board. Shannon was wearing new clothes, a pink cotton top, white shorts, and a pair of Indian sandals with a pattern of red and gold triangles.

She was breathing more easily now but her face was still very white. 'I'm sorry,' she said, 'I'm sorry.'

Kristen put a hand on her arm. 'Have you been feeling unwell or did something upset you?' Shannon said nothing, just kept moving her head from side to side until Kristen was afraid the panic was going to start all over again.

'Come on, Shannon, you can tell me. Is it something to do with the man I saw speaking to you at the bus stop?'

'What?' It was obvious Shannon had no idea what she was talking about. Then she relaxed a little. 'Oh, him. I told you. He said he had a friend who had a boy who came to the classes.'

'Which boy? He didn't tell you his name? You've only ever seen him on the bus?'

'Not *on* the bus.' She screwed up her nose. 'I suppose he goes on a different one, except that's the only number that goes past that stop. He said something about how *you* have a little boy. I think he's a bit funny in the head.'

Kristen wanted to know more. But not now. 'What is it then, Shannon? Did Hugo say something that upset you?'

It was as if she hadn't heard. But a few moments later her head dropped down and she muttered something Kristen had to ask her to repeat.

'They'd say I was a troublemaker and I wouldn't be allowed at the classes any more.'

So it *was* something to do with the college. 'Of course they wouldn't. Nobody's going to blame you. Something's been worrying you for a long time, hasn't it? Whatever it is you'll feel better if you talk about it. Your parents – do they know how upset you've been feeling?'

There was a longish pause. 'Mum said I looked peaky. She thought my periods might have started but I'd have told her if they had and anyway they haven't.'

Kristen waited patiently, wondering what the rest of the group were doing, back in the classroom, wondering if any of them were listening outside the door.

'I told Mum I was a bit tired,' Shannon explained, 'only then I thought she wouldn't let me come here so I said it wasn't that, it was just that I was worrying about when I have to change schools.'

'But that wasn't the real reason.'

She shook her head. 'I thought you'd guessed.'

'Guessed what? Is it something to do with someone at the

college?'

'No!' Shannon's hand went up to her mouth and she started tearing at one of her fingernails. 'He didn't do it. The man the police … It wasn't him. I know it wasn't. I spelled it wrong the first time only it didn't look right without two m's. You know how hopeless I am at spelling.'

'Two m's?' It took Kristen a moment to take in what she was saying. 'The letter? *You* sent it?'

'I saw them. His picture was in the paper. Jackie thought he was really good-looking. She kept going on about what a waste it was.'

Kristen could feel her blood drumming in her ears. 'Who is it you're talking about? You mean William?'

'And Theo was taken away from you. It's not fair. None of it's fair. William and Brigid … Me and my friend were taking Benji for a walk. They were near Oldbury Court – the day he was murdered. I'd have told you before but I thought you wouldn't believe me. You do believe me, it *was* them, I promise it was.'

'You saw William and Brigid together. Oh, Shannon, I think you must have made a mistake.'

'No!' She was on her feet. 'She reached up to kiss him.'

'Go on.' *Did he kiss her back?* But she wouldn't ask. She didn't want to know.

'I heard her shout his name and she started punching him and he shouted that she shouldn't be so stupid.'

Kristen pushed her gently back onto the chair. 'All right, I believe you.'

'Now you'll hate me. Yes you will. I wish I hadn't said but they think someone else did it. I heard her. I heard her shouting. She said she'd like to kill him.'

She was halfway across the room. Kristen raced after her but long before she could catch up Shannon had reached the safety of the classroom.

She said she'd like to kill him. Surely Shannon realised people say things like that all the time. But she had seen the two of them together and ever since Kristen took over the classes she had been fretting, wondering whether or not to tell her.

Obviously, she knew Brigid well, but she had only seen a photograph of William in the local paper. All the same, she knew all about the murder. And about Theo being returned to Ros.

Kristen had allowed time for Brigid to go home and feed the baby. Would Rebecca be asleep now, having her afternoon nap, or was she one of those babies who insisted on being held or played with for large parts of the day?

As she approached the house, she thought she saw Alex's car but it turned out be black, not dark blue, and a newer model. Unlike many academics, Alex dressed smartly, but sneered at people who wasted money on shiny new cars that would lose their value the minute they left the showroom. There was still over a month until the students returned to the university. Some of the lecturers worked at home for part of the vacation, but Brigid had said Alex spent most of his time in his laboratory unless he was writing up research. The time Kristen had seen him on the Downs with the baby he had seemed happy to be looking after her, but since Brigid had led her to believe the reason she sometimes seemed tired and irritable was because Alex didn't give her enough help, perhaps it was a one-off.

When she rang the bell, Brigid appeared at once, holding Rebecca so that the baby covered most of her face. 'Kristen! Come in. I'll put her in her cot and we can have some coffee. Have you eaten? Go through to kitchen, I won't be long.'

What was it about their kitchen that made it feel so uninviting? The large expanse of grey tiles, the shiny hardness of the table? The fireplace had been opened up but since it was summer the grate was filled with a brass pot containing a huge bunch of dried leaves and poppy heads. A framed photograph in the middle of the mantelpiece – Brigid and Alex standing in the garden with Rebecca when she must have been only a few days old – was flanked on either side by a carved wooden bird, placed symmetrically and carefully chosen to blend with the cinnamon walls.

When Rebecca was older, Alex would fix a pinboard to the wall and her first attempts at drawing would be displayed.

Daddy by Rebecca. A bird in a tree. Kristen had loved Theo's paintings when he was little – vivid, uninhibited pictures of her and William, and the puppy he longed for but was never allowed – but by the time he was seven he preferred to draw with a carefully sharpened pencil, tiny figures of soldiers, footballers, imaginary inhabitants of other planets.

'Let's hope she'll settle.' Brigid entered the room then stepped back into the hall to listen for any small cries that might be coming from upstairs.

'Does she sleep through the night?' Kristen asked.

'Mostly.' Brigid gave a huge yawn. 'Although last night she was rather restless. I think she may be getting a cold.'

'I didn't realise they caught colds that young.'

'Oh yes.' Brigid spoke with the authority of someone who has read all the right books. 'It's only for the first few weeks they still have their mother's immunity. Breast-fed babies are less susceptible to viral and bacterial infections. I fed her for the first twelve weeks but there was never quite enough so she had a supplementary bottle.' She broke off, laughing. 'Sorry, it's deadly the way people go on about their babies. It's just – I used to worry so much, but lately she's been more settled, more content.'

'Shannon had a panic attack,' Kristen said.

'Shannon?' Brigid frowned at the sudden change of subject. 'I saw her going home. She looked all right. What happened?'

'She was afraid if she told me what was worrying her she might get into trouble and be stopped from coming to the classes.'

'That's ridiculous.' Brigid bent to pick up a wooden rattle that had been left on the floor. 'You're not going to tell me she's made some accusation against Neville. Someone must have put the idea into her head, all those television programmes.'

'It had nothing to do with Neville. It was about you. She told me she saw you with William – the day he was killed. She said you were having a row.'

Brigid had her back turned, filling the kettle at the sink. 'That's crazy,' she said quietly. 'If you ask me you were right all along, the girl's disturbed, should have been referred to a psychologist.'

'It's not true then?'

'Of course it's not true.' She plugged in the kettle then turned to face Kristen. 'If you must know, Shannon and I have never got on too well. I don't know why she's made up such a silly story but I imagine it must be because of something I said to her during one of the classes.'

'What did you say?'

'Just that she shouldn't be so scathing if one of the others made a mistake.'

'Shannon? Scathing?'

'Don't you find her a bit full of herself?' Brigid's voice was steady as a rock. She was lying.

The baby seemed to have fallen asleep. In the next door garden, someone was whistling part of the Enigma Variations, out of tune, and a child's voice called out, 'Mummy, Max has broken Barbie's roller blades.'

'All right,' Brigid took two cups and saucers from the cupboards. 'Tell me exactly what happened.'

'Hugo mentioned how his grandmother had died of cancer when she was only sixty-two. Then he said something about everyone dying of either cancer or a heart attack, unless they were in a road accident or got murdered.'

'What's this got to do with what Shannon told you?'

'I'm coming to that.' Kristen had a moment's doubt, wondering if Shannon had been lying. But why would she want to do that? 'I was concentrating on Hugo then I noticed – no, Hugo noticed – Shannon was breathing much too fast, gasping for air. Then she pushed back her chair and rushed from the room.'

Brigid gave a short humourless laugh. 'So it wasn't in front of the others that she made this announcement about me.'

'I'm not accusing you of anything, Brigid, there's probably some explanation –'

'But you still think I was with William. Where were we supposed to be?'

'Near Oldbury Court. Close to where he was killed. Shannon

and a friend were taking her dog for a walk.'

Brigid had made the coffee and was attempting to pour it. But her arm seemed to have lost its strength. 'How did she know it was William?'

'She and her sister saw his photograph in the local paper.'

Kristen picked up the jug and poured the coffee herself. Before she came to the house she had been quite prepared to believe Shannon had made a mistake. Now, putting herself in Brigid's place, she tried to imagine how she would have reacted to a false accusation. Not the way Brigid had.

'All right,' Brigid said again, 'we did meet, very briefly. We'd bumped into each other near Broadmead a few days earlier. William wanted to talk but at the time I was in a hurry.'

'What did he want to talk about?'

Brigid swallowed. 'His work. Finding a new job. Someone he'd met.'

'Who?' Kristen tasted the coffee. It was undrinkable. 'Another mythical person who was going to give him some work, or was it just a nice out of the way place where you were unlikely to be seen? Why were you arguing?'

'Arguing?' Brigid said vaguely. 'Yes, I can see how Shannon might have interpreted it that way. William wanted me to persuade Alex to take him on again as a research assistant. I told him there wasn't a hope – Alex was too annoyed about what happened in America – then William tried to turn on the charm and…'

Kristen's eyes were fixed on Brigid's face. 'I don't believe you.'

Brigid shrugged. 'Well, there's not much I can do about that.'

Kristen carried her cup to the sink and poured the contents down the drain. 'William wanted Alex to give him his old job back and you ended up saying you wanted to kill him?'

She expected Brigid to react angrily, accuse her of believing a child's story rather than her own, suggest they both go round to Shannon's house and have it out with her. Instead, Brigid had left the kitchen and when Kristen followed her, she was standing by the open front door.

'I wanted to help,' Brigid said, 'that's why I suggested you for the job at the college, but it hasn't worked out as I hoped. It was too soon, you were too traumatised. When you're feeling better I hope things will be different between us. You should go home and rest. I'll give you a ring later on to see how you are.'

27

Kristen had found Bimbam's in the Yellow Pages and driven there, arriving just after nine when there was still light in the sky. She had expected the club to be for "Members Only", but was unprepared for the hostility of the man on the door.

'What are you, a journalist?'

Presumably it was her appearance, the fact that she wasn't dressed for a night out. Or because she was on her own.

'I'm looking for someone called Pascale,' she told him, 'I need to give her a message.'

'Name?'

'Kristen Olsen.'

When he returned a few minutes later he was shaking his head triumphantly. 'Not here.'

'You know her then.'

He said nothing, just made it clear from his expression that as far as he was concerned the conversation was at an end. Kristen tore a page from her diary and scribbled a note, folding it twice although she knew the man would read it as soon as she had left.

'If she comes in later perhaps you could give her this.'

Back in the car, she sat staring at the passing traffic, trying to decide what to do next. She was reluctant to return to the flat having achieved nothing, and frustrated that she could think of no other way to get touch with the woman. Was Pascale her real name? Tisdall had mentioned something about her being a singer although, according to him, Bimbam's was now just a drinking club and any attempt to provide entertainment had been abandoned.

Switching on the engine, she reversed into the few inches the van behind had left and began easing the car out, watching all the time for the traffic that kept shooting past.

'Wait!' A woman had her hand on the frame of her half-open window. 'Was it you who was round at the club?'

Kristen kept the engine running but lowered the window. The woman was in her late thirties or early forties with a heavily made-up face. She was out of breath, flushed, but there was no trace of resentment in her expression.

'I was looking for someone called Pascale,' Kristen said, and the woman nodded.

'You're Kristen? You wanted to ask about Will? You're just as I imagined you. Strange, isn't it? Listen, we can't talk here but if you gave me a lift …' And when Kristen hesitated, 'Fair enough, you don't know me from Adam, but if I wasn't who I said I was I wouldn't have known your name. Gus on the door gave me your note. How's the little boy? Theo. Is he doing all right?'

Kristen opened the passenger door. 'Where do you want to go?'

'Home. Downend. But not yet. We could drive out towards Yate then round and back through Westerleigh. Give us time to talk. Then later you can drop me off.'

'What about the club? It's only nine fifteen.'

'Place is dead tonight, don't know why I bother. I'm sorry about Gus, I just wanted to be sure you was who you said you were. Thought you might be the Old Bill.'

Serena was staying the night with a friend, a sleepover, Grace called it. Tisdall pretended it had slipped his mind but he had never been able to fool Grace.

'Still working on the same case.' She stood back to let him into the house, treating him like a visitor. 'Bit late, isn't it? Does Julie know where you are?'

'We're looking for a man who was seen hanging about near Kristen Olsen's flat,' he told her. 'Could be nothing to it but a neighbour gave a description and there's just a chance we may be able to trace him through his van.'

Grace switched off the television. 'Your dog man?' Her voice was contemptuous. 'It's Friday, I told you Serena was stopping over at Karen's house.'

'I know. I forgot.'

She gave him a look of resigned disbelief. 'Yes, well, you'd better give Julie a ring, she's probably wondering where you've got to.'

He nodded, hating the way she was able to show concern for Julie's well-being. 'She likes me working long hours, thinks it'll improve my chances of promotion.'

'You don't want promotion.' Grace balanced on the arm of a chair. 'Come on then, let's hear it. What's the problem, what's it all about?'

'As if you didn't know.' He kept his head turned away but she moved to where she could see his face.

'That's just it, I don't, not unless you tell me. All right, so absence makes the heart grow fonder and all that. You know your trouble, Ray, you always want what you can't have, and when you've got it...'

He sat down heavily. 'If Julie hadn't made sure you found out it would all have blown over.'

'So it's Julie's fault now. You wanted a bit on the side but when things started to get out of control ... What about me ... what about Serena?'

'I'm sorry.' He braced himself for her sarcastic retort. *You're sorry. Oh I see, so that makes everything all right.* But it never came.

'Does Julie know,' Grace said quietly. 'Must do, I suppose, just like I knew you were carrying on even though you kept telling me I was imagining things.'

'Don't.'

'At least have the courage to face up to what you've done instead of trailing round like a wet weekend. You made your decision and to hell with everyone else. Now ...' She looked at her watch. 'Serena was going to phone, said she'd let me know what time she'd be back in the morning. I hope she hasn't forgotten.'

'I'd better go,' he said.

'Yes, I think you'd better.' She followed him out into the hall and switched on the outside light.

'Ought to put it on as soon as it gets dark,' he said.

'I know. I forgot.'

'There's been a spate of break-ins in this area.'

'Thanks for telling me. Thanks for helping me sleep more easily in my bed. And don't mention any of this to Serena.'

'Any of what?' He turned to face her but she was picking up a coat that had slipped from one of the hooks on the wall. She gave it a shake, screwing up her nose when she noticed how the loop it was supposed to hang by had come unstitched.

'I love you,' he said.

'Don't.' The sharpness of her voice made him flinch. 'If things have gone wrong between you and Julie it's her you ought to be talking to, not me.'

'How can I?'

'Oh, Ray, I don't know.' She reached out to touch his face and he grabbed hold of her, kissing her hair, her neck, then breaking free and holding her at arm's length.

'I'm such a fool,' he kept saying, 'such a stupid bloody fool.'

'You are that.' Her head was thrown back and for a moment he thought she was going to burst out laughing.

'What are we going to do?' he whispered, and she let go of his hands and started up the stairs.

'I should think that's fairly obvious,' she said.

'Down there,' Pascale said, 'no, sorry, straight on! I meant, that's where I live. Who was it put you on to me, that copper I suppose, old whatsisname.'

'Tisdall,' Kristen reminded her, 'he said you and William were friends.'

'And you put two and two together and made ... If it was like that, me and Will, I wouldn't lie to you, there'd be no

206

point.'

They were passing the Downend Tavern, and a sign told them they were entering South Gloucestershire, although the landscape still looked like North Bristol. The learner driver in front had stalled the engine and was having trouble getting started again. Kristen gripped the steering wheel and tried to prepare herself for what Pascale was going to tell her. Almost certainly not something she would want to hear. 'Why did you agree to talk to me?' she said.

Pascale pushed up the sides of her hair, fluffing it out with her fingers. 'Because of Will. Because you deserve to know the truth.'

'If you knew something you should have told Tisdall.'

She shrugged. 'Will's dead, nothing's going to bring him back. Whoever did it deserves what's coming to them, only sometimes … sometimes I reckon things are best left buried. Anyway, if anyone's going to decide it ought to be you. How's Theo? You never said. Will was ever so fond of him – and of you, of course.'

They passed between rows of shops, a Chinese takeaway, a place selling replacement windows and conservatories. Estate agents, building societies, then the shops gave way to suburban houses with lights in their windows, a red-brick pub, an estate of newly built 'executive homes'.

Pascale started to light a cigarette then changed her mind and pushed it back into the packet. 'Will had this way of making people feel better about themselves. He thought I ought to make something of my life. I do a bit of singing, used to.' She hummed a few bars of an old Shirley Bassey number. 'I can sing in tune all right but that's not it, is it, better to be off key and have that little something extra.'

Kristen opened the car window then closed it again for fear the noise of passing traffic meant she failed to catch something Pascale said. Did she really know something or was she just curious to find out what Kristen was like, to exchange notes about William or 'Will' as she called him? Somewhere along the way would she ask Kristen to stop outside a house then introduce her to another of William's friends that he had never told her about? Someone who knew the man called Steve? Or Steve himself? Or perhaps it would be a woman.

'When was the last time you saw him?' Kristen asked.

'End of May? Couldn't say for sure. Not long after you came back from America. He walked into the club and I thought I was seeing things, we all did. Then he drew me aside, said he couldn't stay long, just wanted to check if I'd signed up for a course in the autumn, which I hadn't. I asked if he was back on holiday but he said America hadn't been what he'd expected, he'd got homesick.'

'Homesick?'

'I know.' Pascale laughed. 'Doesn't sound like Will, does it? The next we heard … I couldn't believe it. If I knew who'd done it, if I knew for sure…'

When they crossed over the M4, most of the traffic was going west – to South Wales or Devon and Cornwall. Kristen watched the receding light of the cars moving in the opposite direction and wondered if Theo had calculated the exact distance from Bishopston to Putney. Ever since she could remember he had loved measuring things, drawing patterns, making maps. In a week's time he would be starting at his new school. When she asked him about it he would say he liked the old one better – because everything he said was designed to make her think he had been happier in Bristol – but it wouldn't be true. Matthew, his friend, had been replaced by a boy called Marcus. John was no good at playing football but had promised to buy him tickets to watch Chelsea. Lately it had even occurred to Kristen that secretly – telling her and William would have impossible – he had always wanted to live with Ros.

The houses gave way to fields, a farm, a private nursing home at the end of a short driveway. Pascale was sitting very still, staring straight ahead. 'That woman,' she said suddenly, 'the wife of the bloke Will worked for at the university.'

Kristen felt her throat constrict. 'Who do you mean?'

'Brigid, her name is, got a baby, a little girl. I've a daughter, Chloe. She's thirteen, looks older more's the pity. Me and two others share this house in Downend, take turns looking after the kids. Don't know about you but I reckon that's how it's meant to be. Blokes are just for having a good time, not to have around you morning, noon and night.'

'You may be right.' Kristen was desperate to hear about Brigid but if she showed her impatience she might have to wait longer.

'I lived with Chloe's father for a couple of years.' Pascale took out a cigarette and this time she lit up. 'After she was born things changed. I reckon it's always the same. Same for Lisa and Dottie. Lisa's got twin boys, one with cerebral palsy only he's ever so bright, and Dottie's girl's a bit younger than my Chloe. Quite a laugh we have when things are going well. Don't know how long it'll last, mind. Could still be together when we're drawing our pensions. I reckon with lesbians it's because they want a partner who understands them, knows how they're feeling, what they're thinking, instead of just asking if the kettle's on. Trouble is, I like blokes.'

She broke off, twisting her head to glare at the car behind that had come up far too close. 'They should have let Theo stay with you, Kristen. He should never have gone to that Ros.'

So William had told her everything. But that didn't explain how she knew Theo had returned to his real mother.

'Copper told me.' She had read Kristen's thoughts. 'Probably believed the more information he passed on, the more he buttered me up, the more likely I was to tell him what he wanted to know.'

'About Brigid Howell?' Kristen checked the petrol gauge. It was only a quarter full. 'Since you keep changing the subject I assume you're going to tell me they were having an affair.'

'Well, you assume wrong. I've never met the woman, well, I wouldn't, would I, but from what Will told me about her there was no way he'd have … There's no easy way to break this to you but maybe you won't see it as such a terrible thing. It's what happened afterwards, that's why I'm telling you now.'

Kristen began to cough and almost missed the sign to Westerleigh then, as Pascale shouted at her to turn right, took the corner too fast and only narrowly avoided ending up in the hedge.

'She wanted a baby,' Pascale said, 'was desperate for one.

Her husband's got something wrong, not enough sperm or they're not strong enough to swim up.'

'Go on.' Kristen had guessed what was coming next. 'So William agreed to oblige.'

'It was all done properly, like at a clinic, except there wasn't a doctor or anything.'

'William told you this, did he?' Kristen said, and Pascale took her tone of voice to mean she didn't believe a word of it.

'Why would he have lied?'

Pictures were forming in Kristen's mind. Rebecca in her bouncy chair. Rebecca on the Downs with Alex. William's nose, his mouth – how could she have been so stupid? People said all babies looked alike but it wasn't true. By the age of three or four months each one was totally different and if you bothered to look you could see, more or less, how they were going to turn out.

'But you still think Will could have made it up,' Pascale said.

Kristen sighed. 'I'm not so sure about the clinical part. Surely sleeping together would have been simpler, and more likely to have had the desired effect.'

Pascale thought about this for a moment. 'But what about her husband? I don't suppose he'd have been too pleased.'

'Alex knew about it? Are you sure?'

'According to Will it was his idea. Will was picked because he was good breeding stock, brainy, tall, nice-looking. Alex couldn't give Brigid a baby and he didn't want to adopt a foreign kid, so as far as he was concerned it was the best arrangement, a fair deal.'

'Fair deal! How could it be a fair deal?'

'William supplied what was needed and Alex found him a job in the States. Trouble was the silly bugger decided to come back to Bristol a few months later.'

They had driven through Westerleigh and were on their way back to Downend. In ten minutes or so Pascale would ask Kristen to drop her off at her house and that would be the last time they met.

'I want to know everything,' she said.

'I've told you.' Pascale lit a second cigarette. 'Didn't want to, not after everything you've been through but I reckoned you deserved –'

'Everything? If you were me wouldn't you want to know the truth however much it hurt? You say you saw William after we returned from Ohio. What did he tell you? Had he been in touch with Brigid, seen the baby?'

There was a long pause. 'She told him having the baby had changed her, made her feel…'

'What?'

'She told him she was in love with him, wanted them to be together.'

'And what did William want?'

Pascale sighed. 'Didn't know what the hell to do, poor bloke. How to get rid of her, stop her getting in touch with him all the time. No, it's true, I promise. And you're right, it is better to know the truth.'

28

As Kristen ran down the steps she heard the door to the ground floor flat open and Mrs Letts call her name.

'Yes, what is it?' She had to phone Tisdall. He was unlikely to be at the police station but someone would contact him.

'Cat's back.' Mrs Letts leaned over the railing. 'Ever such a state it was in, poor thing, half-starved and its fur all matted. Mr Parsons looked all over, all the gardens, but it could've been shut in a shed – or stolen by one of them cat-nappers and managed to escape.'

'Good. I mean I'm glad it's back. I have to go now, Mrs Letts, but –'

'Nothing to do with that man, is it? Hasn't been following you, giving you a fright?'

'No, nothing like that.'

Kristen had left the number on a slip of paper by the phone. It took her a few minutes to find it and when she got through a voice asked if she could hang on.

'No, I can't. It's important. Sergeant Tisdall. I need to speak to him now.'

'I'm afraid he's not here, Madam, but I could –'

'Where is he? Tell him it's Kristen Olsen and I've been talking to Pascale. Pascale from the club. She's told me everything. The so-called dog man had nothing to do with William Frith's murder. I'm at my flat. I'll wait here till he calls back.'

'If you could give me an idea what it's about, Mrs Olsen. There might be someone else you could talk to.'

'Just ask Sergeant Tisdall to call me as soon as he gets the message.'

Later, much later, Tisdall woke and lay on his back, noticing how the street light still shone through the curtains, and remembering how Grace had said they ought to be lined but it was such a boring job she knew she would never get round to it. She was asleep, curled on one side and snoring lightly. He touched her hair, but not enough to wake her, and slipped out of bed and started dressing, cursing under his breath as loose change fell out of his trouser pocket and rattled on the wooden chair. What was he going to tell Julie? He'd had to follow up a sighting of the dog man, hadn't had a chance to phone because he and Brake had left in such a rush. Then what? That it had been a false alarm, that they were no nearer finding who'd killed Frith than they had been a month ago when Liz Cowie had agreed to let him and Brake work on their own for a couple of weeks.

A dark shape was lying on the floor. He reached down and picked up his phone, realising with a jolt that he had switched it off and forgotten to switch it back on. Or had it been what people called "a Freudian error"?

It was nearly midnight and all the lights were out at the front of the house. Kristen had waited for Tisdall to call back, grown increasingly angry and frustrated, and finally decided to go round to the house herself. Now that she had calmed down a little, it occurred to her that Pascale might have got it all wrong. Or that William had invented the story to get her attention. Showing off, making her laugh, except she had not found anything she said amusing. And would William have invented something so preposterous? If she had never met Pascale would she have thought Rebecca looked like William, or was it simply a case of fitting the facts? At the very least, she should give Alex and Brigid a chance to explain.

When she lifted the letterbox, a dim light reflected on the polished pine floor at the foot of the stairs. If she knocked or rang the bell it might wake the baby and in any case the more she thought about it, the less confident she felt that her decision to leave the flat had been a good idea. Tisdall might be round there now. She should have waited till the morning, told him everything she knew and let him interview Brigid and Alex in his own time. He would have spoken to them separately so they had no chance to concoct a story and stick to it.

Turning back to the car she waited for a cyclist to pass and at the same moment the front door opened and Brigid stood there, holding Rebecca. Her dressing gown hung loose, revealing a flowered nightdress, and when she saw Kristen she gave an involuntary shudder. 'Kristen? Are you all right? Has something happened? Alex is asleep. A meeting. He didn't get home until after ten.'

'I'll come back in the morning.'

Brigid hesitated. 'You'd better come in.'

Kristen followed her into a small room at the front that looked as though it was used as a study. Rebecca was whimpering but when Brigid offered her a bottle she jerked her head away. The design of blue and green sheep on her sleep suit was rather like Theo's duvet, and the poppers on the legs were undone as though Brigid had been in the middle of changing her nappy. She must have looked through the bedroom window and seen her standing outside the front door.

'I've been talking to someone called Pascale,' Kristen said.

'Pascale?' Unless Brigid was suddenly an extremely good liar the name meant nothing. 'She and William were friends. No, they weren't sleeping together, or if they were it's irrelevant now.'

Brigid sat down with the baby on her lap. 'Who is she then?'

'She told me about the arrangement you and Alex made with William.'

'Arrangement?' But this time her face showed fear. 'I haven't the first idea what you're talking about. I know what a strain you've been under but –'

'She told me William was Rebecca's father.'

215

The baby had started to slide down Brigid's legs. Kristen reached out to grab her but Brigid managed to catch her under the arms, haul her onto her shoulder, and walk across to the window, where she held back one of the curtains and stared out at the dark.

During the day the temperature had dropped. The room felt chilly. A dead bluebottle lay on the carpet next to a rag book with a picture of a baby donkey.

'It's true.' Brigid still had her back turned but the fear in her voice had been replaced by something like relief. 'I'm sorry, I can imagine how it must make you feel but it was done in a completely clinical way. I expect it goes on all the time. I expect it's quite common.'

Rebecca was clutching her mother's hair in her fist. Kristen looked at the small pink hand and felt a mixture of dislike and longing. 'We weren't supposed to come back from America,' she said, 'least of all to Bristol.'

'William promised not to.' Brigid had her head on one side, listening for sounds from upstairs, but the house was silent. 'Mainly because I was afraid you might find out.'

'How would I have done that? Oh, you thought William wouldn't be able to resist telling me. Or when I saw Rebecca I would recognise the likeness. How often did you meet up after we came back? How many times did William see her?'

'Only once. He begged to see her and I agreed, provided he swore never to get in touch again.' Rebecca was wide awake now and enjoying the unexpected arrival of a visitor in the middle of the night. Brigid let go of the curtain and moved towards the door. 'Can we talk about this in the morning, Kristen, I have to put Rebecca back in her cot.'

'I told you how Shannon saw you and William together, near Oldbury Court.'

'And I told you we just happened to bump into each other.'

'Where was Rebecca?'

'Look, what is this?' Brigid's eyes were very bright. 'I can understand why you're upset but ... Alex was looking after her. I needed a break.'

'You could have walked on the Downs but you chose to

drive all the way to the Oldbury Estate? I came round tonight because I thought you deserved a chance to explain. I could have gone straight to the police.'

'The police!'

'I wanted to make sure Pascale had got it right. Shannon said the two of you were arguing then she heard you shouting.'

Alex was standing in the doorway, fully dressed, and wearing his glasses. 'It was my idea,' he said, 'I bought a speculum and syringe. That's how they do it these days and it's just as Brigid said, a medical procedure involving a surrogate father. It doesn't harm anyone and alleviates the suffering of thousands of childless women.'

'And it worked first time?' Kristen said.

'Why shouldn't it?' Alex ignored the sarcasm in her voice. 'In any case, it's still possible Rebecca's mine. We've never had tests, there wasn't any point. To all extents and purposes she's our biological child. I'm sorry about what happened to William, desperately sorry, but telling people about Rebecca won't help. Think of Theo.'

Up to that moment Kristen had felt unnaturally calm. Now she felt adrenaline surge through her body. 'Who are you fooling, Alex? Brigid was in love with William. All that stuff about a speculum and syringe ... There's an easier way than that to get pregnant. Brigid pestered him for weeks, wanted him to leave me so the two of them ... the three of them could live together. When he refused, she met up with him to have one last try. Then when he still wouldn't agree...'

'Live together?' Alex shouted. 'You're mad, you don't know what you're talking about.'

'I think I do.' But in that split second Kristen knew what had really happened. It wasn't Brigid who had killed William. She loved him and would have done anything to save him.

The veins stood out on Alex's forehead. 'He threatened me,' he shouted, 'even suggested he might be prepared to move away if I made him a good enough offer. And after that? He couldn't even make a go of the job in Ohio. Why should I have believed anything he said? A psychopath, that's what he was, totally without any scruples or morals and –'

'So you killed him.'

'It was an accident. I never meant …' He moved closer to Brigid but she pushed him away. 'Rebecca's the best thing that's ever –'

'You attacked him and he fell from the bridge, then you walked away, or ran I expect, leaving him there, knowing if you'd called an ambulance…'

'No! You're wrong.'

'It must have been a relief when the police came up with their dog man theory. You could relax, you'd got away with it, especially if they never found their suspect. I wondered why Brigid suggested me for the job at the college. Now it all makes sense. Guilty conscience…'

With one quick movement Alex had left the room, and then the house. Brigid pushed Rebecca into Kristen's arms and ran after him into the street, calling his name, pulling at the car door then stumbling and falling to her knees as the car shot forward.

Still holding the baby, Kristen ran down the steps to the pavement and hauled Brigid to her feet. 'Are you hurt?'

'What have you done?' she wailed. 'Where's he going? I didn't know. I promise I didn't know.'

'But you suspected,' Kristen said. And the baby, William's baby, looked up at her and smiled.

29

Alex Howell's car had been spotted in a small parking area just off Brunel Lock Road. Tisdall was there now, leaning against his own car, staring down at the damp grass cuttings that had stuck to his shoes, then letting his eyes scan the horizon, taking in Ashton Park, the Suspension Bridge, The Paragon, the brightly painted backs of the terraced houses in Cliftonwood.

Two divers were searching for the body. Howell had left his jacket on the paving stones surrounding the water: a marker to save everyone trouble, make sure he would be found as quickly as possible?

Shortly after he left Grace, Tisdall's phone had started ringing and the desk sergeant had informed him he had been trying to get in touch for several hours. Muttering something about the phone battery, Tisdall had asked what the problem was and been shocked to discover it was Kristen Olsen who wanted him.

'What did she want?'

'Wouldn't say. Mentioned someone called Pascale. I tried to contact Martin Brake – he'd been working late in the office – but on his way home he got involved in a hit-and-run accident.

Tisdall had rung Kristen's number and when there was no reply driven straight round to the flat, meeting up with her as she stepped out of her car … He had been too late.

Now Brake was shouting his name. Tisdall left the car park

and hurried towards the lock where he was in time to see the divers lift a dripping shape out of the grey water. Without his glasses, Howell looked different. People always did. A polythene bag had been attached to a length of twine round his waist. It was covered in black slime.

'Bricks,' one of the divers said, 'enough to keep him at the bottom.'

Tisdall nodded, staring down at the lifeless face, wondering if anything he had done, or not done, would have made any difference. Kristen Olsen had described the events leading up to her leaving the Howells' house in Redland. If she had been able to reach him on his mobile … If she had waited at the flat … But perhaps Howell had known all along it was only a matter of time.

Where had he found the bricks, and the bag and the twine? Had they been stored in the boot of his car or had he collected them together when he overheard Kristen talking to his wife? Would Kristen feel better now that Frith's killer was dead or would she have preferred it if Howell had been convicted in a court of law? When the facts came out, or Howell's version of the facts, he might have received a relatively light sentence, provided he could convince the jury Frith had taunted him, even attempted a spot of blackmail, and the fall from the bridge had been an accident. The charge might even have been reduced to manslaughter.

Tisdall looked at Brake, who had been crouched over the body but was now standing a few feet away, trying to look as if it was all in a day's work.

'If that woman at the club had told us everything she knew,' he said.

Tisdall shrugged. 'She thought Kristen might not want to pursue the matter.' He was going to add that women were like that, more interested in 'feelings' than in justice being done, but he could imagine how Grace would have reacted to such a remark. 'I can think of one person who's going to breathe a sigh of relief. The dog man, whoever the poor bastard is.'

'Rebecca's just about to have her dinner,' Brigid said. 'Have you eaten?

'Coffee would be fine. I'll make it, shall I?' It was like a repeat of the first time Kristen had visited the house. No, not the first time, that had been with William.

Today was September the third. Theo's birthday, and three days since Alex's body had been pulled from the lock. Brigid looked in desperate need of sleep but Rebecca was in high spirits, sitting in her bouncy chair, waving her arms and legs.

Kristen filled the kettle, glancing at Brigid who had back to her, taking something from the fridge.

'He didn't look any different,' she said. 'He hadn't been in the water very long.'

'I'm so sorry.'

Brigid gave a short, humourless laugh. 'It was Alex's idea. I'd been trying to get pregnant for years.'

'I'm sorry.' Kristen said again, wondering if she and Brigid would keep in touch, even become friends, held together by the past, not wanting to let go. There were so many unanswered questions. Had Alex been the man William had arranged to meet, or had he followed William, seen him go down to the river and decided to plead with him to leave Bristol? And what was the truth about Brigid's relationship with William? Had they slept together and she had fallen in love with him, or was Alex's account of Rebecca's conception the truth but having William's baby had created a bond with him? Why had she said she wanted to kill him? Because she loved him and he had rejected her?

Watching Brigid spoon food into Rebecca's mouth, Kristen knew they were questions she would never ask. Perhaps William would have told her about Rebecca, but she doubted it since he had never told her the truth.

'What will you do?' she asked, and Brigid stood up and moved slowly towards the sink, carrying the empty bowl.

'Go a long way away,' she said, 'probably to Suffolk where my parents live, although they're getting rather old. There'll be an inquest.'

'Yes.'

'It'll be reported in the paper. One day Rebecca may read

about it. Theo might too.'

'Don't think about it,' Kristen said, wanting to touch her, to comfort her in some way, but uncertain if Brigid would like it.

He had forgotten it was Saturday and Julie would be home. She had accepted his explanation of why he had been out all night but complained that he should have phoned her. Now she would be ready to greet him, eager to hear about the night's events.

When he reached the flat she was in the kitchen, cutting up tomatoes and arranging the slices in a bowl, along with the inevitable lettuce, cucumber, and the raw mushrooms she insisted on adding because they gave the salad a bit of class.

'So you caught the man who did it. Liz Cowie will be pleased.'

'Pulled him out of Brunel's Lock.'

'Dead?'

He nodded. He had no idea what Grace would decide but whatever happened he had to move out. Then, provided he gave it time, was careful not to put any pressure, and avoided using Serena as a reason for allowing him to return...

'Now they'll have to let you take all that leave that's owed to you.' Julie gave him a sidelong look that he would like to have interpreted as suspicion, although he knew she thought it was sexy. 'Where would you like to go? Maybe we could afford something a bit more romantic than Spain or Portugal.' She took a quiche from the oven. He hated quiche. 'Anyway, wherever it is it'll be nice to spend a bit of time together at last.'

Vi was coming down the stairs. She stood in the doorway for a moment then walked across to Kristen and enveloped her in a hug. 'What can I say? Nothing that would make you feel any better. Neville called round to see Brigid yesterday but he didn't stay long. The baby will be a help.' She broke off. 'There I go again with another of my crass remarks. How are you? Are you all right? If there's anything I can do.'

'Yes, anything at all.' Neville handed Kristen a glass of wine.

It was the first time she had seen the two of them together.

They were comfortable, relaxed, close friends who complemented one another, gave each other support, and love.

'Rebecca looks very like William,' Kristen said, 'I don't know why I never noticed it before.'

Vi gestured to her to sit down. 'Neville thinks he may be able to find you some A level classes.'

'Thank you.'

Neville fetched the bottle of wine then noticed that Kristen's glass was still full. 'Either at the college, or there are people prepared to pay for individual coaching in their own home. Good pay. It's amazing how much parents will shell out. And not just parents, mature students who missed out the first time around.'

Kristen listened while Neville expanded on the subject, suggesting which subjects she could teach and how the hours could be arranged to suit her needs. They were trying to be practical but what she needed was someone who would listen, just sit and listen. Then listen all over again. She had spoken to Tisdall and the dog man had given himself up. Presumably he felt confident now that his pickpocketing would receive a relatively light sentence. Apparently, his girlfriend's cousin had a boy at Theo's old school and, when he heard how Theo had been returned to his birth mother, he had become obsessed with the injustice of it and felt it his responsibility to uncover the real murderer. Some hope of that but, according to Tisdall, he had confessed to following Kristen, 'wanting to make sure she was safe.' What had he thought Neville was going to do to her? But she could hardly tell Tisdall about the house in Fishponds.

Vi had lit a cigarette and was apologising for the state of the room. 'This weekend I'm going to have a good clear-out. Might even do some dusting. Do you do dusting? I've never seen the point. Sorry, you don't want to hear all this.'

'Yes I do.' Kristen looked round, taking in the sofa and chairs covered in an ugly blue and mauve material, a bamboo bookcase, piled high with old newspapers and magazines, and a large open walnut bureau near the window that held a jumble of papers, sewing materials, and a glossy coffee table book about Marilyn Monroe.

The fact that she knew about Neville's Wednesday evenings didn't seem to bother him at all and if she had been going to stay in Bristol she might have accepted his offer of more work at the college. What was she going to do? Get right away, like Brigid, make a new life for herself. But where? How?

'I don't know what to tell Theo,' she said.

'Just follow your instincts.' Vi leaned forward with her hands on her knees. 'He won't understand, not until he's older, but he'll take in enough to get the gist of it. After all, it's not as if his father did something so terrible.'

'No.' Already Kristen was rehearsing in her head the conversation she intended to have with Ros. *I've told Theo that William and the man he used to work for had an argument, a fight. There was an accident and later Alex was so upset about it* ... 'It's Theo's birthday today,' she said, 'he's nine. Ros's friend John knows someone who's making a documentary about London Zoo. Theo is being taken behind the scenes. He loves animals so he'll really enjoy it.'

Vi and Neville exchanged glances. 'Cameron came round,' Neville said, 'I hope you don't mind but we thought it best to tell him.'

'Only the bare bones,' Vi added, 'he's been up in London, knew nothing of what had been going on.'

Kristen nodded. So he had come back to Bristol and not even bothered to get in touch.

'That dog man character,' Neville said. 'How come the cops latched onto him as suspect number one and ignored all other possibilities?'

'I don't think it was quite like that.' Now was not the time to start explaining how, in all likelihood, it had been the dog man who had told her to go to the house in Fishponds. How he must have been following Neville, thinking he was some kind of threat to her. Whatever had been going on in his distorted mind, it was over with now and best forgotten. The poor guy had probably been trying to clear his own name, pin the murder on someone else.

'I know it's early,' Vi was saying, 'but do let me make you something to eat. You look exhausted.'

Kristen glanced at the clock. It was ten past five. What would Theo be doing now? Still at the zoo or had Ros arranged a party, invited some of the boys from his new school, or the children of her actor friends? 'If you don't mind I think I'd better get back to the flat. I want to give Theo a ring, wish him a happy birthday.'

Neville leapt up, insisting he drive her to Bishopston.

She said goodbye to Vi, who gave her another hug, and followed Neville into the front garden. His car was in the garage and since there was very little space he suggested she wait on the pavement.

'Won't be a tick.'

Vi was standing at the door, shading her eyes. 'Come round again soon,' she called. 'Tomorrow, if you like.'

'Thanks.' Kristen turned her face towards the sun and closed her eyes, letting the heat soak into her skin. She felt light-headed, unreal. She thought about Brigid at home with Rebecca, a child with no father, like Theo. *Exactly* like Theo. In Brigid's situation might she have done the same, been so desperate for a baby that nothing else mattered? Had she and Alex sworn William to secrecy or had he decided not to tell her, partly because he thought she might take it badly, but mainly because it would have brought up the subject of the baby she wanted them to have?

When she opened her eyes, Neville had still not appeared but a white car, one she recognised immediately, was drawing up at the kerb and a moment later Cameron jumped out, pulling off his dark glasses and sticking them in the pocket of his shirt. He looked hot and tired. His hair was damp with sweat and he ran his fingers through it, trying to make himself look more presentable.

'I called round at your flat.' His eyes met hers then moved away. 'I thought you might be here.'

'I'm just leaving,' she said, 'Neville's giving me a lift.'

'What happened to your car?'

'Nothing. I walked, needed some fresh air.'

Neville was easing the Rover through the narrow gap between the wall and a wooden post. He saw Cameron and pulled up, leaning out of his window.

'Come to see us?'

'Yes, but it'll keep. Don't bother with the car, I'll run Kristen home.'

'You're sure?'

He nodded. 'Tell Vi I'll be round later and the news is good.'

Kristen was staring into the distance at the thick woodland on the Blaise Castle Estate. It had rained early on and everything looked fresher, greener. When he was little, Theo had enjoyed playing in the woods, running on ahead and jumping out at them although they had guessed which tree he was hiding behind.

Cameron held open the passenger door and she climbed in like a sleepwalker. 'I wanted to explain,' he said, 'but in the light of what's happened you're probably not interested. I phoned Vi from London and she told me all about it. I'm really sorry, it must have come as a terrible shock.'

'Pity your friend Steve wasn't better informed, or perhaps he knew all along – about William and Brigid. Perhaps you did too.'

'As a matter of fact, I didn't.' The lights had changed to red but he only noticed just in time to pull up before the traffic began crossing from the other direction. 'And I thought you realised there was no Steve. I knew William, knew him pretty well, but it was easier…'

'It doesn't matter.'

'Yes it does. All of it matters. When I phoned Vi she said she'd told you about Eve. It's all right, I don't mind, I should have told you myself.'

She was silent for a few moments. 'Was it William's idea that she give up her medication?'

'It wasn't like that. Eve never took any notice of me or William. I was just as much at fault, made her feel the illness was all in her mind, that she ought to be able to pull herself together. When she died … I suppose I wanted to blame William…'

'I thought you might have killed him.'

226

'What! When? Oh you mean when Vi told you about the overdose.' He looked at her then back at the road. 'Well, I can't blame you for that. How's Howell's wife? No, silly question. Vi said you found out about Neville. And the man who gave you the address in Fishponds, was he the one who sent the anonymous letter?'

'It's a long story.'

'Tell me about it later. So what will you do now?'

'Do?' She was thinking about Shannon. 'Probably go back to London. There's nothing to keep me here.'

'It would be better for seeing Theo, but where will you live? I stay with an old schoolfriend in Richmond, have to sleep on the floor but it's convenient for getting to the West End. Incidentally, the gallery accepted six of Vi's paintings then rang asking for another four.'

'You've passed the turning.'

'Have I? So I have.' He glanced in the driving mirror, reversed a few yards then swung the car round with the tyres screeching.

Kristen thought she could see Mrs Letts standing on the pavement and, when they came closer, a man who she thought at first must be Tisdall until she saw the fair hair and lightweight suit. It was John. Ros's John. Something had happened and he had been sent to tell her. Where was Ros? She hadn't come. She was too much of a coward.

Cameron was trying to park in a space that wasn't big enough. Kristen jumped out of the car and started running.

'John? What's happened? Where is he, where's Theo?'

John smiled, jerking his head back to the house where Theo was coming up the basement steps, carrying Mr Parsons' cat. He was wearing his old jeans and the Bristol City shirt she had sent on to him.

'Lucky he turned up.' He stroked the cat's head. 'Mrs Letts told me.'

'I thought you'd gone to London Zoo.'

He grinned at her and John gave a good-natured sigh. 'We were on our way. Ros told you about the documentary?'

'Yes. Where is she?'

'Audition. Pilot for a TV series. If she gets the part she'll be playing a woman who has a facelift and it all goes horribly wrong! Anyway, as I was saying, we were on our way to the zoo and this little sod suddenly announced he didn't want to see a lot of stupid cameramen taking pictures of animals locked up in cages. He wanted to come down here.'

'Oh, Theo, how could you? Can he stay the night – or two would be better. I'll bring him back.'

'Fine by me.' John nodded to Cameron. 'Let us know when you're coming and I'll make sure Ros is in, or I am.'

So he had moved into the flat. How did Theo feel about that? Perhaps he was relieved, glad it was not just him and Ros. From John's manner, it was clear neither he nor Ros knew anything about the events of the last few days. A man found dead in the floating dock in Bristol was unlikely to have made the nationals. Later she would tell Ros everything she needed to know and they would talk about William, exchange notes about how impossible he had been to live with, leaving out the good part because that would be too painful.

Mrs Letts was still hovering in the background. 'Got a card for you, Theo,' she called. 'Got footballers on it only they didn't have one with the right colour shirts.'

'Thank John for driving all the way from London,' Kristen called, hurrying after Cameron who had started walking back to his car.

'I'm glad about Theo,' he said, 'he's sure to cheer you up.'

'No, don't go.'

'I think I'd better. You and Theo…'

'I don't mind.' Theo had caught up with them, still holding the cat. 'Are you Kristen's boyfriend?'

'Cameron was a friend of Dad's' she said.

'Oh.' He was trying to remember if he had met him before. 'Anyway, I'm starving.'

'In that case we'll tidy you up a bit then go and get something to eat.'

'Is Cameron coming too? Yes, let him, Kristen, it'd be more like a party. John said we should have phoned first but I knew you wouldn't mind.'

She smiled at him and he smiled back, supremely confident that he could turn up at the flat without any prior warning whenever he liked, and she would be overjoyed to see him.

He was right.

Nobody's Baby
Penny Kline

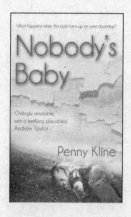

Nobody's Baby is an engaging and eerie thriller about loss, control, and the desperate edge of human emotions.

In the middle of the night Izzy Lomas finds an abandoned baby on her doorstep. It could have been left by any desperate person ... except that the baby's name, pinned in a note to its carrycot, brings back a striking memory from her childhood. *If you had a baby what would you call it...*

If Izzy's suspicions are correct and she tells the police, it could end in tragedy. Allowing herself some time to investigate, she frantically tries to trace the baby's mother, but every twist and turn in her search seems to lead to a dead end. And the longer she stays silent, how many people is she putting in terrible danger?